THE NOOSE

'THE DETECTIVE STORY CLUB is a clearing house for the best detective and mystery stories chosen for you by a select committee of experts. Only the most ingenious crime stories will be published under the THE DETECTIVE STORY CLUB imprint. A special distinguishing stamp appears on the wrapper and title page of every THE DETECTIVE STORY CLUB book—the Man with the Gun. Always look for the Man with the Gun when buying a Crime book.'

Wm. Collins Sons & Co. Ltd., 1929

Now the Man with the Gun is back in this series of COLLINS CRIME CLUB reprints, and with him the chance to experience the classic books that influenced the Golden Age of crime fiction.

THE
DETECTIVE STORY
CLUB

FURTHER TITLES IN PREPARATION

INTRODUCTION

Colonel Anthony Ruthven Gethryn well qualifies for the category of Disappearing Detectives in that, though he was once a highly popular figure, the very last of his exploits appeared as long ago as 1959. This was *The List of Adrian Messenger*, subsequently made into a film which surfaces very occasionally on television. But before it Gethryn's adventures were all chronicled in a cluster of ten which began in 1924 with *The Rasp* and ended in 1938 with *The Nursemaid Who Disappeared*, itself written after a five-year gap.

However, Gethryn deserves to reappear. He is, despite his noticeably stiff upper lip and other marks of the stereotype, a very human character. Witness in this book his plainly amorous, though decently unstressed, relations with his attractive younger wife, Lucia. In *The Rasp* we learnt that he had had a 'good war', rising from Private to his present rank, as well as a stint in Intelligence. 'Oh, I know I'm a filthy spy,' he said, characteristically showing himself as the English gentleman in the tradition of Sherlock Holmes for whom subterfuge is always somewhat to be despised, and at the same time as nicely self-deprecating.

We learnt, too, that Gethryn was rich and could afford to buy into a curious periodical, *The Owl*, which gave him, as here, a squad of useful journalist-spies to do his dirtier work when necessary. And we learnt that he 'read for the Bar; was called, but did not answer', i.e. that he was intelligent enough to have been your 'brilliant barrister' but was unencumbered with legal practice and so free to become the classical amateur detective.

Indeed, he is clearly one of the Great Detectives who came down to us from Holmes and before him Le Chevalier Auguste

Dupin of Edgar Allan Poe. He has that necessary combination of ratiocination (the word was invented by Poe for his hero), indicated by the potential devastating legal argument, and intuition, indicated however symbolically by his 'long sensitive fingers'. Like Holmes, too, there was a double strain in his make-up: he was the son of an English squire and of a Spanish actress and painter. And there is one other infallible sign of the Great Detective in him, to be seen in the pages ahead: his pipe. The pipe is the subtle message to us readers that the great man has gone into that trance-like state in which he will mysteriously combine the discoveries made by his ratiocinative mind with the sudden leaps of intuition, plunging deep into himself (and into us) to produce the entirely unexpected solution. Dr Watson, we remember, spoke eloquently of 'the unsavoury pipe' that was the companion of Holmes's 'deepest meditations' and, after Gethryn, Simenon's Maigret was a pipe-smoke wreather of formidable cloudiness.

Indeed, in the early pages here Chief Inspector Pike is made to exclaim of Gethryn: 'You *can't* be wrong.' The Great Detective, with a notable case or two as exceptions so as to prove the rule, must always in the end be right. And, of course, Gethryn, being Gethryn, also gently mocks at himself as Great Detective. 'We think, but we don't speak,' he says to Lucia. 'We say it's because we aren't *ready* for speech. But . . .' Yet in fact so it is. He is not ready. The pipe is not yet lit.

The mockery comes from a later strand in the history of detective fiction: the tradition springing from Trent in that classic of the genre, E. C. Bentley's *Trent's Last Case* of 1913, a book that set out to deflate the pure puzzle and succeeded in creating the detective with a human face. Or, since Sherlock Holmes is a real human being if ever there was, *Trent* saw the birth of the un-superman detective, the man with feelings to the fore. Thus Gethryn mocks himself; Gethryn genuinely worries for the victim of the plot whom he is striving to save. Gethryn, as we have noted, physically loves his wife.

So what about this adventure of his in particular? It was the first book to be chosen for the Crime Club, that ingenious reader-grabbing scheme hatched by Collins Publishers in 1930, which anyone could join free and be tempted with detective stories chosen by a panel headed by no less a figure than the Headmaster of Eton, Dr Alington. Partly because of this, partly because Arnold Bennett (the Melvyn Bragg of those days) hailed *The Noose* for its 'startling revelation', and partly because the *Evening Standard* bought the rights and heavily advertised it, the book quadrupled MacDonald's sales at a blow.

It deserved its popularity, and still deserves popularity despite the odd dated reference (the 'nine o'clock walk' is the one taken by those about to be hanged; Dean Inge was a notorious 'modern churchman', perhaps today's Bishop Jenkins; a tamasha is Anglo-Indian for a party). It deserves popularity, indeed, despite a comment recorded of it by its author in old age, that it was 'awfully old-fashioned'. I don't think it is. Witness, as a small instance, what Gethryn does to the unmasked murderer at their eventual midnight confrontation: it is an action that is the delight of every violence-merchant of the 1980s.

So, finally, who was the man who so knocked his own early success? He was born in 1899, son of the novelist and playwright Ronald MacDonald, grandson of the Scottish writer, George MacDonald, whose narrative poem 'Within and Without' Tennyson admired. Philip MacDonald, like Gethryn, fought in World War I, then wrote his crime stories and in the early 1930s was lured to Hollywood. There his screen credits included Daphne du Maurier's *Rebecca* but he wrote for himself little other than short stories, ending his days in the Motion Picture Retirement Home. Yet the short stories were of the highest quality. They brought him two Edgar Allan Poe Awards from the Mystery Writers of America and these words of praise from the critic Anthony Boucher:

'MacDonald is at once a craftsman of writing, whose prose, characterisation and evocation of mood (comic or terrible) might be envied by the most serious literary practitioners.'

They are words I am happy to echo of this book.

H. R. F. KEATING
April 1985

CONTENTS

CHARACTERS IN THE STORY

ANTHONY RUTHVEN GETHRYN
LUCIA GETHRYN, *his wife*
DANIEL BRONSON
SELMA BRONSON, *his wife*
EGBERT LUCAS, CB, *Assistant Commissioner Criminal Investigation Department*
CHIEF DETECTIVE INSPECTOR ARNOLD PIKE, *Criminal Investigation Department*
FRANCIS DYSON, *special reporter on the staff of 'The Owl'*
WALTER FLOOD, *special reporter on the staff of 'The Owl'*
ANNIE WILSON, *maid at The Horse & Hound Inn*
JAMES HARRIGAN, *tobacconist and father of—*
TOM HARRIGAN, *prominent witness at Bronson's trial*
ANDREW CONNICOTT DOLLBOYS, *farmer and prominent witness at Bronson's trial*
MRS DOLLBOYS, *his mother*
LT-COL. E. J. BROWNLOUGH (*retired*), DSO, *etc.*
IRENE CARTER-FAWCETT
CAPT A. D. FEATHERSTONE LAKE, MC, DFC
MISS MARGARET BROCKLEBANK
SIR RICHARD BROCKLEBANK, Bart, *her father*
LT-COL. GEOFFREY RAVENSCOURT, VC, *Chief Constable of County*
INSPECTOR RAWLINS, *of the County Police*
DETECTIVE-INSPECTOR FOX, *ditto*
POLICE CONSTABLE MURCH, *ditto*
MRS MURCH, *his wife*
WHITE, *manservant to Anthony Gethryn*

CHAPTER I

THURSDAY

I

THERE was a wet, dun-coloured blanket of fog over London. In the taxi which bore him from Victoria to his house in Knightsbridge, Anthony Ruthven Gethryn shivered. There is no contrast more unpleasant than the suns of Southern Spain and a damp, bleak, fog-ridden London at a November tea-time.

The taxi was slow; slower even, it seemed to Anthony, than the fog's opaqueness justified. He sat and shivered and used bad language beneath his breath. In his ulster pocket, the fingers of his right hand played rustlingly with the telegram which had brought about his return. Again he wondered—as he had been wondering for the past forty-eight hours—what lay behind this telegram.

The taxi jarred to a cracking standstill. The muffled driver left his seat, opened the door and thrust in a dim head.

'This the 'ouse, sir?' He jerked a thumb over his shoulder. 'Should be. But I can't see the numbers rightly. Not in *this*!' His sniff was eloquent of his feelings upon fogs.

Anthony peered; nodded, pulled his coat about him and clambered out, bent double. On the pavement he stretched his long body to its full height and stamped frozen feet. He passed coins.

'Thank'ee, sir,' said the driver. There was a warmth in his voice which told that even fog may bring its compensation.

Anthony turned in at his gate. Over his shoulder he said, 'I'll send out to help you with those bags.'

He went up the flagged path and the steps at the head of

them. Even as his hand began searching for the keys the door before him opened. He said:

'Hullo, White. Skip out and see to that luggage, will you? Where's your mistress?'

White did not answer; there was no need. White went out to the baggage.

In the hall Anthony's wife was in Anthony's arms. When she spoke, she said, a little breathlessly:

'But, my *dear*. You're twelve hours before I expected you. It's . . .'

Anthony smiled. 'Isn't it? But I'm like that.' He took her by the elbow and turned her towards the door through which, a moment ago, she had come.

With his first step, she halted. She said, dropping her voice:

'Not in there, dear. Not yet.' She led the way down the hall and into the drawing-room.

His back to a fire which blazed and crackled and deliciously burned his spine, he put a hand to a pocket and brought out the telegram and waved it.

'And now,' he said, 'p'r'aps you'll explain, ma'am.'

Lucia dropped into a chair. She crossed her legs, left over right, and with the bronze-coloured shoe of the left foot beat a little devil's tattoo in the air.

At the small foot her husband looked down. A smile twisted his mouth. He said:

'And *that* means you're mistrusting your judgment.'

Lucia sat up. 'I'm not!' she said indignantly. 'I *had* to bring you back. But . . . but . . .'

'But you don't know where to start.' Anthony smoothed the flimsy paper of the telegram out between his fingers. 'And I shouldn't think so. Not only d'you jerk me back from a land fit to be lived in, but instead of yourself you send me this.' He crackled the telegram. 'Cancel your passage properly?' He crossed to her chair and perched his length upon its arm.

She looked up at him. Her eyes were very soft. She said:

'You *are* a darling, you know . . . Now let me tell you. It's . . .'

'In the library,' said Anthony. 'Yes? What is it?'

Lucia showed the tip of a red tongue. 'All right, Zancig. It's a woman.' She turned suddenly in her chair. Both slender hands came up from her lap and rested upon his knee. Her tone changed. All lightness went from it. It grew deeper than its usual lovely deepness. She said:

'It's a woman. She wants help. She wants help more than any woman's ever wanted help before. And there's just *one* person who *can* help her.' The white fingers tightened on her husband's knee. 'And that's you, Anthony.'

A small silence fell. Anthony's green eyes looked down into the velvet darkness of his wife's. He said at last:

'It's me, is it. Well, if you say so . . . Where do we start?'

The fingers squeezed gratefully. She said:

'Have you read any papers in Spain? English ones, I mean.'

'The only time I ever read English papers,' said Anthony, 'is when I'm not in England. I have.'

'And did you see anything about the Bronson case?'

Anthony frowned. 'Bronson? Bronson? . . . Bron . . . Oh, yes. Dave Bronson, you mean. The ex-pug who did in a gamekeeper or something. Some months ago. No, I didn't see anything. Was there?'

Lucia's dark head was nodded. 'There was. Not awfully prominent, it wasn't. What it was was the report of Bronson's appeal. Which was what d'you call it—disallowed, anyhow.'

'Rejected,' said Anthony. 'And in *there*'—he nodded in the direction of the library—'is, I gather, either Mother or Mrs Bronson or both.'

'It's the wife,' Lucia said. Her voice was very low again, and with its management she seemed to find difficulty. Anthony, looking down, saw that there glittered in each eye a shining tear.

He put an arm about her shoulders and held her. But he said:

'Anything else to report?'

There was a little movement against his shoulder as once more the head nodded. After a pause, she spoke again. She said:

'Yes. There's been a petition for a reprieve. Signed by thousands of people. I forget how many; but thousands. And *that's* no good. It's been refused by the Home Secretary. And . . . and . . . he'll be hanged in five days. Five *days. Five* days! Unless . . .'

On the last word, her voice broke. Anthony felt that real weeping and much was on the way. Of purpose he grew gently brutal. He said:

'Unless someone does a miracle, you mean?'

'You,' said Lucia, struggling to keep back tears.

'Not my line,' said Anthony, watching her covertly.

'The most wonderful thing,' Lucia quoted, 'about miracles is that they sometimes happen . . . You've got to *make* one happen.' Her voice was under control again.

Anthony shrugged. 'Have I now? You know, a bodkin's far likelier to let a dromedary slip through it than a Home Secretary is to change his mind. And is it right to take a quick death from a man and give him a living one? That's what a twenty-year stretch must be, you know. Again, beginning to remember a little about the case, I'm not so sure one ought to want to get Bronson off. It was a messy, treacherous behind-your-back sort of job, wasn't it? I . . .'

He broke off suddenly. His eyes widened in astonishment. His wife had sprung to her feet. She was facing him now, her great eyes blazing with a light which seemed blent of anger and laughter and anxiety.

'You fool, darling!' she said. 'You darling fool!'

Anthony passed a hand across his forehead. 'Quite,' he said. 'Quite. Most probably. But exactly why?'

She almost stamped. 'Because,' she said, 'you sit there—there you sit—you sit there and think and listen *and* talk, all the time I'm telling you something; and you haven't even *begun* to understand. Not *begun* to . . .'

'If I haven't,' Anthony said, 'I certainly don't.'

'You haven't understood the *main* point. The only point. The point that's the tragedy; the point that's turning that woman's life not into ordinary, everyday horror and pain but into something so much worse that there aren't any words for it. I wonder she isn't mad. *I* should be . . .'

Anthony clasped head with hands. He rocked himself to and fro. He moaned:

'Point, woman, point. If you don't get to it soon I . . .'

His wife came close to him. She said:

'The point is that Bronson did *not* kill Blackatter. *Now!*'

Anthony sat upright with a jerk. He stared for a moment. He said:

'Didn't he, though? Who says? Not the Law, or anyone with weight, or he wouldn't be where he is.'

Lucia came closer still. She set her hands upon his shoulders. She said—and again her voice was different:

'Don't laugh. There *was* only one person who said so. She's in *there*, waiting for you. Two people say so now, and I'm the second. Do something for me, dear. Be the third if you can . . . Will you come now?'

Anthony, silent, rose. Together, they walked across the long room to the door.

II

The library, a square, book-lined room whose height was emphasised by the crowded shelves which covered its walls from ceiling to floor, was lit only by a shaded lamp upon the central writing-table and the red, flickering luminosity of the log-fire.

Anthony, Lucia at his side, paused just within the door. The change from brightness to this illuminated dark took for a moment his eyes by storm. He frowned his sight into submission, and just as clarity of vision came, there came too, to his ears, Lucia's voice. It said:

'My husband is here, Mrs Bronson. Quicker than I thought he could possibly be . . . Anthony, this is Mrs Bronson . . . I think I'll leave you together . . .'

There was a little rustle beside Anthony, and the ghost of a scented breeze. And then the click-clock of the heavy door's closing.

Anthony went forward. To meet him there came, rising from a low chair by the crimson fireside, a tall shape. A hand came out. A long hand and strong, which clasped his with a strength which would have been surprising in many men, but which itself, when felt, was in no way like a man's; and this despite the muscularity of the grip and the roughness—the slight but undoubted roughness—of the skin.

He found himself shaking hands with a woman whose eyes were nearer to being upon a true level with his own than any feminine eyes which in the passage of his adult lifetime he could remember. Even in this half-darkness those eyes impressed upon him not only their intrinsic beauty but an impression of strength and . . . and . . . in his own mind he groped for the word . . . of oddity; of queerness. But of an oddity and a queerness which had nothing to do with irrationality. Rather a *difference* like the difference between the eyes of a woman and a Maeve. He said, suddenly:

'D'you mind, Mrs Bronson, if we have more light?' He turned at the inclination of her head and walked back to the door and pressed one of the switches beside it.

The big bowl-shade hung from the ceiling's centre sprang into soft radiance. The room expanded, gained shape; lost mysterious corners and imagination-giving sudden blanknesses; took on a mellow matter-of-factness.

Almost immediately beneath the light the woman stood. Anthony came back towards her. His idle-seeming eyes were busy. He saw her now.

His first feeling was of checked breathing. He was always to remember that. Only two other women in his life—and Lucia was one—had ever done this to him, and from far different causes. As he drew close to this woman now, his mind searched for a word to fit her. 'Magnificent' came first—and remained to oust the others which came crowding. He never found a better, and yet that never satisfied him.

She was very tall, but her height, for her, was neither over-powering nor grotesque. She was built upon the grand scale, but the grandeur was simple and restrained. There was about her stillness some great urgency; it was as if, not needing voice, the whole woman spoke to him; cried out—not weakly but from one strength to another strength—for aid.

She was hatless, and now, as without speaking he set her chair for her and she sank back into it again, he saw that her hair was of that pale yet vital burnished gold which is purely Scandinavian. He said, wishing to hear her speak:

'It's useless to offer sympathy, Mrs Bronson. Whether or not I can offer anything else remains to be seen.' He smiled at her; a friendly smile which lightened, almost astonishingly, his dark, lean, rather sardonic face. 'It's you to move,' he said.

She replied at once. Her voice was low, and perfectly under control. Yet there was about it a kind of hard, metallic clarity which he would have wagered was not there when she was free from strain. She said:

'My husband is in prison. He has been tried for murder. He has been convicted. He has—what do you call it?—appealed, and this appeal has been rejected. People—ten thousand people—have signed their names on a Petition. This Petition has been rejected by the Authorities. Today is Thursday. On the day after next Monday'—she drew in her breath with a little gasping hiss, immediately controlled—'he will be hanged . . . unless something is done. They tell me there is nothing to be done.' She broke off here, abruptly. The silence seemed to hold a lingering echo of that controlled, vibrant voice, with its armour of hardness and its definite but unplaceable foreignness.

Anthony became astonished at himself and his own emotions; for he found himself speaking merely for the sake of breaking silence. He said:

'They *seem* to be right. If, of course, we could find any way of casting doubt . . .'

He ceased speech. With a single, soundless movement, the woman had risen. He found her standing over him as he lay back in the deep, leather chair. He rose himself and stood to face her. On a level, her eyes of blue fire blazed into his. He saw that, motionless as she seemed, the whole of her was shaking. She said, in a voice so low that barely did it carry to his ears, yet so pregnant with force that every word buried itself like a soft-nosed bullet in his brain:

'Colonel Gethryn, there is only one thing that is to be done. Dan did *not* kill Blackatter. If there can be found, before . . . before . . . before the morning after next Monday morning, the man who *did* kill, then . . .' Her voice ceased; a gesture finished her speech.

Anthony, as straight as she and as rigid, said softly:

'You say your husband did not kill the man Blackatter. You *know*?'

'I know,' said the woman. There seemed no emphasis on the words. There was no raising of that low, hard voice. But Anthony nodded. He said:

'I see. And you have no thought as to who the killer really was?'

'None,' said the woman.

'It was not,' said Anthony, 'yourself?'

'No,' replied the woman.

The tension, instead of tightening, eased at that. For a moment there flickered across that mouth of hers which, thought Anthony, when not set to still its trembling, must be a beautiful mouth, the wan ghost of a smile.

Anthony smiled too. A grave smile, but a smile. He said:
'Sit down again, won't you?'

She sat. He remained standing. He stood, hands thrust deep into his pockets, looking into the redness of the fire beyond it. In his mind logic was receiving its death blow from instinct.

The woman spoke. She said:

'You have believed me, that I know Dan did not.'

It was a statement, this, more than a question. But Anthony said:

'I believed you. And I shan't change.' A sudden smile twisted the corners of his mouth. He became more like himself. 'But why,' he said, 'I believe, I couldn't tell you. Don't know myself . . .'

'It is the strength of my believing,' said the woman.

'And,' said Anthony to himself, 'of yourself . . .'

III

So Anthony once more found himself out in the yellow fog, jolting through it in a crawling taxi. Experience told him that, in fogs, the slowest cab is quicker than one's own car. Up to Hyde Park Corner crawled the lurching little motor, and into St James's Park and across it, and up Bridge Street and round the corner into Scotland Yard.

Up many flights of stone stairs climbed Anthony and knocked upon a door and, getting no answer, walked through this and across a small room to another door. At this he tapped. A murmur ceased; a voice bade him enter. He pushed his head round the door's edge and looked.

'Busy?' he said. 'I can wait.'

'Good Lord!' said Mr Egbert Lucas. 'Look who's here! Come in, man, come in!'

Anthony entered. 'Hullo,' he said to all. 'Lucas, how are you? And you, Pike?'

'Worn,' Lucas said. 'Worn.' His smile was cheerful, even affectionate; his grooming as careful as ever.

The lantern-shaped face of Chief Detective-Inspector Arnold Pike creased with his wide smile. He said:

'*I'm* very well, sir. How are *you*, sir?'

'Full of fog,' said Anthony, lighting a cigarette. 'I'd forgotten what fogs tasted like. I could have borne not to 've remembered. I'm also in a bad temper—so I want to worry you all. I . . .'

Lucas exhibited alarm. He looked at Pike; at his superior Pike looked back, expressionless. Lucas said:

'Gethryn; if you as much as mention the name of Smethwick to me, I'll . . .'

Anthony grinned. 'Don't know him,' he said. 'Don't want to. What I do want is this.' He told them what he wanted.

Pike pursed his lips as if at any moment he might so far forget himself in an Assistant Commissioner's room as to whistle. Lucas sat back in his chair and scratched his head.

'All the stuff we've got,' he said slowly, quoting Anthony's words, 'about the Bronson case . . . Sure you mean *Bronson*?'

Anthony looked at him.

'I see,' said Lucas. 'You *do* mean Bronson. Well, well. It was all done by the County Police, but we should have copies of their stuff.' He looked at Pike.

'We have, sir,' Pike said. He seemed as if he were about to speak further, but suddenly closed his mouth—so tightly that his lips disappeared.

Lucas was looking at him. Lucas said:

'Very discreet, Pike, I'm sure. Gethryn, he wants to ask questions but won't. I will, though. What *is* all this?'

Anthony put back his head and blew a cloud of smoke ceilingwards. 'Only,' he said, 'that Bronson didn't kill Blackatter.'

The two policemen looked at him. In silence for a moment. Then the silence was broken; for, this time, Pike did whistle;

a long low note, forced out of him by astonishment. Lucas, still staring at Anthony, twice opened his mouth to speak, twice changed his mind, and at last said:

'Good *God*!'

'You think,' said Anthony, 'that I'm mad. And so does Pike. Before we go any further, I may as well tell you, quite dispassionately, that you're probably right.'

'But *what* . . .' began Lucas.

'You've been away, haven't you, sir?' Pike spoke with the eagerness of a man who believes that inspiration has shown him, in a flash, the true solution of a problem.

Anthony brought his eyes back from the ceiling at this. He looked first at Lucas, still scratching his head; then at Pike, still eager. He laughed.

'Sorry,' he said. 'But you're both funny. Yes, Pike, I have been away. But I know Bronson's position all right.'

Lucas snorted. 'Position. Hardly a position, is it? I mean, he's breathing and eating, and all that; but no man so near the gallows can be called *alive*.'

'That,' said Anthony, 'is the trouble. What's the one thing that could save him from the nine o'clock walk?'

'Nothing,' said Lucas. 'Man's dead to all intents and purposes. And quite right, too. Nasty, messy, treacherous job that was. And not a shadow of doubt about it. Eh, Pike?'

But Pike pursed his lips, and a worried frown drew his eyes together. They looked, these eyes, at Anthony.

Lucas exploded. 'Good Lord, man! Just because Colonel Gethryn comes in here trying to pull our legs . . .'

'I wasn't,' Anthony interrupted. 'That's too easy, Lucas. I was serious. See it wet and dry.'

Lucas was obstinate. 'My dear man, you can't be. Not *you*, of all people. There never was a clearer case. Never. Why, Bronson left his card all over the place! It took only the *County* Police twenty-four hours to get him inside. It's all too . . .' He broke off suddenly, and sat up with a jerk, gazing at Anthony with sudden intentness. 'Unless,' he said slowly, 'unless . . . you've hit on something that never . . .'

Again Anthony interrupted. 'I haven't. But I want to. I want to badly. Look here, let's get this straight. I'll tell you how mad I am, and then you needn't worry your heads with me any more. I've been away. Instead of my wife joining me, she sent me a cable which told me to come back. So I came back. I found, this afternoon, that with my wife was Bronson's wife. Foolishly enough, my wife had allowed the woman to persuade her of Bronson's innocence. I didn't scoff aloud, being an intelligent husband, but I scoffed all right. I then had half an hour with Mrs Bronson. And now I'm not scoffing any more. I'm having half an hour with you, being convinced myself—'

He got up and crossed to Lucas's table and dropped his cigarette stub into Lucas's ashtray. 'And that,' he said, 'is the true and rightful history of my madness. Very sad, you know. Decline of a great intelligence. But there it is. Now d'you think, peaceably to rid yourself of the raving guest, you could let me have that dossier?'

There was a silence. Lucas looked at Anthony; Pike looked at Anthony; Anthony looked at the steel-engraving over Lucas's head. Lucas was the first to speak. He said:

'Tell me this, Gethryn. What was it Mrs Bronson told you that gave you this conviction?'

'Easy,' said Anthony. 'She told me, with her voice, that she *knew* Bronson hadn't done it. She told me, with herself, that if she *believed* this, this was so.'

Lucas lay back in his chair. He made a little helpless gesture with his hands. 'May Jupiter,' he said, 'aid me! I need aid.'

Pike said nothing. He looked still at Anthony, and his right hand rubbed at his smooth, almost rectangular jaw.

Lucas tried again. He said, his tone pleading:

'What *is* this, Gethryn? Damn it, if it was anyone but *you* I'd just laugh or send for a doctor. But . . . but . . .' Again he made that helpless gesture.

Anthony took his eyes from the picture. He smiled suddenly and said:

'I'm worrying you. And it's a shame. But you mustn't be worried. I've told you everything. Nothing up my sleeve nor concealed beneath the 'anging covers.' He got to his feet with a movement, for him, curiously jerky. He began to pace up and down between window and door. 'The best thing for you people,' he said, 'is to give me the papers I want and forget all about me until you hear of my certification . . . Why worry your heads?'

At Pike Lucas glanced, shrugging his shoulders. Pike said, looking at Anthony:

'Speaking for myself, sir . . . and possibly for Mr Lucas'— Lucas nodded with a sort of wearied agreement—'we're worrying our heads because it's *you*, sir. As Mr Lucas said just now, if anybody else . . .' He shrugged, and his shoulders spoke his contempt. 'But with you, sir, it's different. We've got into a kind of way up here, as you might say, of thinking you *can't* be wrong. Not even if you were to *try* . . .'

Lucas sat up. 'Good, Pike! That *is* it. Since the Hoode show and then the Lines-Bower business, you've got us on velvet. You're a sort of ju-ju.' He almost groaned, shifting uneasily in his chair. 'I wouldn't mind so much if you'd *anything* to base this preposterous belief of yours on. You see, if you had, we *might* come in with you. Give you an official blessing, anyhow; but as it is we can't—how could we? We're Bobbies here, not mediums! And what's giving me a pain in the tummy's the truly dreadful thought: suppose, by some appalling coincidence, A. R. Gethryn was right! It'd come out, you know, that the Police had done nothing. *You* wouldn't say so, but it'd come out. And it wouldn't be a bit of use telling 'em you just had a hunch and that we're not here to back hunches . . .' His voice trailed off, a little querulously, into silence. Perhaps he had realised that he was complaining without exactly knowing what his complaint was.

Anthony ceased his pacing. He halted in front of the table, so that he directly faced Lucas, and at Lucas he stared, smiling.

'The trouble with you,' he said, 'is that you're too much of a man to be The Perfect Bureaucrat and too nearly The Perfect Bureaucrat to be a man. You want, you know, jam on both sides of the pancake. You want to be out of this if I *am* mad, and in it if my apparent madness *should* turn out to a sort of super-sanity.' His smiled robbed his words of any but the mildest sting.

Lucas glared for a moment, then suddenly laughed. 'You're an irritating devil!' he said ruefully . . . 'Well, I'll let you have the Bronson file. But more I can't do.'

'Nobody,' Anthony murmured, 'asked you, sir, she said.'

Lucas looked at Pike. 'Could the file be got at now?'

Pike nodded and was gone. Anthony and Lucas smoked and chatted. But the pleasant small-talk of Lucas was a trifle wandering; and the eye of Lucas, though obviously against its owner's will, was not free from a worried, speculative look. Anthony, noticing this look, interrupted suddenly his own discourse upon the less oily type of Spanish cookery. He said:

'You don't trust me, you know. And it occurs to me that there is one small fact I've not mentioned . . .'

'Ah!' Lucas sat up at once. His fingers drummed upon his blotting-pad. 'Yes? Yes?'

'Just,' said Anthony, 'that it wasn't the idea of her Dan's killing a man that Mrs Bronson scouted. It was that her Dan should kill a man that way—by stealth and treachery, from behind—*that* was what made her *know* this was no work of Dan's.'

'Oh!' Lucas's tone was flat again. Once more he sank back into his chair. 'Oh—ah. Yes. Quite. What almost any hitherto happily married wife 'd say, isn't it?'

Anthony replied with another question. 'Ever met Mrs Bronson? Ever seen her even?'

Lucas nodded, with a little less apathy in his manner. 'Yes. She's been here. Magnificent creature . . .' His tone changed.

'But they all come here, you know. Poor devils. What they hope from it, God knows!'

'If,' said Anthony, 'you've met the woman and talked with the woman and yet see no significance in what I've just told you she said, there's nothing more for me to say.'

Lucas once more sat upright. His open hand came down with a slap on the table-top. 'Look here, Gethryn,' he began; then ceased abruptly as a knock came upon the door and, hard upon the knock's heels, Pike.

Under his left arm Pike bore a bulky foolscap envelope from the open end of which protruded the edges of an orange-hued folder. He came to Anthony and presented this burden. He smiled as he handed it over, but his glittering brown eyes were sharp with a curiosity at once avid and restrained. He said:

'That's the lot, sir.' And turned to Lucas as if awaiting orders.

Lucas lifted his eyes. 'Thanks,' he said. He glanced at the small clock upon his desk. 'Better be getting off, hadn't you? Don't want to miss that train. If you do, something might turn up to stop you again.' He said to Anthony: 'Pike's got leave. And about time, too. Hasn't had a holiday for two years. Pike, buzz off!'

'Yes, sir,' said Pike. But he stood a moment after the words had left his mouth. He looked down—a trick he had when thinking deeply—at the very polished toe-caps of his very shiny boots; but after a moment, with a visible jerk, pulled himself away from whatever thought had held him. He said:

'Very good, sir. Thank you. I'll say goodbye, sir.' He turned to Anthony. 'And goodbye to you, sir . . . And . . . and . . . good luck.' The door closed, softly but crisply, behind him.

Lucas looked at it. He laughed a laugh which was half snort. 'Good luck indeed!' he said. 'Pike's got you and your marvels on the brain, Gethryn. Since the Lines-Bower show he's damn near deified you.'

Anthony stood up, the bulky envelope held firm beneath one arm. He said:

'Pike's too good a man to do any deifying . . . So long, Lucas, and thank you.' He tapped the envelope. 'These'll be safe. And don't you worry. If I were you I should think I was mad, too. I do now.'

The door closed behind him. Lucas was left alone. He sat in his chair and stared at nothing and chewed an unlighted cigarette until the sting of wet, stringy tobacco on his tongue brought him to himself.

IV

The dark, shapely head of Lucia Gethryn looked round the edge of his study door at her husband. He sat astraddle upon a small chair and gazed down over its back and his folded arms at the carpet.

Lucia followed her head. 'I thought,' she said, going to him and laying a hand upon his arm, 'that you weren't *ever* going to stop using the telephone. And your coffee got cold. And you didn't have any port. I've told White to bring . . .'

'What *I* want to know,' said Anthony, 'is how in the name of the Seven-fingered Septuagesima an ex-bruiser got a woman like *that* woman . . .'

Lucia crossed to the writing table and upon it perched herself. She said:

'I knew that would make you wonder. It did me. There's a good story behind it, I should think. She adores him, you know . . .'

Anthony raised his head. 'Make it "loves". It means more, and it's what she does . . . Know her beginnings?'

The dark head nodded. 'Just a little. She's told me one or two things. She's a Dane. Her father was Captain of a sailing-ship. She was at sea with him from when she was a baby until he died. After his death she couldn't get to sea any more. She said that at one time she thought she'd go mad with being on land. And then she met Dan. And she hasn't worried about the sea any more.'

'Curioser,' said Anthony, 'and curioser. One should meet Dan, I feel.'

'Probably,' said Lucia softly, 'Dan isn't Dan except to her.'

Anthony raised his chin from his hands. He lifted his head again and looked at his wife. He said:

'Sentimental. But very probably true . . . I'll tell you what D. Bronson, ex-pug, is though. I have, as you know, been telephoning. The receiver is still hot upon my ear. I have telephoned to old Lansmoor and to Betty Partridge and to two old friends of mine called Spiky Skinner and Flatty Wilson. And also to Myerbeer. *And* to Dick Dybar . . .'

'Please!' Lucia said. 'Stop the roll-call. Except for Lord Lansmoor, I don't know even the names . . . And who's Betty Partridge?'

'Betty,' said Anthony, 'is no bird, except for the name. Betty was once the best heavy-weight in this country. But he would try to train on beer. He's now the hall-porter at the Senior Imperial. Spiky Skinner and Flatty Wilson are the best seconds in the country; they also happened to be in the first platoon I ever had. Myerbeer's the man who runs the Olympic Sporting Club and Dybar's that friend of Archie's who's lost more money promoting fights than his father made printing Bibles. Point of contact with A. R. Gethryn—Daniel Bronson. I knew they'd all know a lot *about* Bronson; but they were even more obliging—they all *knew* him. Even Dybar.'

'But what . . .' began Lucia; then, 'sorry, darling.'

'Granted,' said Anthony, 'no sooner than asked. I was checking the opinion of Mrs Bronson. You can say it didn't need checking, and probably you'd be right. But check it I did. No dissentients.' He put his chin again upon his folded arms.

Lucia looked down at the head of her husband. She waited, but he did not speak. She leaned forward then and between finger and thumb took as much of his hair as was convenient. She pulled, and the silence was sharply broken.

'That,' she said, 'is for being a Master Mind. Explain. What were there no dissentients about; exactly?'

Anthony rubbed at his scalp. 'What else, woman, than the character of D. Bronson in relation to the killing of Blackatter? That woman said to me this afternoon: 'Dan might kill, but he wouldn't kill like *that*!' Blackatter was shot, you know, at close range, through the back of the head. The telephone has just said to me, in six voices and six different ways, that it seems incredible, not only that D. Bronson should kill like that, but that D. Bronson should kill at all.'

'Oh!' said Lucia. 'But she would be right, you know. I mean, if she says he "might kill", he might.'

'Very true,' said Anthony, 'but nothing to do with the case. Several tra-las. What we *have* got—put in its lowest terms of value—is confirmation of the great unlikelihood of Bronson's killing a man behind his back . . .' He fell silent.

There came a knock at the door, and after it White bearing a tray upon which were a coffee-cup, two wine-glasses, and a decanter. Lucia moved from the writing-table. But Anthony sat motionless, his head upon his crossed arms, his half-closed eyes looking down, over the chair-back, at the carpet.

White went. To Anthony his wife brought coffee. He did not move until she touched his shoulder. Then, absently, he straightened his body, took the cup and drained it and, almost in one movement, gave it back to her. Back went his arms along the chair-rail, and down again upon those arms went his head.

Lucia poured port. One glass she picked up and held out towards her husband. His eyes cannot have been really closed, for his hand came up and his fingers closed about the glass's stem and took it from her.

He drank. With a sudden movement he straightened his body and, reaching out a long arm, set down the half-empty glass, with a little smack upon the writing-table's edge. He said, with an explosiveness most foreign to him:

'It's idiocy! It's damned, fat-headed, raving foolishness! It's worse than that, it's waste of time! *And* it's cruel to that woman!' He got to his feet and began to walk up and down the long room. With anxious, wide eyes Lucia watched him. She waited for him to speak again, but he paced in fiery silence. She said at last:

'What . . . what . . . d'you mean that . . .'

He interrupted her. He halted to face her. He thrust his hands deep into his pockets. He said:

'I mean that it's hopeless. I mean that I ought to be shot for not having said so from the beginning and gone on saying so. Read *that!*' He flung out an arm, pointing. Lucia's eyes followed the finger; brought their gaze to rest upon a bulging, rusty-orange-coloured folder which lay upon the writing-table.

'In that,' said Anthony, 'is the case against Bronson. It's a cast-iron case. And Bronson's been tried; and Bronson's appealed; and Bronson's had a very strong petition for him put up. And he was found guilty, and his appeal didn't work; and his petition's been turned down. And he's going to be hanged in a hundred or so hours from now . . .'

Lucia stood now, close to him, facing him, her lovely head thrown back a little so that her eyes could meet his. She put up a hand to her throat. She said, in a low voice which gave evidence of her difficulty in producing it:

'You mean . . . you mean to say, after *all* you've said . . . you mean to say that you . . . Oh, Anthony!'

He looked down at her. His eyes softened. He said:

'I mean that not even Gabriel could get the man off. See: there's one way, and one way only, to get that man off. And that's to produce, within four days from this minute, utterly conclusive proof that not he, but some definite other person, killed Blackatter. Understand? Look what you're asking, you women! You're asking that now, months after the thing was done, when even witnesses' memories are getting hazy and any scent there might've been at the time's vanished long ago— you're asking that now, within less than a week, a man's to dig up a murderer who in the first place covered himself so well that no one got even a hint of his existence. It's Merlin you want, Unlimited . . .'

He broke off. For Lucia was smiling at him; smiling that particular one of her smiles which always had, and always would, make him catch his breath a little at its beauty. Smiling, she was! Yet, a moment ago, when she had jumped up to face him, she had been tense and white and her eyes had been dark pools of anxiety. She said softly:

'All right, dear. All right. I'm sorry. I didn't understand. D'you know, I thought—just for a minute—I thought you were going to say that you wouldn't even try. I *am* a fool sometimes.'

Anthony looked at her. 'Sure you weren't right the first time? Because, you know, you were.'

She shook her head, with a slow, decisive mockery. 'Don't tell *me*!' she said. 'You went off the deep end because you *knew* you were going to try but you were frightened—and *are* frightened—horribly frightened, that you mayn't succeed. And *that's* right, whatever you say! Isn't it?'

Anthony kissed her. 'If there's anything,' he said, 'more annoying than a woman who knows she's right, it's a woman who is.' He reached out and plucked from the table the orange-coloured dossier. 'Here, you take this and go to bed and read it. I want to think.'

Lucia took the folder gingerly. 'But think about *what*, dear? I mean'—her brow puckered—'where are you to *start* thinking?'

'That,' said Anthony, 'is what I've got to think about.'

v

The little cell was suddenly full. The Warden looked down at the man who sat upon the edge of the small and narrow bed. The two warders were at attention; the man who had come with the Warden hovered loosely in the background. The Warden said:

'It's late, Bronson. But I'd given you my word I'd let you know, so soon as I had official notice, about the Petition. I'm sorry, Bronson; the Home Secretary has notified the Petitioners that he cannot make any recommendation to the King.'

The Warden's voice was soft, and deep and rounded. It seemed to roll murmurously round this room which was a box of stone.

The man who sat upon the bed's edge looked up. He nodded apathetically. His great shoulders were drooped, and his head seemed sunken between them. He said:

'Thank you, sir.' His voice was low, lower even than the Warden's, but it was rough. There seemed to be harsh, uneven edges to it.

The Warden looked down at the speaker. He seemed about to say something; checked himself; turned on his heel. The warders stiffened. The man in the background opened the cell door. Within its frame the Warden turned. He said:

'Is there anything I can do for you, Bronson?'

The man on the bed did not look up. But his head, down between those great shoulders, moved slowly from side to side.

'No,' he said.

'Good night, Bronson,' said the Warden.

From the prisoner's down-bent head came the beginnings of an answering 'Good night'; but only the beginnings. It was as if, halfway through the familiar words, he realised, possibly for the first time in his life, their meaning.

'Good . . .' he began. 'Ha!'

The one deep note of the little laugh seemed to break itself against the close walls so that discordant pieces of it went on jingling inside the listeners' heads long after the sound had died.

CHAPTER II

I

A BREEZE had risen in the night and the fog was no more. Pale-gold, seven-o'clock-in-the-morning November sunshine lighted a white-rimed London. In Stukeley Gardens the great square houses had roofs like pantomime palaces, and the shrubs and trees were fantastic white jewels enclosed not by sullen railings but a hedge of bravely glittering spears.

At three minutes to seven o'clock Anthony's new car—an open, very low, very black and very wolfish car—purred away from Number 39. Anthony drove. By his side was Lucia, a fur bundle from which peered, every now and then, a delightful nose which the frosty air whipped to a most unusual pinkness. At the back, an ulster and a cap making of him a barely animate-seeming bundle, was White. He cowered back into his seat, and beneath the pulled-down peak of his cap his eyes were closed. The Guvner's driving—as frequently White said to his cronies—was OT.

The big car devoured the almost empty London streets; tossed them throbbingly, contemptuously behind it. London began to fade; streets straggled; ceased, began again patchily; tailed off into fields. They tore up over Fordley Common, swung right by the new bridge over the Bale and came out on to the smooth dun-grey riband of the arterial road.

'Ah!' said Anthony; and his right foot went down.

'Oh!' muttered White. He pressed his body still further back into its corner.

Lucia was silent; from her nest of fur her eyes stared out

at the speedometer-needle. They opened wide as they stared; then wider. They shifted at last from that needle and its story and cast one oblique glance at the grass-edging of the road. And then, like White's, they closed.

And so they came at last, having turned off the arterial road at New Fordwich, first to the town of Greyne and then to the village of Farrow and The Horse and Hound Inn.

Before the porch of The Horse and Hound Anthony brought the black car to a smooth and silent standstill. He looked at his dashboard clock and was satisfied; afterwards, Lucia was heard to refer to the time taken for the journey as 'sinful'; White's only comment, at this time or any other, was a shake of the head and a rigid compression of the lips.

Stiffly, they got to ground. Up the steps of the porch Lucia ran and beat upon the door's knocker. White began to unload luggage. Anthony looked at The Horse and Hound and was gratified. It is one of the few real Inns left to the land of Inns. It is a building of real half-timbering and white plaster, and leaded windows most pleasing to the eye. And beyond its western end is a stable-yard where still horses are stabled. And there is a garden. And beneath the very proper sign showing a Horse only a little less gaudy and unbelievable than its companion the Hound, is, among others, the word Bait.

Anthony, blowing upon stiff hands from which he had peeled the gloves, went up the porch-steps in the wake of his wife. The door stood open and Lucia was inside it. Upon the threshold he paused for an instant while he read, over the lintel, the words 'FREE HOUSE—D. BRONSON—LICENSED TO SELL BEER, WINES, SPIRITS AND TOBACCO'.

He stepped across the threshold and stood in a low, black-beamed, white-walled, sweet-smelling hall-place. Upon each side were doors, four upon the right and three upon the left. Before the first upon the right, which stood open, was Lucia. She was talking with someone within the room. Anthony went forward. He stood behind his wife and over her fur-clad shoulder saw Daniel Bronson's wife. He bowed; he found himself, most surprisingly, without words. In answer the fair head was bowed. She stood in full flood of the hard winter sunlight which streamed through a window behind her and to her right. He saw her as paler than he had thought, but perhaps that was fatigue. Yet there was nothing sickly about this whiteness of her; rather was there a vivid, vital sort of ... of ... he groped in his mind for a word and found *transparency*. And he saw her as even taller than the picture his mind had kept—but perhaps this was a matter of clothes, for today her garb was white and black—black from well-shod feet to admirable waist, white from waist to chin, beneath which was a bow of silken black which held together, gracefully and gratefully, the collar of silken white.

She said to him:

'You are good. I have said to your wife how welcome you are. They gave me this morning your telegram which you telephoned. I have said to your wife that there is, now ready, breakfast for you. After, if you wish me, I could be at your service ... perhaps I mean to answer your questions. Or to tell things which you might wish to know.' She came closer, up to the doorway upon whose other side Anthony and Lucia stood. She pressed a bell upon the wall and there came within half-a-minute a neat maid. To this girl she said:

'Show Colonel and Mrs Gethryn their room, Annie.' And to Anthony: 'You will not forget. If you wish me, at any time, I am here.'

Upstairs went Anthony and Lucia then, following the silk-clad and very shapely legs of the girl Annie, who presently opened a door without which their bags already lay and stood aside to let them enter. A most pleasing room, though of no great size. Its windows looked out over the garden and beyond the garden to a country wide and rolling where wintry browns were broken by the thin tracery of hedges, the black and red and silver of trees and the steely glitter of the river which twisted sharply down the Kare valley.

The maid hovered in the doorway. She murmured:

'If there's anything, ma'am . . .'

Lucia turned from the window and that view. 'Nothing, I think, thank you.' She looked at her husband.

Anthony shook his head. 'Nothing for me.' He smiled down at the girl. The girl smiled back; an odd smile, compound of shy and willing servitude, challenge to the male, and . . . something else. Anthony's mind noted that smile, tucking it away in the back of his brain. He said, as she reached the door:

'Many other people staying here?'

The girl turned. She was not smiling now. 'Oh, no, sir!' she said. 'There's . . . they . . . sometimes we're full this time o' year, sir, for the hunting . . . but *now*, sir, they . . .' She stammered, grew red in the cheek, lost her tangled threads and ended with: 'No, sir. Only one other gentleman. He came last night, sir, late. Don't know how long for, sir, I'm sure. He seems a very quiet gentleman, sir.'

'Thanks.' Anthony nodded to her very evident desire for exit. The word was barely out of his mouth when the door closed and Annie was no longer with them.

'That,' said Lucia, 'is a *very* pretty child.'

'It is.' Anthony remained looking at the closed door, as if his eyes were still watching the small figure in its charming uniform. After a moment he shrugged, frowned and turned away. 'What about this breakfast? Going to wash?'

They washed. They went downstairs and into the door marked Coffee Room. The clock upon the mantel showed the time to be nine-forty-five. In the far corner of the long, low room there sat, behind the *Morning Post,* a man. Otherwise the room was empty of humans. At the foot of their table, which was close to the fire of apple-logs which flamed and crackled in the arched brick fireplace, lay a sleepy Dalmatian who cocked his head at their approach, surveyed them, passed them, and put his head down again and once more slept.

'He's rather a dear,' Lucia said. She sat at the table and turned her chair and bent down and scratched the broad, black-spotted head.

'He's a gent,' said Anthony. 'And he's asleep.' He spoke very low. 'So *he* won't listen. But what about the "quiet gentleman"? Damn him, he's late over his breakfast. I want to talk. I must talk. I've got to that stage when I can't think straight unless I think aloud.'

'You can't,' said Lucia, 'whisper like that and talk.' She touched the bell by the fireplace and presently came an aged but brisk waiter.

It was a good breakfast. They dealt with it fairly. And over it, when they did talk, they talked of matters which a thousand quiet gentlemen might without damage have heard. At intervals, Anthony glared into the far corner, but always and only to see the *Morning Post*. Lucia, affected, turned to glare too. She saw the *Morning Post*. Tacitly, they put a wish on this quiet gentleman. But he remained rooted. No sound came from his quiet and gentlemanly corner save—and this very occasionally (strangely seldom, Anthony thought)—quiet and gentlemanly rustles of the *Morning Post* behind which he remained, semi-visible and apparently wholly content.

They gave him up as a bad and a very bad job. They relapsed themselves into silence. Anthony behind creased brows went round and round that circle of his thinking. Lucia, behind eyes grown suddenly sad and afraid, thought of the woman whose house they now were in.

They reached the end of their meal. Anthony took out his case. They lit cigarettes. They still were silent with their thoughts. There came a loud rustle from the *Morning Post*, a real rustle; but they paid no heed. Then, following the rustle, came the sound of a chair being pushed back and following that sound, footsteps.

Anthony heard, but did not look up. He waited for the quiet gentleman's complete going. But the footsteps, instead of passing by, upon the room's far side, came across towards the fireplace and Anthony's table. And they stopped. And there came the sound of a cough, deliberate and apologetic.

Anthony, his brow furrowed by a scowl, calculated to scare the quietest gentleman who might wish to pass the time of day, did now raise head and eyes.

His frown went and his eyes widened. He said, softly: 'Great Scotland Yard! Pike!'

II

They sat about the fire in the Smoking Room—Anthony and Anthony's wife and Chief Detective-Inspector Arnold Pike of the CID.

'But why,' said Anthony, 'oh why, and oh why, my Pike, did you hide so long? Why entrench yourself behind that paper? You've wasted time, you know? Why not declare yourself?'

The smooth-shaven, rectangular face of Pike changed in hue from its normal healthy tan to a dull, glowing red. But Pike is no coward. He said:

'Thought you'd think it was cheek, sir. My pushing in. Had to screw up my courage.'

'Cheek!' said Anthony. 'Good Gad!'

'Mr Pike,' Lucia said, 'there's one thing I want to say to you. It won't take long. It's just—thank you!'

Anthony nodded. 'Many hears! Pike, you're the original good scout. To give up a two-year late holiday and come down here to help in the wildest and saddest of wild-goose chases . . .'

Pike cut him short. He said, his face flaming once more:

'Haven't given up anything, sir. Pleasure to be allowed to work with you. I *am* on holiday. I don't look like a policeman now, do I, sir?' He looked down, not without complacence, at the worn tweeds and brown shoes which had replaced the dark suit and black boots of his official life.

Anthony laughed. 'You don't!' Laughter faded suddenly from his voice and manner. He said: 'I'm going to take you at your word. You're in on this. So *now* we'll get on. We've got to realise one thing—and keep on realising it, holding it in front of our noses. Time! That's what's against us.' He got to his feet in a sudden movement. 'We've got to *start*—and when we've started we mustn't stop . . . Pike! What *d'you* know about the business?'

'All the paper stuff.' Pike's voice was crisp and quick. 'That's all.'

Anthony nodded. 'Me, too. And my wife. And what would you say, Pike, in ordinary circumstances, after reading those papers?'

'Guilty,' said Pike.

Again Anthony nodded. 'Exactly. A very nice, straight-forward case, with all the flats neatly joined . . .'

'*Flats*, sir?' Pike's eyebrows went up in query.

'Theatrical term, Pike. No loose ends about . . . Yes, a very tidy job . . . So tidy, in fact, that it is in me to wonder whether it isn't too tidy. Very rare to get a murder case utterly straight-forward—if you except killings in quarrels.'

'Which this, sir,' Pike put in, 'might have been. I mean, there were these two in that wood. No love lost between 'em, and that Blackatter, from what we can make out, one of the nasty, sneering sort.'

Anthony ceased his pacing. He turned sharply. He said:

'Yes. But we must start at the other end. We're prejudiced, because we've got to be or we shan't get anywhere. We're assuming that Bronson, though he might kill a man, would not kill that man by blowing the *back* of his head off at a range of twelve inches. We're more than assuming that, we're telling ourselves that we *know* it. Because if we didn't *know* it, we should neither have a real jumping-off place nor, if we did get a starting-point, could we have the necessary ardour even to attempt to do the miracle we're straining after. Understand?'

Pike nodded; but his nod was slow, and there was a pause before he spoke. He said then:

'I see the . . . theory, as you might call it, sir. Whether I can . . . can get into the skin of it . . .' He broke off with a little shrug.

Lucia spoke now. 'If Mr Pike,' she said softly, 'were to talk to Mrs Bronson . . .'

Anthony swung round to face her. 'Top of the form!' he said. 'He shall. Pike, you've *got* to get the point of view! If you don't, fifty per cent of your usefulness 'll be missing. And I want a hundred and ninety-nine per cent of it.'

Pike smiled. 'I'll do my best, sir. And I will, if she'll see me, talk to Mrs Bronson . . . And I'll stay and help anyway . . . But whether I'll . . .' Again he broke off his sentence; again shrugged.

Anthony dropped into the armchair facing his wife's. He stared a moment at the fire. 'You shall see Mrs Bronson,' he said. 'In a few minutes. Just now we'll go on talking. And if you can't believe yet, Pike, please assume. Now to get back: and don't forget we're working upside-down. As Bronson did *not* kill Blackatter at all, therefore Bronson did not kill Blackatter in a quarrel, and, therefore also, Blackatter was not killed in *any* sudden quarrel by anybody but was killed at the climax of a highly polished plan whose partly achieved object was *two* deaths, Blackatter's *and* Bronson's.'

There was silence then while Pike, his long smooth-shaven jaw cupped in his palms, considered this. He looked up at last. He said:

'I don't like it, sir. It's clever; but it doesn't seem to me to fit. This new murderer of yours; as I see it, if he wanted to get rid of both Blackatter and Bronson, all he's got to do is to get 'em both up there in that wood the way he must've done in your version and then just shoot 'em both and clear off. Much easier than running the risk of just leaving Bronson there stunned when Bronson *might* 've seen him and been able to split.'

Pike came to an end a little breathless; he had spoken very fast. His colour was heightened. He was arguing with Colonel Gethryn, for whom, ever since the Lines-Bower case, he had borne a respect amounting as near to reverence as a man of his sort might manage to attain.

Colonel Gethryn smiled at him a friendly smile. But Colonel Gethryn shook his head.

'That won't do, Pike,' he said. 'You've not seen all round it. Your argument holds water up to a point; but only up to the point that X *could* have killed both men; for obviously it was either due to X that Blackatter and Bronson came together in that wood that night; or else X knew that together there they would be; or else he took one, or both, there himself. That's right, then, that he *could* have killed both. But to go on from there and say because he could and didn't proves that he doesn't exist, is all wrong . . .'

'*May* be all wrong, sir,' Pike muttered rather than spoke.

'*Is* all wrong,' said Anthony. 'You've forgotten the starting-point. You've forgotten it because you can't—not yet, anyhow—force your mind to begin from it. Anything, Pike, that proved or was used as possible proof that X, the unknown killer, has no existence *must* be wrong. Because our starting-point is the knowledge—*knowledge*, Pike—that Bronson did not kill Blackatter. It's established, therefore, that X killed Blackatter. My next step is to say that X has endeavoured to kill Bronson as well, the method chosen for Bronson being a rope instead of a gun. Because, if X had merely desired a scapegoat, then he could easily have found a more plausible one than Bronson. Read through that dossier again, or remember all you read in it—and *into* it—of Blackatter's character. Not a nice man, you know. Not at all a nice man. A man with a very hazy occupation—he's called, variously, farmer, horse-dealer, independent-means, pensioner and smallholder, with a final consolidation, probably for convenience, on *smallholder*. He was, no doubt, all of these things a little. But he was equally obviously a bad hat in one way and another—poacher on a large scale for one thing, I should say. Definitely a wife-stealer and daughter-spoiler; equally definitely a bully. That man must have had enemies in thick clusters over half the county. *Real* enemies, I mean. And yet, before the night of the murder, his only visible point of contact with Bronson is Bronson's refusal to have him in this pub or anywhere near it. No, X could have found a hundred scapegoats easier to plant it on than Bronson. But he chose Bronson. Therefore it was a double-death he was after—a particular double-death, Blackatter's and Bronson's . . . That all right?'

Pike smiled; a slow and rather worried smile. 'You know it is, sir.'

'Why the harrassed air, then?'

Pike hesitated. 'It's just . . . it's just . . . if I look that, sir, it's because I'm *almost* getting to the point of view you want.'

Anthony smiled. 'It's all a question of Coué, Pike. If we all say, and keep saying, and you say to yourself: "We *know* Bronson did not kill Blackatter," you'll find it comes to you. But it oughtn't to make you care-worn . . .'

Pike sat up. He said, with a vehemence so unusual, so unexpected and so fierce as to make Lucia Gethryn visibly start:

'Oughtn't it, by Willy! I say it ought, and I say it will! *If* it's right that Bronson didn't do it, there's a man in prison, waiting for a rope which he hasn't earned. Waiting! And p'r'aps going to get it. Oughtn't to *worry* . . .' He broke off. He was sitting forward, his hands gripping the arms of his chair with a grip which made white islands of his knuckles. He stopped speaking, in the middle of that sentence, and sat with his mouth open while there visibly swept over him realisation of his words and tone and attitude. For the third time that morning the colour streamed up to his long face. He shut his mouth and opened it again to begin, looking anxiously towards Lucia, a stammering apology.

But she would have none of it. She smiled at him a smile which took away his breath with its beauty and its friendliness. She said:

'Mr Pike. There seems to be only one thing this morning for me to say to you. So I'd better say it again, hadn't I? . . . Thank you!'

And Anthony said:

'I thought your worry was academic. But thank God it isn't. Now you kick me for a fool and everything in the garden will be beautiful.'

Pike beamed. He let the beam fade and said:

'You were saying, sir, that X was after a particular double-death. Have you gone on from there at all? In thinking it out, I mean to say.'

'Thus far,' said Anthony. 'That though X must have known and been known to Blackatter, as at least a potential danger, he cannot have so been known to Bronson. Get me, Steve? I hope so, because *that*, in its implications, is very rummy indeed. So rummy that presently I'm going to be drawn to a conclusion which is very chancey, extremely improbable and yet the only answer I'd care to bet on.'

'I get you, sir,' Pike said. 'At least, I think I see how you got there. You mean that, if X had been known as possibly dangerous to Bronson and not to Blackatter, then the murder would 've been planted t'other way round.'

'And,' said the soft, deep voice of Lucia, 'that if Mr (or Miss or Mrs) X had been known as a potential murderer *both* to Blackatter and Bronson, *then* he'd 've *had* to kill both for fear that any alive one left about would say—'

'"Twarn't me,"' said Anthony, '"it was 'im!" Exactly . . . . Marriage is a funny thing. Until this moment, dear, I've never

suspected you of logic . . . But you're right. And so was Pike.
So what are we faced by? By the fact that X is a man who
feared both Blackatter and Bronson but who knew that
Bronson would not associate him, in his ordinary self, with
the death of Blackatter and his (Bronson's) apparent connection with it . . .'

Lucia held up appealing hands. 'Stop! Stop! And say that
again, *much* more slowly.'

Pike grinned at that. 'Can't say I'd mind a repeat myself,
sir.'

Anthony sighed. 'We are faced with this,' he said, with slow
solemnity, picking each word: 'That X feared Blackatter, so
much that he had to kill him; that X feared Bronson, so
much that he had to arrange, too, for Bronson's death; that X,
however, although he did fear Bronson, could *yet* afford to let
the Law, in all its slowness and with all its chance-giving to
an accused, kill Bronson for him.'

'Yes?' said Lucia. Her hands covered her eyes. 'Go on,
quick. Don't stop—if there's any more.'

'With you, sir.' Pike's tone was cheerful. 'Maybe a bit ahead,
but I wouldn't like to bet on it.'

'Right,' said Anthony. 'This, if you look at it, is a rum situation. Let us all look at it. Let us, in turn, expound theories
as to how such a situation might be.' He looked at his wife.
'You first, ma'am.'

Lucia took away her hands which had been clutching her
head. She was silent for a long moment. She said at last:

'Bronson might have known something, but not have known
that that something was about the X whom he knew . . . That's
very badly put . . .'

'No, no,' said Pike quickly.

Lucia sent him another smile. '*Again*,' she said, 'thank you.
But it was. I ought to 've said: Bronson might've known
something about somebody, but not known that that somebody was X—while X knew all this but was frightened of

Bronson finding out some time that he (that is X) was the
person Bronson knew the something about.'

'Ninety-five,' said Anthony, 'out of one hundred. Now, you,
Pike.'

Pike spoke at once. He said:

'Bronson might have known something about X in the past
and known the present X was the same man, but, not associ-
ating X in any way with Blackatter, would not see any bearing
of this bit of knowledge on the death of Blackatter. That's
assuming, of course, that he didn't know X was frightened of
Blackatter.'

'Ninety-eight,' said Anthony, 'out of one hundred. The extra
three's for neatness. Both are possibly right; but I'd plump
for a bit out of each, plus something you've both left out. I'll
put it the other way round and make a story out of it. Thus:
Blackatter in the past discovers something discreditable about
X. The same thing (it's straining coincidence too much to
assume a different thing), the same thing is discovered by
Bronson. Blackatter remembers everything. Bronson—another
sort—forgets, perhaps everything, certainly all save the incident. That's the past. Now present-day: Blackatter and X
and Bronson are, certainly by accident upon the part of X and
Bronson, probably by design upon the part of Blackatter, all
in the same part of the world. To X Blackatter discovers his
knowledge. X says, after the first shock, "Well, what about it?
It's only your word against mine." But Blackatter says: "Ah!
No, it isn't then. What about D. Bronson?" because Blackatter
knows that Bronson knows. "Oh," says X, "he's in this with
you, is he?" Blackatter says, "No, he isn't. But he'd be with me
if it came to proving. He'd have to be. He's an honest man."
X thinks about that and says, sooner or later in the tale, "Meet
me in the wood." He then does in Blackatter and plants the
killing on Bronson. Back in our recent style, *that* leave us like
this . . . I'll write it so that we can keep the formula and not
get rattled by having to think back over the steps.'

He took a pencil from one pocket and a slim notebook from another. From the book he tore a sheet. He wrote:

'X knew that Bronson knew the something; *but* X knew that Bronson—
either
   (a) did not realise that he knew it,
or
   (b) certainly did not connect X, in this or any other way, with Blackatter,
or
   (c) a + b.'

He handed this first to Pike and then, when he had got it back with a decisive nod, to his wife. She was longer over it than Pike. But she raised her head at last. She too nodded. Her dark eyes were wide; they shone with a mingling of effort, excitement and affection. She said, in a breathless, small voice which was almost a whisper:

'I say! We've got somewhere, haven't we? I mean . . . it seemed as if there wasn't *anything* . . .'

She looked first at Anthony with those shining eyes, and then at Pike. And Anthony, for a brief moment, wished that Pike were elsewhere. And Pike, for a brief moment, was disturbed within himself by a strange and beautiful pang which seemed blent of delight and pain and longing and comfort.

'What we *have* got,' said Anthony, 'is one of the stations on this line we're trying to get at. First stop, Blackmail.'

Pike nodded. But he said, a little hesitantly: '*If* you're certain, sir, that the motive was fear.'

'Must be,' said Anthony. 'Look at it. Fear's the only possible motive when you've got two opposites like Blackatter and Bronson as the victims. It can't be jealousy; it can't be gain; it couldn't be any of the others except pure, unreasoned blood-lust. And if it's that we're done anyhow—you can't run a motiveless murderer to earth in a couple of days. No, fear it is. Fear it's damn' well got to be!'

'You're right, sir.' Pike's voice was decisive. 'And as it's fear, Blackmail's the first card.'

'It's the only card we've got yet.' Anthony's tone was almost savage. 'But we've got to start playing and get the rest of the deal as we go. Now, how do we play?' He got out of his chair and began to pace the room. He went to the window and stood at it, looking out. From that window one may just see, over the hedge round the garden, the bend in the road which brings one abruptly into the narrow, leaning, main and only street of the village of Farrow and the Inn of The Horse and Hound.

He seemed to be watching this corner for something; and there was a silence in the room. But at last he turned again. He said:

'Yes. How do we play? Look for anyone and everyone in this half of the county who might be a blackmailer and a murderer? That means, even if we confine ourselves to people *obviously* worth blackmailing (which might lead us right off the line), that means a good six months' work for five people. And we've got three days and a bit. How do we play? Interview all the turnips who gave evidence? They'll either 've forgotten or say what they said before. By God! Where *do* we start? It's eighty-five haystacks and one needle we don't know the look of, which may be in the barn after all . . .' He fell silent and prowled back to the window and once more stood watching the curve of the road.

Pike was huddled into his chair. His hands were clasped round his knees and his small, dark eyes gazed upwards at the ceiling. In her chair Lucia sat relaxed. Her eyes gazed into the fire, and from them had gone—with this change in Anthony from gaily-fierce concentration to savage, prowling, chafing discontent—all their eager sparkle. If there were sparkle in them now, it was of a sadder kind. Her thoughts were back with another woman; a woman who was in this house but who had in this house, though it was their own, no husband . . .

At last Anthony spoke. He said, slowly and almost lifelessly, without turning from that window:

'What we must do first is look for oddity. Follow me? Split ourselves into units and look for oddity, queerness, anything sub- or super-normal in anyone remotely connected with this business. P'r'aps it's not so difficult as it sounds. I found one small one this morning . . . Not that that'll be much. And there's another I must look into—only *that*'ll probably turn out a mare's nest. You others must . . .'

'Others?' Pike put in. 'You said *five* just now, sir. How did you make that?'

Anthony still stood at the window. Still he spoke without turning. He said:

'You, me, my wife—three. The two men Spencer Hastings is lending me—five.'

Pike changed his position abruptly. His head came down; his hands unlocked themselves from his knees. He sat erect, rather as if something had stung him.

'Will that,' he said, 'be two men from the Special staff of *The Owl*,* sir?'

Anthony nodded; and with the nod suddenly stiffened. He went a half-pace nearer to the window, until his face was almost touching the glass. 'And here,' he said, 'they come.' He sighed— a sound of relief. He turned from the window now and came back to his chair and dropped into it.

* *The Owl* is a weekly Review of which Colonel Gethryn is half-proprietor. His friend Spencer Hastings is half-proprietor and editor. *The Owl*, besides its ordinary weekly edition, runs 'Special' editions whenever there is 'Scooped' any news sufficiently exciting to warrant these. In connection with the Specials a Special staff is employed. Full description of the paper and its methods was given in *The Rasp*.

Pike fidgeted. He pulled out a cigarette-case; opened it; shut it again; did the same with his mouth. But no sound came from him.

From the depths of her chair Lucia said:

'You didn't tell me, dear.'

Anthony smiled at her. 'Didn't I? Must've forgotten. I telephoned Hastings last night. There's nothing doing for the Special staff just now, so we're getting the two best. They may be useful; they've got to be . . . They haven't lost time, anyhow . . .'

The last words of this sentence were, despite the room's closed windows, almost drowned in a swooping burst of noise from without the house; a noise like a testing-garage run mad. Lucia covered her ears with her hands. She looked amazed inquiry.

Anthony grinned. Something of his almost savage hopelessness of the past five minutes seemed to have dropped from him. The noise died in a screeching wail of brakes through which there came, a blasting obligato, the explosive coughing of a motor-bicycle's exhaust. There was a silence which seemed a large round emptiness.

Lucia took down her hands. 'What on *earth*?' she said.

Anthony lit a cigarette. 'The rest,' he said, 'of us.'

There came a tap upon the door and then, through it, the girl Annie. She said, fixing her eyes upon Anthony:

'Two gentlemen, sir.' She then was eclipsed.

From behind her there came, to hide her completely, two young men in a hurry. The first of these was tall and thin and stooping, and was habited in the stained and weather-marred leather affected by that sort of motor-cyclist whom drivers of fast cars forever try, not often successfully, to catch. He was without a hat, but from his gauntletted hand there dangled a leather helmet and a pair of goggles. Coming out from the folds of an ancient woollen muffler of the colour of wholemeal bread, his head seemed like that of a large and ferocious bird with a sardonic sense of humour. Lank black hair, which seemed, as some hair does, only loosely attached to his scalp, tossed and flopped as he walked. Black tortoiseshell-rimmed glasses of the largest size were athwart his fierce nose and behind them were large heavy-lidded eyes which yet gave an impression of amazing, almost impudent, alertness. The long, thin fingers of his ungloved right hand were stained with tobacco and petrol and ink and yet somehow conveyed that they were washed as frequently as might be. This was Mr Francis Dyson.

Behind Mr Dyson—but only a little way behind, and with something in his gait which suggested that, though he wouldn't show this for *worlds,* he was striving to get in front of Mr Dyson—came a man as different in appearance from Mr Dyson as well might be; a young man whom, at first glance, one might have put down as anywhere betwixt eighteen and twenty-three but who, one saw very soon, was much more likely to be ten years older than this; a young man with a round, smooth, freshly and rather highly coloured face, very sleek fair hair, very correct plus-fours, a nice taste in linen, round, rather prominent, light-blue eyes and a thick solidity which made him seem shorter than his actual five feet and eight inches. A picture of unspoiled, healthy, pleasant but rather foolish young Englishman with very little to do and rather too much time in which to do it—until one looked carefully at the mouth; a good mouth enough though stubborn, but a mouth with lines of experience about it and something of that same hard, sardonic humour, differently reacting, as was expressed in the whole of the head of his companion. This was Mr Walter Flood.

They came across the room fast. Anthony rose to meet them. Mr Dyson halted within a foot. Mr Flood drew level and halted too.

'Dyson,' said Mr Dyson crisply. 'Sorry be late.' He gripped the hand which Anthony offered.

'I,' said Mr Flood, 'am Flood. I hope we aren't late. We pushed along as well as we could. We were both a bit late getting to the office this morning.' He shook hands in his turn.

Dyson nodded. 'Pity!' he said.

'Be introduced,' Anthony said, and to Lucia presented them. She smiled upon them, and they bowed, Dyson with a quick, bird-like out-thrusting of his head, Flood with a rather florid grace.

'And this is Mr Pike,' said Anthony.

Pike, who had so sat back in his armchair that its wings had kept his face obscured, now got to his feet. He said:

'Mr Dyson and I know each other all right!' There was an odd note in his voice—a blend of humour and wrath. 'I've met Mr Flood too.'

The faces of Messrs Dyson and Flood showed their owners to be as near to astonishment as may come any follower of their profession.

'Strike *me*!' said Dyson. He cocked his head to one side and looked at Pike as might a benevolent vulture uncertain as to the amount of kick left in his intended dinner. Pike, his hands in his pockets, his long lower jaw out-thrust, stared back.

Flood regarded them with evident delight. He said, in a thick and unctuous voice:

'Shake hands, my men. Shake hands. Then box on.' He turned to Anthony and dropped his voice to a stage whisper. 'The whole CID's after Dyson's gore. The last "Special" we did—that scoop on the Blattner diamond job—none of that ought to've come out when it did. At least, that was the Yard's idea. Old Mogul—Dyson—thought differently though. What he did to that Insurance laddie and the busy to make 'em spill the story, nobody knows. But he got it. And he got it right. The Yard hasn't forgiven him yet . . . Look at 'em. Old Master—Fur and Feather!'

But Pike made up his mind. He said:

'I'm not a policeman; I'm on holiday, Mr Dyson.'

He took his right hand from his pocket and held it out.

Dyson shook it. 'Good. Nothing I may say'll be used in evidence.'

Flood stepped forward. 'Kiss me too,' he said.

Anthony looked at his watch. 'Listen,' he said. His voice was low but its tone brought the gaze of eight eyes round to him. 'It's 11.10. Lucia, will you take Mr Pike to Mrs Bronson? He should see her.' He turned to Flood and Dyson. 'You two,' he said, 'must stay with me. I'm going to tell you what I've asked you to come for. And we're up against time.'

III

The clock upon the Smoking Room mantelpiece showed 11.30. Anthony, in twenty minutes, had been over the ground covered just now with Pike and Lucia. He said:

'So that's where we are. And remember—keep remembering—the essential attitude. You must *believe*—whether you really do or not—that Bronson didn't murder. It may be difficult, but . . .'

Dyson raised his eyebrows, his long face wearing a look of almost anguish.

'We're *journalists*!' he said.

Flood nodded. 'Beliefs,' he said, 'to order.'

'Made-to-measure,' said Dyson. 'Or off the peg . . . My trouble is: I'll have to waste time reading. Hardly remember case at all. Wasn't interested.' He nodded in Flood's direction. '*He* knows it.'

Flood shook his head. 'I'll have to read it up too. I did do the inquest and part of the Magistrate's Court, true enough. But I was on the Minkwell business at the same time. And that was such a long chalk more interesting—at the time—that I took precious little notice of this one. It'll come back all right . . .'

Anthony interrupted. 'I'll tell it you. Quicker, brighter, better. And good for me. If you clothe a thing in your own words, sometimes you see what you've missed and would go on missing . . . Have a drink?' He pressed a bell beside the fireplace.

'Oh, *yes*!' said Dyson.

'Please,' said Flood, 'I will.'

'Forgive,' said Dyson. He hoisted his lankness out of the chair and stripped himself of leather coat and overall leggings. He stood revealed in a battered tweed jacket and what Flood has always taken oath are the oldest pair of grey flannel trousers in the world. 'Hot,' he said.

Again Anthony pressed the bell. This time it was answered. By a round and nervous and rustic young woman who said:

'Ay'm soary, sir. Has yeou roong twice?' And went off into mutters about 'that *Annie*'.

At Dyson Anthony looked inquiringly; then at Flood.

'Oh, *beer*,' said Dyson.

'And beer,' said Flood.

The rustic was quick. While she was gone there was silence. Anthony's eyes were fixed upon the door through which she had vanished. Dyson filled an enormous pipe with very black tobacco. Flood lit a new cigarette from the stump of its predecessor.

The rustic returned and went away again, leaving behind her two full tankards and a glass of sherry.

The sherry was a pleasant surprise. The glass was half-empty before Anthony spoke. He said:

'Here it is then: At just after three in the morning of the 18th of May last, the village constable here was turned out by a youth called Harrigan. Harrigan stated that he had found, in Bellows Wood, two dead men. The constable found one dead man, Blackatter, and one man just recovering consciousness from a knock on the head. This was Bronson. In Bronson's hand was Bronson's gun. It had been fired, and recently. Both barrels. The back of Blackatter's head did not exist. The middle of his head was full of shot. He had been dead some hours. According to the Crown, what happened was this. Bronson and Blackatter meet in the wood, Bronson having followed Blackatter there as Blackatter went homewards from Farrow at about 10.30 p.m. They quarrel, mainly over Blackatter's attentions, or intentions, to Mrs Bronson. They do not come to blows. Blackatter, probably with some final insult, turns away, where upon Bronson, seeing his chance, ups with his gun and at about six inches range blows off Blackatter's head. Bronson has not, according to the Crown, done this in blind fury but (though he was doubtless passionate) in deliberation. What, says the Crown, he intends to do is to leave Blackatter's body, go quietly home, and having cleaned his gun sit down and be Brer Rabbit. The killing will then be put down to one of those indeterminate poachers of whom Bellows Wood and the surrounding coverts have for a long time been filled o' nights. But, says the Crown, afire with a fine indignation and a due marvelling at the slickness of Divine Providence, his intentions were not to be. On turning away from his victim, he catches his foot in a very tough bramble. He slips, staggers and, covering two yards in a stumbling run in endeavour to keep his balance, falls heavily, rolls back down the bank and strikes his head with great force against the jagged stump of a recently-felled oak. He is stunned—he is, in fact, suffering from minor concussion. And so there he lies, his empty gun still clutched in his hand, to be the chief evidence of his own crime.' Anthony broke off; he finished the sherry.

Messrs Dyson and Flood were silent. Each held in his right hand a nearly-emptied tankard. Otherwise, their attitudes were in direct contrast. Flood sat upright, his eyes open and fixed upon Anthony; his legs were neatly crossed, his thick body in easy alertness. His bland face was empty of expression. Dyson lay sprawled in his big chair so that from untidy head to bony knees he was almost a straight line. His arms—a tankard at the end of one—were loosely and almost wildly abroad. His eyes were fast closed. But there was not, curiously, any suggestion of sleep, nor even repose, about him.

Anthony set down his empty glass upon the mantelpiece. He said:

'Now for supporting evidence. When Bronson, still concussed, was searched by the Bobbie—Police-Constable Murch—there was discovered, among the usual cag in pockets, a note in Blackatter's writing. This note was dated the day before. It said: "We had better meet to settle this once and for all. If you think you can bluff me you're mistaken. Meet me in the new clearing, Bellows Wood, at 10 tomorrow night." It was signed J. Blackatter. There was no doubt as to the letter's authenticity. I think I'm word-perfect in it, too . . . That was the first bit of corroborative evidence. And pretty damning. The second was that, on the evening of the murder, Blackatter—at 7.30 to be exact—paid his first visit to The Horse and Hound for two months. At his last previous visit he had to be ordered out by Bronson, and told by Bronson that he would only show his nose inside the door again at the gravest risks to itself and also to the rest of his body; in fact, three witnesses at the trial had it forced out of them that Bronson, in reply to Blackatter's "answer-backs" had said that if he *did* have to set about Blackatter he was just as likely to kill him as not, *and* that, if he did kill Blackatter, it wouldn't worry him and would probably give pleasure to a great many people. The sort of remark, you will notice, which while possibly a perfectly ordinary, justifiable and even, in certain circumstances, faintly humorous remark, is a dangerous sort of remark to make.'

Suddenly Dyson spoke. His grating voice came out of a thin-lipped mouth which barely moved. And his eyes remained fast closed. He said:

'Why did he make it?'

Flood nodded once. Anthony, too, nodded. 'Bronson swore,' he said, 'that it was because Blackatter was a general nuisance in the bars. Mrs Bronson says: because she, once and almost inadvertently, had remarked that Blackatter was unpleasant and a nuisance with his loudness, bullying and would-be gallantry which had extended, once or twice, even so far as herself. The Crown said, and ostensibly supported it by evidence, that the reason was far graver and larger than either of these; was, in fact, either some ill-doing with which Blackatter and Bronson had been jointly connected (Crown, you see, did not even attempt to whitewash Blackatter); or else Mrs Bronson, on a serious plane. Or else a bit, as it were, of both.'

Flood spoke now. For the first time he took his unwinking blue gaze from Anthony's face. He looked now at a little notebook which, with its pencil, he had taken from a pocket. He said:

'"Ostensibly supported by evidence," you said. Whose? What?'

Anthony said: 'Tittle-tattle. Mrs Bronson's a very striking woman. The sort that either you will revere, or hate with that most dangerous type of hatred—the hatred inspired by a hopeless, helpless certainty of the hater's inferiority to the hated. I say "tittle-tattle". I mean, exactly, that the Crown never brought into the case any direct question or answer upon this point of to what extent Blackatter and Mrs Bronson might have been associated. But Counsel, using all the little pieces, venomous, well-intentioned, and merely verbose, which fell from the mouths—generally feminine—of the witnesses on both sides, did a very pretty bit of hinting. Most effective it must've been in Court, for a good deal of it got over in cold-blooded shorthand transcripts. To answer your question directly: there does not appear, from the dossier, to be any witness who deliberately set out—even under Counsel's incentive—to get Bronson convicted. There's one'—Anthony's eyes strayed for a moment towards the little table by Dyson's chair, upon which the orange-coloured folder lay—'who seemed more anti-Bronson than most. A man called Dollboys—farmer. But he seems honest enough . . . To get back. This visit here, on the night of the murder, by Blackatter, was a very strong link in the Crown case. He walks in, slightly, one gathers, bolder than brass, goes into the Private Bar and orders a drink.

In the Saloon Bar—from which one can see, if one is in the right position—is Dollboys, who *is* in that position. The Private Bar is empty. Blackatter calls for a drink. The barmaid—new since the Blackatter veto—serves him. Blackatter begins his usual fascinations. For a bit the girl's amused; then, as Blackatter gets warmed up, a little nervous—p'r'aps on her own account, p'r'aps on her place's. Anyhow, she drifts away and, in a moment, there arrives Bronson. Trouble. In his evidence Dollboys says he'd never seen a man "look nastier" than Bronson. Dollboys is the only witness as both the Saloon and Private Bars were empty at the moment except for these three men. Apparently, however, all that Bronson *did* was to lean both hands on the bar and say: "I've told you not to come in here. Get out. I'll give you a minute." He was, says Dollboys, very quiet—but, apparently, all the more dangerous-seeming for that. Dollboys says—he didn't seem to like Blackatter any more than he did Bronson—that Blackatter, though he tried to put a face on it, was scared. He gulped down his drink—his third large whisky in ten minutes—and made for the door. Bronson did not move, only his head turned to watch the exit. At the door Blackatter paused. He turned the handle and pulled the door open. And then he said, over his shoulder: "It's all right *now*. But don't forget the night's not over." And he went . . . That's the case against Bronson, then, in its essentials. He's found, fallen and stunned, by Blackatter's body. Blackatter's head's half blown off and in Bronson's hands Bronson's recently-fired gun. In Bronson's pocket a note from Blackatter making an appointment for this night at this place. Bronson has been agin Blackatter for months—no one *quite* knows why—and has forbidden him this house, at the same time saying—jocularly or not—that he wouldn't mind killing him. On the evening of the night of the murder Blackatter comes, for the first time since the veto, to the Bar here and is again turned out, but before he goes he makes his little speech which refers to the appointment.'

Dyson squirmed in his chair until he was almost upright. He opened his eyes. He cocked his head to one side and looked at Anthony. He said:

'Convincing too. Only obvious flaw seems lack of connection. Bronson won't have Blackatter near the place. That goes on. What's the hidden trouble about? Any connection earlier?'

Flood answered that. 'It's all,' he said, 'coming back to me. There didn't seem any earlier connection between the two men.'

'But,' Anthony said, 'Bronson was a walker, with or without gun. And Mrs Bronson isn't a walker. Bronson was always out and about by himself. Blackatter was always out and about by himself. Suggestion: they met a great deal more often than the country knew.'

Dyson closed his eyes again. 'Anyone see 'em ever?'

Anthony nodded. 'One witness *thought* he had . . .' He broked off as Dyson, with another squirm, shot bolt upright. He looked down at Dyson and he shook his head. 'No,' he said, 'it was *not* Dollboys.'

For a moment the heavy-lidded eyes behind the huge spectacles of Mr Dyson opened wide in something like astonishment.

Flood laughed. 'Don't get too clever about here, Mogul. You're giving away weight, laddie.' He seemed to enjoy the glare which came at him.

'Not Dollboys,' Anthony said. 'The lad Harrigan, who found the dead Blackatter and the unconscious Bronson . . .'

'And,' said Flood, grinning at Dyson, 'you needn't theorise about Harrigan equalling X. Because Harrigan's potty. Not there. What the rustics call a Natural.'

Anthony turned quick eyes on the speaker. 'He is, eh? Evidence might've been just an ordinary clodhopper's.'

'To read perhaps,' Flood said. 'Not to hear, though. And when you see him—' A shrug finished his sentence.

The door of the room opened. Lucia came in, and behind her Pike.

Flood and Dyson got to their feet, the first with a neat though solid alacrity, the second with a writhing, protesting wriggle of his thinness.

Lucia smiled at her husband, a smile which somehow included his companions. But the smile was short-lived. She was pale. There were faint lines beneath her eyes and faint marks of misery about her mouth. Anthony set a chair for her and in it, without fuss, settled her. He looked then at Pike. He said to Pike:

'Well, you've seen wife of D. Bronson. How's the belief?' The words were light, but not the tone.

But Pike did not answer. He shook his head in excuse. In silence he sat. He lit a cigarette but after one inhalation threw it away. Anthony watched him. The long face seemed longer; certainly its tan had now beneath it very little colour. The jaw was set; at either side the knotted muscles showed tense.

Lucia broke the silence. 'What have *you* done?' She looked up at Anthony.

He shrugged. 'Put us all level. And found an oddity.' He surveyed the four. He took the cigarette from his mouth and flipped it into the grate where it lay smouldering beside Pike's. He said, with once more that tone which brought all eyes to bear upon him:

'We're going to start. But before we start, I want one thing clear. You're going to work on your own, as you find best. But the line of your working's to be what I say. That clear?' He did not look at Lucia. His eyes rested first on Pike. Pike nodded. The glance went to Flood.

''Course!' said Flood.

The glance went to Dyson. Once more Dyson was asprawl in his chair. His eyes were closed behind the grotesque glasses. There was a silence.

'Dyson!' said Anthony.

The eyes opened, unwillingly it seemed.

'Oh . . . *all* right!' said their owner.

'That,' said Flood to Anthony, 'is OK, you know.'

CHAPTER III

THE AFTERNOON OF FRIDAY

I

THE sun worked round in its course. A pale, bright shaft like the sword-blade of a god stabbed through the high, square, small window in the wall of stone. The man who lay upon the bed stirred and opened his eyes, for the sword-blade had touched them. He muttered to himself, for he had been in something which nearly was sleep and sleep he desired with a great desire. For a while he lay motionless, a great forearm flung up and over his face so that in this little darkness he might strive to catch once more that first soft wave which, loosening a man's consciousness, tells him delightfully that oblivion is about utterly to dissolve him . . .

But presently the arm was lifted from the face. The softness—that blurring of all the edges of all things—was not to be recaptured. He was awake and wide awake. But still he lay, flat upon his back. His eyes moved—little by little, until, just within the edge of their field of sight, there crept what he had known he would see but forever hoped that he would not . . .

They were there, as they had been there since the beginning. They sat, square and stolid, in their stiff blue uniforms, upon stiff, awkward little chairs.

His glance flickered secretly over them. They seemed curiously unreal. He took his eyes from them and lay looking up, along that bright stairway of the sun-ray, full of a myriad dancing things, to the small window. He stared at the window, frowning because the brightness hurt his eyes. He went on staring at the window, for he knew that if he stared long enough there would

49

form, in that small sky-backed square, a faint, quickly-fading picture.

He stared until his eyes ached and a savage little pain behind them carved deeper the lines of the little frown between them. And then, mistily, he saw her . . .

II

Bronson's wife looked out from a window upon a world bathed in a flood of hard bright sunshine which poured over the land like golden wine. But she saw neither land nor light. She saw a square stone box and inside that box a man . . .

She stood upright. Her arms hung down at her sides. She was motionless. She seemed scarcely to breathe. And her face was like a dead face—save for the eyes. And these eyes burned with a steady blue fire.

The window before which she stood was open and through it came that fierce wind whose breath was ice. Her own breath hung upon the air in little white clouds.

She stood there, and her eyes sent out their gaze. But they saw nothing that was there for them to see. They saw only that square box of stone which stood in her mind.

Sounds from outside, beneath the window, brought her back to herself . . . She shivered. She found herself to be aching with cold. She peered out of the window. She saw, coming out from the door beneath, the tall figure of the man who had believed her. A sudden energy seized upon her. This man and the other men that were with him—they were working for her . . . The image of the box of stone grew less in her mind and lesser. She shut the window and moved away from it and once more moved about the house.

III

Anthony was on his way to the village. Anthony swung along with his lazy-seeming stride at a pace which many men would have found impossible. His feet beat out a clanging rhythm on the frostbound road. His pipe, wedged in a corner of his mouth, sent up blue spirals to blend with the white clouds of his breath.

He came to the corner by the church and swung round it, over the little white bridge across the river and so into the one street of the village of Farrow. He slackened his pace. His hands dug themselves deeper into his pockets. His eyes glanced this way and that as he walked. Halfway down the narrow, cobbled street, they saw what they had been seeking. A small, low-windowed, frowning little shop, over its door the word J. HARRIGAN— TOBACCONIST & NEWSAGENT, in its window an untidy raffle of newspapers, pattern-books, pipes, jars of bullseyes and other more violently-coloured sweetmeats, sheets of 'transfers', tins of tobacco and threepenny stories of Buffalo Hill.

He went up the three worn steps and, bending to save his head, into the shop of J. Harrigan. A dim and dusty place, as vague and characterless, despite its age, as the man—presumably J. Harrigan himself—who, slowly and with a fussy deliberation, served him with two tins of tobacco, a torn *Morning Mercury* and a packet of matches.

Anthony tendered a one-pound note. At this the dim and dusty man stared a moment. He mumbled over it and at last shuffled off, through a droopingly-curtained doorway. From behind the curtain came more mutterings; more shuffling; the rattle of a cash-box.

Anthony sat himself down upon the edge of the deal counter which held the sorry-looking booklets and papers. He opened his *Mercury* and became apparently engrossed.

The curtain swayed, sending out a little cloud of dust. J. Harrigan returned. He counted out, with much frowning analysis, the change from the note. Anthony pocketed this, and folded up his paper with weariness. He said:

'Nothing of any interest *there*. Seems very little doing just now.'

Mr Harrigan mumbled. He was lean and bent and wrinkled and very tired.

Anthony, surveying him, decided that finesse was unnecessary. Anthony said:

'No fires; no frauds; no murder cases. The last interesting murder was that one about here . . .' His eyes took veiled stock of Mr Harrigan. Was this too crude?

It was not. Mr Harrigan, with the words, became a different man. A light came into his face. He seemed straighter and younger and almost alive. When he spoke, it was no longer to mumble but to issue words with a high-pitched and squeaking clarity.

'Ah!' said Mr Harrigan. 'You're right there, sir.' His accent showed him an exiled Londoner. 'You *are* right!' He seemed about to say more, but shut his mouth firmly. His little eyes, now bright with interest, seemed to implore that the subject should not be killed.

Anthony began to fill his pipe. He took his gaze from Mr Harrigan's face. He said idly:

'Yes. That was an interesting business for a student of these things. Straightforward enough, of course. I mean there was no doubt as to Bronson's being guilty. But there were interesting points. At one time I thought of going into it and working it up for my next book. But I was away from England and missed the trial. And everyone's forgetting all about it now—even about here, I should think. I couldn't get any first-hand stuff worth having, so I dropped the idea. Pity, in a way. It would've been a contrast to most of the other cases where there's doubt as to guilt.' He finished his pipe-loading, and began to strip the cover from his packet of matches. He appeared bored, and felt shame. The crudity of all this was offensive; but where crudity will serve crudity means speed.

Mr Harrigan snapped joyously at the fly. He said, in that high and rattling voice:

'D'you write *books*, sir? Detective tales, sir?'

Anthony, busied now with getting his pipe alight, shook his head. 'Not detective stories,' he muttered round the pipe-stem. 'Not *fiction* at all.' The scorn for fiction which his tone implied was great. 'No, I write upon the psychological, philosophical and physiological aspects of criminology.'

'Oh!' said Mr Harrigan. He added, hesitantly, that he saw. And then there fell a silence. Anthony made little movements indicative of departure. The eyes of Mr Harrigan shone with something like agony. Very little, except a continual and increasing failure to make both ends meet, had happened in Mr Harrigan's existence of sixty years except the killing of Blackatter and his vivacious connection with that killing. For weeks he had lived in the centre of a drama; for weeks he had been listened to and consulted and honoured, and then, little by little, this prominence had seeped away until now his life had become again that grey, shiftless struggle—only now it was greyer, more hopeless, by reason of his knowledge of higher states. And here, miraculously, hope had come again, in most superior guise, into his life. He could not bear to see it so swiftly depart. Beneath the counter his old hands clenched until his nails dug into the palms. He said, in a little rush of words:

'P'r'aps *I* could 'elp over the case, sir, I've not fergotten nothink of it. Nothink. It's all as clear in me 'ead as if it'd 'appened only last evening. It is that! And *I* was connected, you might say, most intimate with the 'ole affair. I . . .'

Anthony exhibited a sudden and intense surprise. He became most excitedly animate. 'Harrigan!' he said. 'Harrigan? Harrigan? That's the name over this shop. Harrigan! . . . I say, are you the man who discovered the body?'

Mr Harrigan smiled his smile of triumph. He strove to repress it, but out it came, irradiating him. He nodded impressively. He let that nod sink in before he spoke. And then he said:

'Well . . . it wasn't me exactly, sir. It was my boy Tom. But it comes, you might say, to the same thing. Or more so, like. Because Tom—it's our cross, sir, Mrs 'Arrigan's and mine—our boy's . . . well, Simple's what we call it. An' so you see, sir, I reely knows, you might say, more about things than what he does.'

'I see,' said Anthony. He was standing now, and the air of weary boredom which Mr Harrigan had noticed about this gentleman at first was still most noticeably absent. The gentleman was, in fact, Mr Harrigan saw, all excitable-like. And the gentleman proceeded to make a proposal to Mr Harrigan which filled with joy Mr Harrigan's heart. For not only did it mean that Mr Harrigan was—for this gentleman at least—a centre of interest, but it also put five pounds into Mr Harrigan's very empty pocket. The only fly which Mr Harrigan could find in all this pleasing ointment was the gentleman's reply to Mr Harrigan's last question. He had said:

'I don't think so, Mr Harrigan. No. Very kind suggestion on your part, but not one I'd care to accept. We criminologists'—here the gentleman had coughed—'we criminologists you know, are accustomed to dealing with all sorts and conditions. Of course, after I've been up there with the boy, I may want to ask questions of you. And again, of course, I shan't hesitate to do so . . . Now, if you wouldn't mind fetching the boy . . . Thank you.'

And so the boy was fetched. Through the lopsided, dust-ridden curtain Mr Harrigan led him, and Anthony saw that the word 'boy' was applicable only in description of a mental age. For this Thomas Harrigan was perhaps thirty years old. He seemed as he came in, towering over his little wisp of a father, a giant. He was actually a man over the middle-size and holding himself so that the most was made of his height and thickness. He walked solidly, and yet with something of that shambling uncertainty which marks the mentally-underdeveloped. But his face—a brown, open, mild and weather-beaten face, was unlined as that of a twelve-year-old. His blue eyes were wide and round and astonished. To Anthony the old man said:

'I've told him, sir, what 'e's got to do. He understands all right. Don't you, boy?'

Tom nodded. He kept an unwinking gaze upon the stranger, who smiled at him with a friendly and uncondescending openness. Tom smiled back, showing teeth of a dazzling white.

Anthony looked at the father. 'Far to go?' he said.

Old Harrigan shook his head. 'Little under a mile, sir. He'll take you there the shortest route, Tom will. Won't you, boy?'

Again Tom nodded. 'Tom knows *all* quick ways,' he said. His voice was high-pitched, like his father's, and it carried, too, the queer uncertainty of a child's.

Old Harrigan stood in the little, low doorway of his shop and watched them go. That smile of delight could now have free play. And it did; it creased his old face with a hundred new wrinkles. Once more he tasted fame; the interest of fellow-creatures. His eye followed the tall gentleman, walking beside his boy. He saw that the gentleman was talking to Tom and that Tom was looking eagerly towards the gentleman and nodding in that way he had when pleased. The lad had taken to the gentleman. That was very good. He watched the two figures until with their rounding of the corner by Maston's they went from his sight.

Beside Anthony, Tom Harrigan jerked and scuffled and swung his arms; hut he made good progress. Anthony, watching from the corner of his eye, saw that his pace was not distressing. Every now and then he spoke, and always Tom answered eagerly, like a child who is anxious, because he is himself pleased, to give back pleasure.

They came to the village's end and walked now between bare hedgerows. A hundred yards of this and Tom halted. He spoke for the first time save in answer. He pointed to a gate in the right-hand hedge.

'Through there,' he said. 'We go through there. The quick way. Through there.' He unlatched the gate and they were in a field of rough pasture across which a footpath wound, mounting the field's steep slope and disappearing into the darkness of a copse which fringed the skyline with bleak, black tracery. To this Anthony pointed.

'Bellows Wood?' he asked.

Tom nodded violently. 'Yes. Yes. Bellows Wood. Where Tom found the men lying. Yes.' He swung his arms like an excited child. He hurried on.

They made good pace across the field and up its far slope. At the top the path ran along a small plateau which led to the edge of the dark trees. Tom broke into a shambling run, very little faster than his walk. But it was a gait which expressed almost furious energy. He shouted:

'Come along! Come along! Nearly in the wood. Nearly! See where Tom found the men lying. Clever Tom!'

Anthony did not increase his pace. He said:

'Yes. We'll see in a minute, old chap. I can't go as fast as you can. Is this the way everyone comes to Bellows Wood?'

Tom ceased his run. He walked again. 'Yes,' he said. 'Yes. All come this way from home. Some go round . . . round by road. But *all* come this way. Quick way.'

They were in amongst the first trees now. Once more Tom began his run. Anthony put out a hand and gripped an arm and halted him.

'Steady,' he said. 'Steady. We'll get there all right. You mean: *some* people come here right round by the road, but *most* people by this path?'

Tom went through his violent nodding. 'Yes. Yes . . . Come and see where Tom found the men lying. Nearly there now!'

Anthony released the arm; let him run on ahead. It was very dark in this wood, and very cold. It was quiet, too. No bird sang, and there was not that subtle rustling of life unseen that most woods will give.

Round a huge oak which blocked the little track, Tom disappeared. From behind it came his voice. 'Here! Here! Tom found the man here.'

Anthony strode on and round the tree. He found himself in a small clearing through which the path still ran. Over this clearing was a carpet of fallen and rotting leaves, with every here and there sticking up out of this carpet like distorted fingers, sharp stumps of felled trees.

Immediately behind the great oak knelt Tom. He looked up at Anthony with a curious twist of the neck and tilting of the face which for the first time gave Anthony that little involuntary pang of disgust with which the sight of idiocy affects the sane. But he went close to the kneeler and looked down at him. He said:

'Which man, Tom? Which man lay here? Blackatter?'

'Yes. Yes.' The violent nodding again. 'Yes. Man with blood on his head. He was here, lying quiet. Tom found him. Tom found him. Clever!' His face broke into a wide, staring smile. A little white froth flecked the corners of his lips.

Anthony nodded. He picked up a twig from the ground and idly played with it. He said:

'And where was the other man lying, Tom? Over there?' He nodded to his left. He saw the little bank the reports described; it sloped up and away from the clearing. And at its foot was just such a stump as a man, climbing up the bank in the dark and with haste, might, if he lost his footing, fall back to strike his head upon.

Tom wriggled to his feet. He ran, nodding, to this stump. He shouted:

'Yes. Yes. Other man lied here.' He pointed down at the stump. 'Tom show you. Tom show you.' He ran back to Anthony, covering the ground in long, leaping, unsteady steps. At Anthony's feet he flung himself down, panting. 'First man,' he said, 'lie here . . . Like this!' He squirmed over upon his face, twitched his arms and legs this way and that—and then was immovable. Not even, it seemed, did he breathe. Every line in that big body spoke of death. Anthony's eyes, which had seen as much death as most men's and more, widened for a moment, then narrowed as he bent his head to stare at the body.

It was very cold in the wood, and there was no sunlight; no sound. Anthony put out a foot and stirred the body. He said sharply:

'That'll do now. I've seen.'

The twisted thing lay in slack, lifeless abandon. Anthony stared at it. For a moment a cold doubt was born in his mind; born of man's instinctive belief in that which he cannot understand. But he pushed this doubt from him. He said again, and now with an edge to the sharpness of his tone:

'That will do now. Get up. I've seen.'

Under his eyes life flowed back into the sprawling heap. Tom wriggled, and was upon his back; squirmed and was sitting up, his knees under his chin, his arms clasped about his knees. He raised his head to look up at Anthony above him. To his cheeks and nose and forehead were sticking clots of loam and mouldered leaves. His mouth was drawn down at the corners and its lips trembled. His eyes were like the eyes of a whipped and reproachful dog. He said, his high voice trembling with tears:

'Tom only showed. The man lied like that. Tom only showed.'

Anthony, on a sudden, dropped to sit beside him. He said quietly:

'That's all right, old chap. You showed me very well. Like to show me how Bronson lay? The other man.'

Tom was on his feet in a whirling rush of arms and legs. 'Yes. Yes. Tom show you.' He ran the few yards to the stump at the bank's foot. Again he cast himself down. But this time he lay upon his back. His feet pointed up the bank; his head lay, lolled to one side, near the black tumulus of the stump. He was inert, but there was not about him now that look of deadness. His right hand was clenched loosely, as if it were holding some invisible thing.

Anthony rose. He walked over and stood looking down at this strange mummer. He said, after a moment:

'That'll do, Tom. Thank you. Sit up now.'

Tom sat. Once more he huddled his knees beneath his chin and clasped about the knees and arms. But now the face which he turned to Anthony was bright and proud. He put up a hand and brushed from his cheeks and nose and forehead those black patches. Beside him, Anthony once more himself sat down. He still played with the twig, and presently from a pocket he pulled a glittering penknife and began to whittle. He kept his eyes upon this task but out of the corner of the left saw the eyes of Tom fixed upon the little knife with a gaze of hopeless and almost lustful longing.

He went on whittling. He said, his tone as idle-seeming as his actions:

'How was it you found them, Tom? It was late, wasn't it? Night-time. Are you often here at night?'

Tom kept his eyes upon the knife. 'Pretty!' he said. 'Tom always here at night in summer. Often always.' He stabbed a pointing forefinger towards the wood's dark heart. 'Little house there,' he said. 'Tom sleep there. Sometimes often. In summer. They let Tom sleep there. They know Tom.' His eyes never left the knife. He said again: 'Pretty! Pretty!'

Anthony said: 'Little house? What house is that, Tom? A hut, is it?'

Tom nodded. His round head rolled and jerked on its short, thick neck. 'Yes. Yes. Hut. Mr Appleby's hut. But he lets Tom sleep there often always in summer sometimes.'

Anthony was carving the twig now. It was a short, gnarled, thickish twig. Under the strokes of the penknife's blade it was taking on the shape of a dog's head. He held up his handiwork the better to see it. He said:

'That's going to be a nice dog, isn't it?'

Tom took his eyes from the penknife at last; they grew round in wonder at the penknife's work. Once more his head was set jerking and rolling by his nod. Anthony said:

'So you were sleeping in Mr Appleby's hut. What waked you, Tom? Was it the gun going off?' His tone was smooth, but not his mind. He remembered the verbatim reports of Tom's evidence, and in that evidence there had been nothing of this hut, nor of the habits of Tom in summertime. He went on carving. He waited.

This time Tom did not nod. Tom shook his head. 'No, not much. Tom heard gun.' He lifted his great shoulders in a shrug. Then eagerly: 'But Tom saw!'

Anthony's mind was once more back with the papers in that

dusty-orange binding. He said, suddenly and with a change of tone:

'When you went into the Court and they asked you all those questions, were you frightened?'

Again the rolling head showed dissent. 'No. Not afraid. Dadda was there. Dadda tell Tom how to say.'

'He did,' said Anthony to himself, 'did he?' But the words had no sound. He said aloud: 'Would you show me your little hut?'

There was a scraping, heaving rustle as Tom got to his feet. He did not speak, but his nod was violent and delighted. Anthony rose. He shut the shining penknife with a snap.

'Have you got a knife, Tom?' he said. Beside his companion he began to walk, away from the clearing and the path, towards what seemed the densest part of the wood. Tom said:

'Yes. Got a knife. Big, ugly knife.' He put his hand to his side pocket and brought it away gripped about a large and battered pruning-knife.

Anthony swung the little penknife by its ring. 'Would you like this one?' he said.

Tom's eyes grew round and rounder. He did not speak, but he nodded a series of nods. Anthony said:

'I'll give it to you. If you're a good lad and help me. You tell me what I ask, Tom. Will you?'

Again the nodding. 'Yes. Yes. Everything. And then Tom have the pretty knife.' He strutted and jerked along with swinging arms and loosely-working legs.

The going was rougher now and brambled undergrowth tore at their clothes and clogged their steps. They fell into single file, Tom leading. They came through dense trees to another clearing. A hut of tarred planks was there and Tom changed his walk to a shambling run. He threw open the latched door and proudly pointed.

Anthony, stooping, went in. Tom came at his heels. It was dark in the hut, but enough light came through the small window for Anthony to see that here was nothing to be seen. He went out again and before the hut stood looking about him. He found that, through the trees, he could just see that other clearing. He turned and touched Tom upon the shoulder. He said:

'You were in here, Tom, when you heard that bang?'

Tom shook his head. 'No. No. Tom didn't hear. Tom was sitting on box. Tom saw.' His tone was apathetic. His eyes were shining; but they were fixed upon the knife in Anthony's fingers.

Anthony put the thing into a pocket. 'You'll get that,' he said, 'when you've told me what I ask you.' His tone, by contrast with that of a moment before, was stern almost to harshness.

Tom's lower lip thrust itself out. His whole mouth quivered. Tears sprang sparkling into his eyes. He hung his head.

Anthony, his hands thrust deep into his pockets, strove for patience. He was cold in body but his mind was afire. He tried another gambit. He said:

'*Show* me, Tom. The way you showed me the men were lying. Show me everything you did when you saw. Understand me?'

Tom's sheepishness left him. He drew himself rigidly upright. He nodded his jerky, lolling nod. He did not speak, but turned and went into the blackness of the little hut, and came out bearing a topless sugar-crate. In the hut's mouth he set this, and himself atop of it. He sat sprawlingly, as if he were tired, and leaned his back against the rough pole which was the door-jamb. His eyes were half-closed; his head began to sink towards his chest as if sleep were coming to him . . .

He sat on a sudden bolt upright, lifting his head sharply. He jumped to his feet with a quick, clumsy movement which sent the box crashing on to its side within the hut. He ran forward three paces, thus passing the silent, watching Anthony. He stood still, his head out-thrust, staring between the trees towards the clearing . . . He began to walk, rapidly, not going by the easier way they had come but straight down the avenue of vision. He stepped high through the tangled undergrowth. His arms waved and flapped.

Anthony followed. He went slower. When he came to the

clearing, Tom was by the big oak and kneeling, his hands running this way and that, like clumsy moths, over an invisibility. Watching those hands, Anthony could see the body slack and limp beneath them.

Anthony stood still, Tom scrambled to his feet, looked down, looked up, looked this way and that . . . As he looked down at the body which was not there there was no emotion save astonishment upon that round and red and staring face, but as he looked up fear came—fear which made the lips gape wider and the eyes roll and a little trickle of saliva drool from a mouth corner. And the looks this way and that were looks which sought escape . . .

A deep frown carved a V between Anthony's eyes. But he waited motionless. Tom looked up again, right up, it seemed, at the tree-tops—and then, turning, began to run. He ran as Anthony had not yet seen him run; he ran with that wild speed which terror alone will give. He ran until he reached the foot of the small bank where there stood, sticking up black and malignant, the stump by which had been found the unconscious Bronson . . .

And as the wild, leaping, grotesque yet compelling figure reached that stump, so Anthony saw another body which was not there. For the feet of Tom met something, which was not there, and over that something Tom fell asprawl upon his face. For a moment he lay motionless; then scrambled to his knees and swung round and once more began his fluttered pawings. And then he stood. And then he looked back, across the clearing, to the big oak and what lay beneath it. And then he stared at what was beneath his hands. He stood, once more, fearfully, craned his neck back to look right upwards, and then walked up the bank and made off through the trees and was lost to sight. But as he went he did not run. He walked, and with only his normal oddities of gait.

Anthony did not move. The frown was deeper yet between his eyes. He looked not after Tom, nor at the foot of the big oak, nor across at the stump at the bank's foot. He looked straight ahead at the trees with eyes which did not heed them.

Tom came back. Not by the way he had gone. He came through the trees at the far end of the clearing. He trotted with a shambling, happy trot. There was a loose, expectant smile upon his face.

Anthony roused himself. Tom came near and halted and held out his hand. He was not acting now. The wood seemed not so dark, not so cheerless, not so cold.

Anthony took the little penknife from his pocket and dropped it into the outstretched palm. Tom's fingers closed lovingly about it. Down at its glitter he gazed happily. He did not move until Anthony took his arm. He started then. Anthony said:

'We'll go back, Tom. Take me the other way. The road way.' And was led then in the path of Tom's recent disappearance. Past the stump they went, and up the little bank and through more trees, quickly thinning, and were on a rutted cart-track. The whole distance from the clearing was not more than thirty yards. And yet, in that clearing, one seemed deep in a small forest.

Anthony's brows went up. He was surprised. And then that frown of concentration came again.

At the other side of the cart-track a hedgerow ran. Looking over it Anthony saw a road; a narrow but well-conditioned road probably marked upon maps as of the second class. Fifteen yards to his right there was a gate. Tom led the way to this, and over it, for it was locked with chain and padlock.

Over the gate he turned left and, Anthony beside him, began to walk down Pedlar's Hill to Farrow. For the first quarter-mile they walked in silence. After that Anthony spoke. He said:

'Tom, do you like birds?' His voice was idle; but his eyes, glancing sideways to catch the first reaction to this question, were hard and bright and keen.

Tom gave his epileptic nod which was many nods, diminishing. 'Oh, yes! Yes. Tom love the birds. They like Tom.' He began to whistle. The cold air was filled with the song of a thrush.

For a while they talked of birds and the ways of birds, from sparrow to plover. This talk brought them to the foot of the hill and the two lone cottages which were Farrow's only straggling. Anthony let the talk die. He spoke again as they turned the corner by Floxon's Mill. He looked up at the three great elms by the road's edge.

'*That*'d be a tree to climb!' he said. 'Ever climb trees, Tom?'

Again the nodding, delighted. 'Yes. Yes. Tom climb. Often always. See long ways. Everything small.'

Anthony was busy with his pipe. He halted a moment while he tapped it out against a lifted heel. He said, more idly yet:

'Many men climb trees here?'

Not the nod this time. A negative shaking instead. 'Only the boys. They climb. They take the eggs. Bad! Bad!'

The last rap of Anthony's pipe against his heel sounded almost savage.

They walked on. Near to the little shop over whose doorway was the name of Tom's father, the footsteps of Tom began to lag. Anthony sensed reluctance. But he was silent. He feared that time, perhaps, had been wasted. Not that he had learnt nothing. He had, definitely, learnt something. But—he smiled wryly to himself—what was it?

Tom's steps grew slower. He liked this gentleman. A kind gentleman. He did not want to leave the gentleman. And then the gentleman, who had been walking faster than Tom liked, came to a sudden stop. And he asked Tom another question. He did not ask it lazily, he asked it quickly and sharply, rather in the way that other gentleman in the Big Place—the gentleman with the odd hair—had asked him questions. This new gentleman stopped walking and caught hold of Tom's arm and looked straight into Tom's eyes and said:

'It's nice in the moonlight, isn't it? . . .'

Anthony's third shot, this. And his last. No more were needed. A clear bull's-eye.

Tom shivered. Tom's eyes seemed, even while held by those

of his questioner, to cringe. His body shrank. His lips worked. Little twitches of fear worked like ripples over the smooth blankness of his face.

Anthony released the arm. He smiled. He said kindly:

'That's all right, old chap. Don't like it myself. I tell you what, you come and have tea with me. Like buns and jam?'

Tom straightened. Tom grinned happily. Tom nodded with rather dreadful vigour.

Into The Horse and Hound by its back entrance Anthony led his guest. As they entered, the big clock at the stair's foot chimed four o'clock.

IV

So also did the grandfather clock which towered dimly in the corner of the parlour of Ashvale Farm. A dank and airless parlour. Clean enough, but with, permeating it, the feel and odour of the room which is never used. It was very cold here, and the grey dusk of the winter afternoon seemed intensified.

Mr Flood pulled his overcoat more closely about him. He strove to keep his shivering to himself. A notebook lay upon the oak table before him, and in the blue fingers of his right hand was a pencil. Facing him, the width of the table between them, was a short, square man of a stolid solidarity; a man whose age was not less than thirty-five and not more than fifty; a man whose tanned face seemed neither harsh nor gentle, intelligent nor stupid, interested nor interesting. His eyes were of a pale, slatey grey and the trick he seemed to have of keeping them all the time widely opened—so that no lid was ever visible—was the one remarkable thing about him. His clothes were like the rest, neither one thing nor another, neither the garb of a farmer, nor of a quiet 'country gentleman', nor of a man who followed business in a country town. His curt manner was neither civil nor boorish, patient nor impatient.

For nearly an hour had Flood been in this room . . . and an

hour had been his time. He made a final, flourishing note and
beneath it dashed the line of a finale. He shut the notebook and
clipped the pencil back into its pocket. He said, with the bluff
yet very courteous heartiness which had been his from the beginning of the interview:

'Very many thanks, Mr Dollboys. Sorry to've kept you so long.
Very good of you to be so accommodating. Very good!'
He flipped open his notebook again and scanned its pages. He
nodded decisively. 'It'll make a very good article,' he said. 'The
stuff's all there. It'll be Number Three in the "Famous Trials
by Witness" Series. And so soon as my Editor's received it,
he'll send you a cheque, Mr Dollboys. No need for you to
worry over that. By being so courteous to me for an hour, and
answering all my questions, you'll very likely be fifty guineas
or so the richer.' He laughed with hearty delight; very friendly
and yet respectful was Mr Flood.

Dollboys made a sound which was neither word nor grunt.
He shifted about in his chair a little, as one trying to get another
to terminate himself his visit.

Flood got promptly to his feet. He thrust the notebook into
the side-pocket of his tweed overcoat. He rubbed his cold hands
together and announced his departure.

Dollboys muttered in his throat. Something about a cup of tea.
He was not enthusiastic; neither was he surlily dutiful.

Flood shook his head. 'I thank you,' he said, 'no. I've got to
get along.'

Dollboys rose now, and led the way out into the dark square
hall with its stone floor and gloomy iciness. He opened the
door as Flood took from the table his hat and gloves. He said
to Flood:

'Well . . . evening, Mister. And glad you an' me's done each other
a bit o' good. Not that *I* knew much about yon business . . .'

Flood smiled with good-humoured reproach. 'Now, Mr
Dollboys!' he said. 'After all, you *were* the principal witness. And
the only one, *I* should say, who had any head on his shoulders.'

The flickering ghost of a smile for a moment gave semblance of life to Dollboy's face. He said:

'Well . . . I s'pose there's no denying that . . .'

Flood shook his bland head. 'There isn't, Mr Dollboys. Not a bit . . . Good afternoon, and many thanks. If all the people one interviewed were as pleasant over the job as you've been, my life 'd be a lot easier.' He put on his hat and passed out through the door which his host held open for him; held neither fully open nor so nearly closed that egress was difficult.

Flood's first ten strides across the railed-in yard towards his little car were brisk and decisive. The tenth took him half of his way. And then, in gait and demeanour, there came a change. He checked in mid-stride, as a man will check who suddenly has remembered something of import; he hesitated; he went on towards the car, but he went on with a shorter pace, doubtful and hesitant. It was very well done. Dollboys, motionless in the doorway, watched him with, it seemed, neither curiosity nor idleness.

Flood reached the car; opened its door; lifted a leg to enter; put the leg down again. As a man who has on a sudden taken a decision, he shut the car door again, turned briskly about and went back to the square house-front and the house's owner. He smiled apologetically as he drew near—apologetically but with the inoffensive pride of one who does a kindly deed. At the house door he stood awhile with Dollboys. He talked earnestly, and with a little gesticulation. Twice Mr Dollboys nodded, neither emphatically nor wearily: no expression crossed that wooden face . . .

'So I thought I'd mention it,' Flood said. His tone was not without the tinge of nervousness which seemed suitable. His round, rather youthfully florid face wore a look of gravity. His blue eyes were candid, and innocent without foolishness.

Dollboys nodded. 'Much obliged,' he said, 'I'm sure.'

'Right,' said Flood. 'Thought I'd better mention it. You've been very patient with me and one good turn deserves another. That's

what *I* always say.' He turned to go. Over his shoulder he said:
'You can't mistake him if you do see him, that's one thing . . .
Goodbye again.' He ran towards the car.

'Evenin',' said Dollboys. As the little car shot out of the gateway
he closed the door. The cold dusk of the grey afternoon filled
the yard. The square house stood solid, looking blankly out over
its bare fields.

Flood's car bumped its too rapid way down the farm-lane to
the high road; slowed; swung right in the direction of the four-
mile distant Farrow; was off at speed. But halfway to Farrow it
slowed and, almost stopping, swung into the obscurity of the
little, perpetually overgrown lane which runs, between high and
wooded banks, from the main Greyne road to Finchmere and
the Hunt Kennels. A hundred yards up the lane—which is nearly
as far as a car can penetrate—a figure came out of the left-hand
hedge and halted him. A lean, leather-clad psittaceous figure.

'Whoa!' said Dyson.

The car jerked; stopped. Flood pushed out his head. He
grumbled:

'Came far enough up the alley, didn't you? Where's the bike?'

Dyson jerked his head at the hedgerow behind him. 'Where
d'you think! Seen him?'

Flood nodded.

'Go all right?' Dyson came closer. He thrust out his beaked
faced. Behind the great spectacles his black eyes gleamed in
the half-light. Flood said:

'Like a dream! I worked him carefully. Made real notes 'n
everything. He thinks he'll see his name all over the middle
pages of Belton's monthly. And get . . .'

Dyson interrupted. 'Cut it out! What's he like?'

Flood grinned. 'Keep civil, you toad. Mr Andrew Connicott
Dollboys is like nothing. So much like nothing that he makes
you quite uncomfy. Most nondescript, non-committal stick *I've*
ever rubbed against. Bit too much so, p'r'aps. Or p'r'aps that's
my imagination. Quite ready with his stuff on the case, though.

No hesitation, no biases, no awkwardness—in fact, quite entirely straightforward . . .'

Dyson cut in again. 'Right!' he snapped. His thin-lipped mouth seemed to disappear on the word. 'Do the rest?'

Flood nodded. 'I should say I did! You can tell the whole world that I gave Mr A. C. Dollboys such a picture of Mr Francis Dyson that he'd know you a mile off. Know you—and *probably* fight shy of you. You're a shark, Mogul; an interfering, cold-blooded, most unpleasant, persistent, thick-skinned, utterly unpopular stick-at-nothing crime reporter. You are famous among those who know. It was really you who solved the Billington case, the Shop Murders, the Liverpool Arson ramp, and the Greenford poisoning job. The Police—probably by bribing you—took the credit. But all Fleet Street—though they hate you like hell—know the truth. And your name—though quite probably you'd give a different one—is Marable. And I've seen you in the district today and have wondered what you're showing your beak round here for and think it just *might* be something to do with the Blackatter murder. And so I've just warned my pal A. C. Dollboys to have nothing whatever to do with you, you being . . .'

'That'll do!' Dyson waved a gauntletted hand. 'Going back?'

'Yes.' Flood started his engine and put his gear into reverse. Before the car moved he said: 'Put the gust right up him. *Might* hook something.'

Dyson's mouth appeared again. He smiled; a curious distortion of his face. He stood a moment watching while Flood backed down the lane. He turned to the hedge and his motor-cycle . . .

It was at five o'clock precisely that the chill peace of Ashvale Farm was disturbed for the second time that afternoon. A stuttered roaring drove fowls in a squawking storm. A motor-cycle came up the rutted lane at thirty miles an hour. A lean man in leather brought this to a standstill before the oaken door.

He did not wait, this man, even to push up upon his helmet the talc goggles which were over his eyes. He fell upon the door and beat it with its heavy wrought-iron knocker. Thunder ensued.

The knocker was still in play when the door was flung open. Almost the man who knocked fell into the house. But his rush, voluntary or no, came to an end upon the chest of the house's owner.

'What the blasted? . . .' began Dollboys. His face, for that first instant, was not the neutral mask which Flood had seen. A mask, perhaps, but a mask of white, cold rage. But the pallor went, and the rage, immediately. It was as if an unseen sponge had been drawn across it, leaving it calm and controlled; neither this nor that.

A voice came from beneath the goggles; a rasping, rough-edged voice which said:

'Mr Dollboys? My name's Dyson. Press man. Want a few words with you. Spare a moment?' A gauntletted hand went up to the leather-cased head, pushing the goggles up and away from the fierce dark eyes magnified by the great glasses before them.

Dollboys stared; a flicker of some emotion—the ghost of an expression—crossed his face. He stared unwinking. The wide-open, seemingly lidless eyes took stock. They saw the bird-like face, the great glasses, the wisp of black hair straggling out from beneath the forehead-piece of the leather helmet; the stoop of the shoulders and the out-thrusting of the head between them. Dollboys stared. Dollboys said:

'I think y'r name's not Dyson. I've been told of you. You're Marable.'

The thin lips in the beaked face twisted into a snarling smile. They said:

'Possibly. Want a word with you. Spare a moment?'

'No!' said Dollboys. In Dyson's face the door shut with a controlled bang.

Dyson smiled. A real smile this time, not without triumph. He was enjoying himself. He stood looking at the door for a full minute. He then turned on his heel and went back to the centre of the yard and stood, legs astraddle and hands on hips, scanning the front of the house. Its blank-seeming windows, closed one and all, reminded him of the eyes of their possessor. He made a parade of his scrutiny. He saw the corner of a curtain twitch and something moving behind it. This was from the only lighted window. He gave no sign of having seen. He shrugged ostentatiously and turned back to his motor-cycle. In a moment the fowls again were storming in all directions. The roar of the exhaust receded down the lane.

At fifteen minutes past five Dyson, on foot, came through the copse behind the farm-house. At seventeen minutes past the hour he turned the handle of the farm-house's back door. It gave. He stood in the scullery. Facing him was a door, ajar, between the edge and jamb of which showed a line of soft yellow light. He stripped off goggles and helmet. He tiptoed to this door and softly pushed it until it stood wide. He slipped across its threshold and was in a wide, brick-floored kitchen. A great range showed its glowing fire between thick bars. Facing it stood a dresser of black oak. Two chairs and a table completed the furnishing. Food was on the table and a man and a woman in the chairs. The woman faced Dyson as he entered. The sitting man's back was Dollboys' back.

There was a clatter on the brick floor. The woman, jumping to her feet, had overturned the wooden chair upon which she had sat. She was an old woman; tall she was, and thin, and out of her pinched and many-wrinkled face stared terrified eyes. She put up a hand to her breast. She stared at Dyson and stared, No sound came from her. Dollboys, slowly, began to turn in his chair. He made no move to rise.

Dyson spoke to the old woman. He smiled at her a smile doubtless intended to he reassuring. He said:

'Sorry trouble. Want a few words with Mr Dollboys. Spare a moment?' This last sentence was to Dollboys, who now, his turn completed, sat and looked up, his wide eyes still unblinking, at the intruder. For perhaps the half of a second there had been in the unlidded eyes a glare. But now they were calm again; blank; emotionless.

Their owner got slowly to his feet. He put the chair from his path with a quiet and strong steadiness. He came three steps towards Dyson. He said: 'Get out. Quick.' His voice was level and quiet. There was no more feeling in it than that of a man who tells the hour to a stranger.

Dyson shook his head. His lank black hair tossed and flopped with the movement. He twisted his mouth with the snarling smile he had used just now at the other side of the house. He said:

'No. Only few words. I'm a press man. Want to talk to you about the Black . . .'

'Get out.' Dollboys came two steps nearer.

'Andrew!' The old woman's voice went up in a high, cracked note of fear. Dyson shot a quick glance at her. Why the fear? He said quickly:

'About the Blackatter case. I . . .'

Dollboys turned a shoulder to him. Dollboys said:

'Mother, you'd best run off. I'll get rid o' this.' He jerked a thumb at Dyson.

The old woman shuffled to the door. A creak and a rustle, and she was gone. Dollboys turned to face his visitor again. He said, not moving:

'Get out. I want none of your sort here. Shovin' your way in . . .'

Dyson sat down upon the table's edge. '*I* know,' he said wearily. '"Without so much as a by your leave." Say it. Then we'll get to business.'

Dollboys, without a word, turned his back. Without haste he crossed to the door through which the old woman had gone. He opened it and passed through, leaving it wide behind him.

Dyson sat where he was. He fumbled in some hidden recess in his overalls and brought to light his vast, black pipe, with it a tattered pouch of oilskin. He began to fill the pipe. He whistled—a painful, tuneless noise—between his teeth.

There came the sound of Dollboys' steady footsteps on the flags of the hall. The man came in. In his left hand was an old but well-kept fowling-piece. He halted three paces within the door. He said.

'Will y' get out? Or do I scatter some pellets into y'r legs?' His voice was as level and unemotionless as ever.

Dyson started. He looked at the weapon, then at its holder. His face expressed astonishment but no fear.

'Good God!' he said. 'Bit old-fashioned in your methods. Don't be silly. Put the thing away. Give me a moment. Want a few words on the Blackatter case. Press man.'

Dollboys did not speak. He slowly raised the gun towards his shoulder. Dyson said, sharply:

'Don't be a B.F. Put the thing down. Get into trouble, you will.' He suddenly leaned forward, bracing his hands at each side of him, on the table's edge. His shoulders were bowed, his neck and head sunk down between them. His beaked face seemed to thrust itself out towards Dollboys. Behind the spectacles the black eyes shone with a sudden and ferocious glitter. He stared. The eyes of Dollboys did not drop their glance; but the left hand of Dollboys lowered itself until once more the shotgun was harmlessly trailed. Dyson, still staring with forward-thrust head, spoke again. He said:

'I'm a press man. My paper's got hold of a story. Someone's saying the Blackatter case wasn't handled right. I'm on the job. Get me? So I'm digging up all the witnesses. You're one of the first. You're the one I want to talk to most. You're the chief witness for the prosecution. You're the man whose evidence put the rope round Bronson's neck. So you can help me. Maybe. I want a talk with you.' He broke off. In his tone there had been much which was not in his jerky, ambiguous-seeming little sentences. An undercurrent, savage and laden with suggestion.

A momentary flicker of feeling, untranslatable, passed over the wooden face of Dollboys. Dyson, glaring still, thought he perceived at work within the man the tales of Flood. He said, suddenly thrusting himself upright:

'Going to talk?'

Dollboys was once more expressionless. 'Why?' he said. 'Newspapers 're none o' my business. Not what they do, nor what they think.' His words came very slow; perhaps he was picking them with care; perhaps merely emphasising. He said: 'My duty, I did in the Court. You've no 'thority. Why should I waste my time on you and your newspapers?'

'Might,' said Dyson, stabbing the air with his pipe-stem, 'do you a bit of good. Financially . . .' He paused there; then added: 'Or it might not. But what *won't* do you any good's to refuse to talk. *That* . . .' Again he broke off. He shrugged. Dollboys saw the black, staring eyes narrow until they were slits. He said:

'Don't rightly see what you're talking about. But if you . . .'

But Dyson was looking at his watch upon his wrist. He said, cutting across the other's speech:

'Didn't know it was so late. Must cut along. I'll come back for that talk. Tomorrow say. Just a few words.' His glance swept over Dollboys, taking him in from head to foot. He thrust his pipe into his mouth and went out by the way he had come. As he closed the back door behind him he smiled. A thoughtful smile. Mr Dollboys was negative indeed. And steady enough. But Mr Dollboys had very soon ceased his gun-play. And at the last Mr Dollboys' forehead had been glistening with sweat.

Dyson went slowly across the fields to his cycle.

v

Mrs Murch was wroth. It was after five o'clock when the slow thudding crunch of Mr Murch's boots was heard upon the little gravel path leading to the cottage. And Mr Murch's tea had been waiting since four-fifteen.

Mr Murch entered the kitchen. In his policeman's uniform Mr Murch was not without a certain impressiveness, when helmeted. He took off the helmet now. A bald and pinkly-flushed scalp gave him at once the look of a self-important infant who from somewhere had procured, and stuck on none too skilfully, a moustache of gingery crepe hair.

Mr Murch aimed at the cheek of Mrs Murch a kiss. But it bounced on air, for Mrs Murch saw it coming. She said, with asperity:

'Nice time to come in! And you with nothing 'cept the Malldene licenses to 'tend to!'

For a second Mr Murch debated within himself the advisability of a tale of sudden and dramatic duties. But his invention—and he knew it—was not equal to this. He fell back on truth. He pulled up a chair to the table. He sat in it heavily. He loosened the collar of his tunic and said:

'Sorry, Mother. Met a chap an' got talkin'. Int'restin' chap. Bin in P'lice. Stayin' 'ereaways for a 'oliday. Fact 'e's up at the 'Orsenound. Name o' Spike or somep'n. Very int'restin' chap. Lot o' tales 'e 'ad . . .'

Mrs Murch laid before her husband, with a force which swayed the solid table, a plate of toast. She said:

'An' you told 'im some back, I'll lay. Fairy tales.'

'If y'want to *know*,' said Mr Murch with dignity, 'on'y one of my 'speriences I told 'im of was the murder.'

Mrs Murch banged down the teapot now. 'An' 'ow you enjoyed that talk!' she said. 'Since I forbid any more on the subjec' in this 'ouse a couple o' months since, this must be the first chance you've 'ad. An' I'll wager you made the most of it. *And* I'll wager your p'lice friend didn't hurry off neither!' She poured tea into a great cup.

Mr Murch took a draught from that cup. He sighed and wiped his moustache. He said:

'If you want to *know*, 'e was int'rested, very *much* int'rested. 'E's a intelligent 'uman bean. *Of* which'—here Mr Murch inhaled more tea—'there are precious foo about.'

Mrs Murch sniffed. But as ill-temper abated, some slight curiosity took its place. She sat down to face her husband.

'Why should 'e be so full of int'rest. Don't they 'ave any crimes round 'is way?'

'Plenty.' Mr Murch plainly resented this slur upon his acquaintance's usual environment. 'More,' he said with much emphasis, 'than the general publick knows of. Lot more . . . An' bafflin' crimes at that . . . But what 'e was int'rested in was the p'lice aspeck o' Blackatter's murder. 'Ow we 'andled such things down in the country. An' such like.' Mr Murch chuckled; a gratified sound. 'An' I told 'im . . . 'E was int'rested. As neat an' quick a job, 'e says, as the London p'lice could of done . . . Ay, 'e said that.' Mr Murch leaned back in his chair and looked out through the window with a far-away look.

'Which,' said Mrs Murch, now again her pleasant self, 'is only what they said down here. The very words the Chief Constable used.'

Mr Murch nodded. 'That's right; so 'e did. But 'e's not a *p'liceman*, as you might say, Colonel Ravenscourt isn't. Pleasant to 'ear the same words from a man *in* the game . . .' He drank more tea, with an enjoyment by no means silent.

'Ar!' said Mrs Murch in agreement.

VI

Anthony stood in the inn's porch and watched the thick and shambling figure of Tom loll, slouching, off into the evening darkness; a full Tom and a happy Tom, the richer by one shining penknife and an equally shining coin.

Anthony turned on his heel to re-enter the inn. But he did not. For there came to his ears the sound of his own car. He waited. With a white, hard glare of headlights it swung, throbbing, into the yard, White at the wheel. It slowed; stopped. Lucia came from it. Anthony went down the steps to meet her. She said, clutching at his arm:

'I'm cold, cold, cold! . . . *Did* you bring tails or only a dinner-jacket?'

Anthony put an arm about her. 'Come and get warm. I brought both. Why?' He led her in silence into the house and upstairs to their room where a fire of coal and logs shot blue and orange flames halfway up the chimney.

She stood before this blaze and let him slip the fur coat from her. She said:

'Why d'you want tails? Because we're going to a party. Yes, we are! Tonight!' She turned to face him. Her hands came up and gripped each a lapel of his coat. Her eyes were shining. Her breath came quick. Her lips trembled a little with excitement. 'Oh, Anthony!' she said. 'It seems . . . it *does* seem . . . there is *something* helping us. There is! Listen: When you sent me to the Marstons', I thought—I really did, darling—I thought you were just being kind and *finding* something for me to do; something I couldn't make a muddle of because it wasn't really anything to do . . . No, it's no good starting to say you wouldn't do such a thing, because you're perfectly capable of it and it's quite likely! . . . But whether you intended it that way . . . all right, you didn't then! . . . Whether you intended it that way or not, I think it's been useful. Darling, *everybody* was there, this afternoon of all afternoons. You remember what you said to us after lunch, about being certain that we should only find anything by looking among "the gentry"? . . .'

Anthony groaned. 'Woman, woman! I said nothing of the sort. "Certain" is a word I'm careful with. I treat it tenderly. I said, in almost these words: It won't pay us to ignore the local heads. The nobs. The only possible link between our X and Bronson and Blackatter is blackmail. And you don't blackmail someone who's got nothing. We should ignore the lowly in riches and go for the middle and highs.'

'You said,' said Lucia with a fine and illogical indignation, '"particularly the highs".'

Anthony grinned at her. 'Very probably. Because highs are worth more than middles. And because they're more improbable. And if there's any answer to this riddle, it's an improbability. Go on, now.'

She made a small grimace at him. She said:

'Betty Marston was charming to me. Nice of her, I thought. We've only met about half-a-dozen times. It was her At Home day. I babbled. I didn't know I could be so terribly unlike me so easily. I was *the* talkative wife. I took you at your word, darling. You said: tell the world what we're at. And I *did*. I really did. They'd *all* 've thought I was mad, if it hadn't been for your name. They all knew about you. Betty began to tell them, but they all knew. I looked down my nose and literally simpered. When I'd told them what you were in this part of the world for, there was a noise like the parrot-house. I've always wondered what "a sudden hum of conversation" meant. I know now, only "hum's" not a loud enough word . . . But it was wonderful luck! You wanted the news spread. And instead of it taking a day and a night and perhaps more, here it is simply bubbling over the whole county. *And* you wanted—didn't you?—to see the local high-lights. And here am I, with an invitation to both of us which'll let you see them—*all* of them—all at once and tonight. I . . .' She ceased abruptly. A soft rapping had come upon the door.

'Come in!' said Anthony.

The door opened. Bronson's wife stood in the doorway, just beyond the bright circle of light cast from the globe in the ceiling. She stood tall and straight and still. In that stillness was a tension which had about it something terrible. It was untold by outward sign, yet to the watchers it was the more apparent for its invisibility. It held them motionless too—for a moment which seemed minutes.

Lucia went towards her at last. With a smooth rush, like something released, suddenly, from powerful bonds which spring.

At this approach, Selma Bronson moved. A sudden movement; a movement which was like the reaction of an automaton to the pressing of a switch. She thrust out an arm. At its end the hand stood up almost at right angles, palm forward, fingers rigid. She said:

'Don't touch me!' Her voice was low, and hard. It was as if each word were cased in metal. And then: 'I am sorry!' she said, 'I did not think. I was afraid that you might touch me. You would not, I know. But I was afraid.'

Lucia looked at her dumbly. Anthony, with a savage little flick, hurled his cigarette into the fire. He came forward. He said:

'Did you want us, Mrs Bronson?' The words were meaningless, but in his voice was an inflection which brought the dark eyes of Lucia round to him in a sudden gratitude.

Selma Bronson bowed her head. In the half-light in which she stood, the smooth, ash-blonde hair glinted as if it were silver. She said:

'I wished to ask, is there . . . anything? Yet? . . . It is foolish of me, I have tried not to come; to worry. But I have come . . . Is there . . . anything?' She finished. Her hands, dangling by her sides, clenched suddenly into white fists. That was her only movement. Her eyes were upon Anthony.

He met their gaze with his own. The green eyes looked into the blue. He said, slowly and with a deliberation:

'Yes. There is more than I had any hope for.'

A small sound came from the white throat. The tall figure swayed. A slight movement. Instantly it was still again and erect. Its impassive rigidity told of a strength of will and body almost more than human. Lucia sobbed, once.

Anthony spoke again. He said:

'You can help. You must tell me a thing. On that night, was there bright moonlight?'

There was a pause. Her throat moved. She said at last:

'There were clouds. Black clouds. And a high wind. There was moonlight, but not all the night. Early it was a black night.'

'Until—?' said Anthony.

'Until,' she said, 'at least the half an hour after ten.'

Anthony bowed. He smiled a grave, small smile. He said:

'And that has helped me too. It was what I wanted to hear. Unless you wish it, I won't explain now. There are other things I shall want to ask you. In the meantime . . . we do what we can. Everything we can.'

'I know,' said the woman. 'I cannot thank you. But I do thank you.' She turned. There was a little, eddying draught. And then a soft click as the door closed.

Lucia sat, heavily, upon the bed's edge. She covered her face. Anthony put a hand upon her shoulder. She showed him a face drained of colour. She said:

'My God! Before she came in, I was laughing. *Laughing!* My God, I *laughed* before she came in. I *laughed*. I was *laughing*!' Her voice broke on a sob. The sob became another sob and that sob laughter not good to hear; a choked, rising crescendo.

Anthony took her by the shoulders. He shook and went on shaking. He said, in a voice which grated:

'Stop that at once!'

The sound ceased. The shaking ceased. His wife leaned her head against his body.

'I'm sorry,' she said. 'I'm sorry.'

'So am I,' Anthony said. 'I'm a brute. But well-intentioned with it . . . Where, my delight, is this party you're so proud of?'

Lucia dabbed at her eyes. 'General Brownlough's. He's rather a dear . . . I think.' She looked up suddenly at Anthony. 'It *is* useful, this chance of meeting them all at once, isn't it?'

Anthony nodded with decision. ''Course. You're right, luck's with us . . . so far.' To a new knocking upon the door he said: 'Come in!'

It was the pretty and diminutive Annie, who said that below were three gentlemen who asked for Mr Gethryn. Mr Pike and the other two gentlemen who . . .

'I'll come down,' said Anthony, cutting her short.

But she lingered. She seemed to be about to shut the door upon herself but did not. Her charming gaze sought Anthony's. Her negligible weight was shifted from one foot to the other.

Her small face was a dull and angry red. But her eyes were bright and a little furtive. Anthony said, slowly:

'I—will—come—down.'

She went then. Anthony looked at Lucia, Lucia at Anthony.

'Merely your beaux-yeux?' said Lucia.

Anthony shook his head. 'I fancy not. Something worries the chit. What is it? What's the tangled web she weaves. Or isn't there one. D'you know, I could bear to know all about this.' He pointed a finger at his wife. 'Your job, Corporal.'

VII

They went downstairs then, to find in the Smoking Room Pike and Flood and Dyson.

'Pike,' said Anthony when they were settled, 'open the ball.'

Pike did not lose time. 'I spent most of the afternoon, sir, with the local PC—Murch. He's the ordinary blockhead; not so stupid as some nor so clever as others. I got a deal of information. What use it may be, *I* can't tell. But I'm ready with it, sir.' He tapped thoughtfully upon the notebook in his pocket. 'It'll likely come in when we least expect it. After Murch and I went on a general sort of gossiping tour, as you might say. On the lines you suggested, sir. I got the tone of the district, I think. And it's just what you might expect—and no more. All very surprised they were—at the time. Didn't seem possible that Bronson could be a murderer. But there it was; no denying the facts and all that . . .' Here Pike hesitated, to add at last: 'Can't help feeling, sir, if I may say so, that I must've caused more talk than I got, if you follow me. I was tactful all right. But that's no matter. If they haven't got on to it already that there's some sort of something doing in the Bronson case, they very soon will . . .'

Anthony interrupted. 'And that, Pike, I don't mind about. Not one little bit. In fact I'm glad. I've said before, we're working this business upside-down, so we may as well be thoroughly inverted. Instead of keeping quiet, we'll be noisy—(a) because owing to the time-limit we couldn't be quiet even if we wanted to, and (b) because it'll pay us. If we beat round the pool hard enough and loud enough we may scare something up. Someone may show his hand through fear. Whereas if he didn't know there was any bobbery going on, he wouldn't. And our object is, primarily, to save Bronson from the nine o'clock walk. Our ends won't be met if we let them hang him and *then* catch the real It . . . No'—he looked round at his listeners—'make a noise by all means, even when there's nothing real to make a noise about. Only keep the noises sinister . . . Anything more, Pike?'

Pike shook his head. His long face was set and sad. He said:

'Nothing, sir.' Again he tapped the notebook in his pocket. 'Not until my notes *re* Murch's talk come in useful.'

'You found,' asked Anthony, 'no feeling, nor any suggestion of any feeling, that anyone you saw thought there was even a possibility of Bronson's innocence?'

Pike shook his head. 'None, sir. None whatever. I think the general run of ideas is that Blackatter'—he dropped his voice suddenly and looked over his shoulder at the closed door—'is that Blackatter *was* mixed up with Mrs Bronson.'

'Which,' said Anthony, 'is the natural and easy thing. It explains everything for them. It's the line of least resistance for their atrophied minds.'

'That,' said Lucia, 'also seems the impression in the upper circle . . . *Fools!*'

Pike shook his head again, slowly and hopelessly. He said:

'If you ask *me*, the job's impossible. *Can't* be done. Not in the time. Even if there *is* a job . . .'

'Mr Pike!' said Lucia.

Pike jerked himself upright in his chair. His face flushed. 'I'm sorry!' he said.

Lucia smiled at him. He flushed yet more darkly and became busy with pipe and pouch. The silence was broken by Flood. Flood said, in a brisk and matter-of-fact voice:

'Half the trouble—if not all of it—is that defence of Bronson's.

He or his counsel or both ought to be spanked. Look at their case. Just look at it—or the mess they made of it! All "no's" or "don't-knows" is what it came to. "Did you go to meet Blackatter that night?" "No." "Why did Blackatter seem to refer, in your bar that night, to a possible meeting that night?" "Don't know." "Did you hear what he said?" "No, he said something, but I didn't catch it." "Did you see Blackatter in Bellows Wood?" "No." "How did you come to be lying, stunned, where you were found?" "Don't know. Something hit me." "You didn't fall, then, and strike your head against the tree-stump?" "No. Something hit me." "Were you aware that traces of blood and hair from the wound in your head were found in that tree-stump?" "No." "If you didn't go to Bellows Wood to meet Blackatter, what were you doing there?" "Nothing. Walking home." "Had you been shooting?" "No. I'd taken my gun to Blackfan coverts but I hadn't used it." "Were you trespassing, or poaching, in Blackfan?" "No. I have permission to shoot there." "Do you *generally* do your shooting at *night*?" "No. Hardly ever. But I always carry the gun." "Why?" "I don't know." "You had not fired the gun that night or during the day?" "No." "How then, was it found with a recent discharge from both barrels?" "Don't know." "Were you acquainted with Blackatter before he came to live in this district?" "No." "Had you any dealings or meetings with him other than those to do with your inn?" "No."'

Flood paused for breath. He had spoken all this very fast. He said now: 'And so on . . . *and* so on. It's pitiful. It's dripping! Bronson's counsel ought to've been shot.'

'He couldn't,' said Lucia in a low voice, 'do anything with Bronson. Bronson said: "I'll tell the truth and the truth is that I don't know anything about it." And there it was . . .' She stared into the fire.

'No,' said Anthony, 'it wasn't too good. It was, in fact, bad and damn' bad. It wasn't a Defence; it was a sort of Rider to the Prosecution.'

Dyson came to life. He said to Flood:

'The worst of these "No's" was the one you left out. The one you told me this morning. They say to Bronson: "Did you ever receive a letter from Blackatter?" "No," says Bronson. "Then how do you explain this one found in your pocket, ordering a meeting for that night in Bellows Wood?" "I don't," says Bronson. "You've never seen it before, I suppose?" says Crown, very nasty. "No," says Bronson. "Oh!" says Crown, nastier . . . And that's that!' Dyson let his head drop back to rest against his chair. His eyes closed again.

Anthony, who had been sitting, rose to his feel with a jerk. He began to pace up and down between the glowing fire and the curtained window. His pipe was in the corner of his mouth and clouds of its smoke hung about his head in the room's warm air. He came to a sudden halt and said:

'And now Dollboys.' He looked from Dyson to Flood; from Flood back again to Dyson. 'And that's *not* inapposite.'

Dyson opened his eyes. 'No?' he said. Then: 'P'r'aps not.' He turned his spectacles upon Flood. Who said:

'Report: At 3 p.m. I called at Ashvale Farm and interviewed its owner, Andrew Dollboys. I told him I represented Belton's Magazine, which was anxious to include an interview with, or a story by, him in its "Famous Trials by Leading Witnesses" series. He fell for it. I was with him just over an hour. We got on very well. In the hour, I prepared him; his mind was full of the Blackatter case again, but he wasn't worried about it. Nothing in my behaviour to worry him. Just as I was going I remembered something and let him see me remembering it. I remembered I'd seen'—he waved a hand towards the sprawling Dyson—'another journalist in the district. Not a nice journalist. In fact, a reporter. A crime reporter called Marable, who had the reputation of unravelling all mysteries and generally seeing justice done—and being very unpleasant in the course of it. I thought it unlikely that Marable was here to see Mr Dollboys, but just mentioned it in case. I strongly advised Mr Dollboys to have nothing to do with Marable (I described him) whatever name he happened to call himself. Of course, there was no suggestion that Mr Dollboys had anything to worry about. How could he? But Marable wasn't a desirable person to have poking round. I then left, having done all I could to put Mr Dollboys in a suitable frame of mind.'

Dyson sat up again. He said:

'Bit later *I* turned up. Dollboys very short. Heard about me. Shut door in my face. I went away. Returned to back door. Walked in. Great scene. Mother Dollboys sent away—very nervous. Dollboys fetches old shotgun. I'm very sinister. 'Tisn't what I say, it's the nasty way I say it. Dollboys thinks better of gun. Eventually I say I'll come back tomorrow. I go. Dollboys left. He was sweating. Literally. I want to know why. Why sweat? If there's no more in him than meets the eye, why sweat over a newspaper-man? Even me. 'Specially as Flood's seen he didn't object to the press . . . No. We're in luck. We wanted to find Dollboys fishy. And fishy he is.' Dyson fell silent, but now he did not lie back in his chair again. He still sat upright, and from one to the other of the group he darted glances, like a proud and sardonic but very untidy vulture.

Anthony looked at him. 'Dyson,' he said, 'is pleased with himself. And not without reason. He ought to be. And Flood too . . . It's all very heartening, this fishiness of Dollboys'. Let us consider Dollboys . . . It was Dollboys who heard what Blackatter said when Bronson turned him out of this house on the evening of the murder. Bronson did not hear it. Dollboys said that at the door Blackatter turned and made that remark at least suggestive of a pre-arranged meeting. And, if you look at that *private* bar, and remember that Dollboys was at the *saloon* bar, you will realise that Dollboys was some six feet farther away from Blackatter than was Bronson. And Bronson said—and stuck to it—that at the door Blackatter turned round and "muttered" something . . . Bronson is not deaf; he's as quick of hearing, I'm told, as anyone. And Bronson—never forget our hypothesis—is truth. *Ergo* Dollboys is lying when he said he heard. And now Dollboys sweats over what would, to a maculate soul, be at the worst an annoying experience.' He turned suddenly upon Flood. 'What,' he said, 'is the material worth of Dollboys?'

Flood shrugged. 'Very difficult to say. Impossible, almost, without inquiry. From what I saw of the menage, he might be living above his income, or inside it, or just making it balance.' He looked at Dyson. 'What d'you think, Mogul?'

Dyson shut his eyes. 'I say he's comfortable. No more. And his idea of comfort's not everyone's.'

Anthony looked at Pike. He said:

'How about it?'

Pike nodded, got swiftly to his feet and was gone. Anthony looked at the closing door with a smile of approval. He said:

'It occurs to me that if Dollboys faked the spoken message, he might know more of the written one . . .'

'Meaning?' said Dyson.

Flood took on the manner of a Sergeant-Major. He muttered: '*Wait* for it! Wait for it!'

'Meaning,' said Anthony, 'that it occurs to me to wonder if the letter from Blackatter, found in the pocket of Bronson, may not have been addressed, actually, to Dollboys. Speculation that, and perhaps impure.'

'You're saying,' Flood cut in, 'that Dollboys is X.'

Anthony shrugged. 'I'd like to think so. P'r'aps he is, but I can't feel it. I can feel, though, that he's in the equation somewhere.'

Dyson said: 'He could be X, that cove. It's in him to do what's been done . . .'

'And then,' asked Anthony swiftly, 'sweat at shadow-threats?'

Dyson was silent a moment. 'Maybe,' he said, eventually. There was no great conviction in his tone.

'Mr Dollboys,' said Flood softly, 'is frightened. Hadn't he better be frightened more? A lot more.' His round face seemed youthful and mild as ever, but Lucia, looking at him, shivered a little within herself when she saw his eyes. With the sudden illogicality of the female, she felt sudden pity for Dollboys. She strangled this emotion.

Anthony nodded. 'As much,' he said, 'as you like. P'r'aps more.'

The door opened. Pike came in, closing it swift and soft behind him. He came across the room to the fire. He said, looking at Anthony:

'I've had a word with Mrs Bronson. She knows all about Dollboys. Enough anyhow. He comes here a lot. He did before, and he does still. And that shows something of the man, I'd say!' Pike's eyes were slits, his long jaw was thrust out. 'But she says Dollboys has nothing. A little competence, and a small farm which would be neglected if it wasn't for the man's brother. As it is, it just pays. The man's got enough to clothe himself and feed himself and have a quiet drink when he wants it.'

'Has he,' said Anthony quickly, 'got a car? Or a motorbike? Did she say that?'

'Car,' said Pike. His jaw seemed to stick out farther. 'Tell you how I know, sir . . . He's here now!'

'Eh?' said Dyson, sitting really upright.

Flood whistled.

'As I was talking to Mrs Bronson, sir,' said Pike, 'she stopped suddenly. We were in that little office at the other end of the passage, behind the saloon-bar. She said: "That sounds like his car." And she looked out. It was. He always leaves it round the back.'

Dyson, his head to one side, was looking at Anthony like a speculative bird. He said:

'Why d'you ask, has he got a car?'

Flood nodded.

'Because,' said Anthony slowly, 'of what I learnt this afternoon. I spent most of it with T. Harrigan. You know the name. T. Harrigan is an arrested-development case. T. Harrigan at thirty has the mind of a boy often. And not an advanced boy at that. I went up to Bellows Wood with T. Harrigan. He showed me where and how he found the dead man and the unconscious man. He is an excellent actor—or mimic of himself. He can *re-live* an act. An asset; sometimes rather a grisly one. He re-lived for me and a pocket-knife. I thought I was going to get nowhere. But then, acting himself finding the men, he did a thing I couldn't understand. Twice, three times, he looked straight up, either at the tree-tops or the sun through them. And when he did, fear caught hold of him . . . It took me half an hour and all my brains to get at that. It wasn't any good just *asking* him point-blank, you see. That might have put him right off, or frightened him so that he wouldn't say. Or, asked definitely, he might not have remembered. His acting's not so much a memory—in fact I'd swear it isn't done at all from "memory" as we know the word—as the reproduction, by his body, of an unrealised cinematographic picture in his tiny mind. Garbled, that, but the best I can do . . .

'Anyhow I got at this thing that puzzled me by a series of question and answer. Animal, Vegetable or Mineral technique. I got it—*at* last . . . T. Harrigan is terrified of the moon. Though he spends much time alone at night in the woods, that time, if there is bright moonlight, is spent in shelter. He won't go out into moonlight. The wildest horses wouldn't make him. The very word makes him tremble. Quite a usual thing with that mentality. *But*—have you heard any mention yet of this failing of T. Harrigan's?' Anthony broke off. He let that sink in. There was silence, broken only by a little hissing whistle from Flood. But Pike was staring, and Dyson once more was bolt upright in his chair. Lucia, her dark eyes lakes of bewilderment, looked from one man to another.

Anthony, too, looked at the three men, 'Yes,' he said at last. 'It is like that, isn't it?'

Dyson relapsed again into an ungainly heap. '*If*,' he said, 'he didn't have a torch, or a lantern, it is.'

Anthony shook his head. 'He had neither torch nor lantern. *And* he left his little hut where he sometimes sleeps to go and investigate. But it wasn't a shot which made him investigate; he hears too many of those to worry about them. And he heard no cry. *And* there was no moonlight . . . He investigated because he saw a light. A great light and a strong light. That light pleased and intrigued him. He went towards it as a moth might go. He was halfway through the undergrowth and in full view of the clearing, when the light went. But Tom kept on. He had seen something, which had driven the light's existence out of his small head. He went on and found it. Blackatter. And when, after making sure the moon was not likely to blaze out from behind the cloud-wrack, he started off for help, he tripped over Bronson . . . *That's* why I'm asking about cars. The great, bright light. He described it to me.'

'A car in a wood!' grumbled Dyson. His eyes were fast closed. His mouth opened only at one corner to let out the words.

'See here,' said Anthony. He took from his pocket pencil and paper and sketched rapidly a little plan. 'Look at that.' They came and crowded round him. 'There's the wood, there's the clearing. This is the hedge along the road, that here's the gate. If that gate were opened, a car could get along the cart-track— here—and its headlights could blaze right into the clearing . . . Suggestive. Yes?'

'My Winkey!' Pike's strange and childish oaths were sure sign of excitement in him. He said: 'But *why* didn't this come out, sir? Three times that lad gave his evidence. Coroner, Magistrate, Assizes . . .'

'Exactly.' Anthony nodded. 'And it didn't vary a word. Why?' His lean dark face took on a savage look. 'Why? Because *Dadda* told him what to say. Tom wasn't frightened, *Dadda* was with him. *Dadda* had coached him. *Dadda* was at his elbow. Blast Dadda! *He* ought to be hanged, if you like. And the Defence didn't cross-examine the boy. You can't cross-examine a virtual lunatic. And anyhow there seemed nothing to cross-examine about. T. Harrigan was in the wood. T. Harrigan found the bodies. T. Harrigan, having told Dadda, told the policeman. And the policeman goes up there and there the bodies are. Quite obviously no need to do anything with T. Harrigan except the formalities. It . . .' He stopped in mid-sentence. Lucia had sprung suddenly to her feet. Her face was white, her eyes wide. But she spoke quietly. She said:

'Unless . . . unless . . . No. I suppose it's impossible . . . But he isn't sane, this Harrigan . . . Could he? . . .'

'No,' said Anthony. 'No. I toyed with that idea. But only for five minutes. You haven't seen him, dear. I have. And he's *sane* enough. As a child is sane. No; this thing's a plot and T. Harrigan's not the plotter.'

'Nor,' said Dyson suddenly, 'the plotter's thumb?'

Anthony laughed. But still he shook his head. 'T. Harrigan's square. A small square, but a right-angled one. The only crooked thing about the boy is the boy's father. And even Dadda *meant* no harm! Didn't even know he was doing it. The most dangerous kind, that. And his harm's irreparable.'

Lucia dug her fingers into her palms. She said, in a voice whose very control showed the strain upon her:

'But can't *we* do something about that? Can't we? If evidence was withheld and we can prove that it was withheld, doesn't that . . . wouldn't that be enough to . . . to make them? . . .' She broke off. Her eyes were fixed upon Anthony's. He said:

'No, dear. Even if we could show that there had been with-holding of evidence—which I doubt—where are we? A looney boy saw a bright light in a wood. And *then* found the two bodies. Put that little crumb against the Prosecution Cake. Because the boy's looney, his asinine but doubtless well-intentioned sire rehearses his evidence and omits to make him tell of the bright light. That doesn't alter all the rest of it. *We* say it does because we know what the other side don't—that Bronson's innocent. But put yourself in the place of the Prosecution and you'll see there's little to it. Nothing doing. No. It's helped us. But it doesn't finish our job. Far from it. Agree, Pike?'

'Absolutely, sir. It's nothing—unless you're doing what we're doing—the whole case over again, upside down.'

'What we *can* now do,' Anthony said, 'is to make X the owner of a car or motor-cycle. What I mean is: pay less attention in our eliminatory searches to persons without one or the other of these.'

'Except,' said Flood, 'that X might've had an accomplice to do his dirty work. E.g . . .'

'Dollboys,' said Dyson quickly.

Anthony surveyed them. 'Quite. We're on to Dollboys. We're following him up. But that doesn't mean we've finished. You can use one path and then another in the ordinary way; but we've not got the time. We've got to go down 'em all at once. I mean this: that, looking for other strings, we can make car-owning, if not an essential, at least a guide.' He looked at his watch. 'My wife and I are going, almost at once, among the heads. Dyson and Flood: you stick, on any lines you think fit, to the Dollboys' scent. Pike: use your own judgment about what you do. I've no suggestions. We'll all meet here at—' He looked at Lucia. Who said:

'We ought to be back by 1.30 at the latest, I should think.'

'At,' said Anthony, 'two o'clock then. This room. I'll fix it up with Mrs Bronson.'

Dyson wriggled back in his big chair until once more his body was a long pot-hook. He said:

'If we sleep, where do we sleep?' He jerked his head to indicate Flood. 'Him and me? Mean: is it wise to billet here? Might put Dollboys wise that we're in with you. Better find 'nother place. What?'

Anthony shook his head. 'No. No; you're wrong. What's our scheme with Dollboys? To scare him. Well, if he does smell a rat, so much the better. The more rats and the higher smell the merrier. You and Flood put up here.'

Lucia rose, and with her the three men; Pike alertly; Flood with a solid grace; Dyson with a protesting scramble. Flood crossed to the door and held it open. She smiled upon them all and went, Anthony at her heels.

CHAPTER IV

THE NIGHT OF FRIDAY

I

THERE was much light in the usually dim house of Colonel Brownlough, and music of a sort, and many women of whom a few had pretensions to beauty.

And there were flowers and ferns and sofas in the great hall, and along the corridors which from it ran east and west. And in the conservatory at the end of the western corridor— through the billiard-room—were chairs and soft-shaded lights. And in the library, along the whole length of the far wall, was a white-draped buffet, on and beneath and behind it bottles, bottles and yet more bottles.

And the whole house of Colonel Brownlough, usually so silent a house that in it a sneeze unrepressed would assail the ear like the shattering of a bomb, vibrated now with the droning hum of a hundred ceaseless voices which wove their sound, against the background of the dance-music, into a changeless yet ever shifting pattern by no means unpleasant.

Anthony's car, its low headlights cutting the blackness with a pure hard beam, swung through Colonel Brownlough's gates. It throbbed its slow, repressed way up the curving drive and came to a halt, near an orderly mass of other cars, before the house.

Anthony switched off lights and engine. 'Out you pop!' he said. But Lucia sat. She laid a hand upon his arm.

'These,' she said, 'are the first words from you in twelve miles. Most unusual! . . .' Her voice changed. 'Darling: what are you thinking? Tell.'

'I can't,' said her husband. 'It's always like that with these great detectives. We think, but we don't speak. We say it's because we aren't *ready* for speech. But it's really because we don't know what we're thinking about.'

He felt, in the darkness, soft fingers make strong, gentle pressure upon his arm. 'Tell!' said Lucia.

He smiled. But when he spoke there was to his voice the rough edge of worry. He said:

'If you must know—it's a link I want. Not the surface link of blackmail, but the one *behind* that. Tell me something— anything—which *could* even in the remotest possibility, link Bronson with Blackatter and both—*both* mark you—with X. Tell me! You can't. Nor can I . . . Now out you pop!' He stretched a long arm across her and opened the door.

They were barely within the house when its owner, brushing aside a manservant, surged upon them.

'Good of you!' coughed Colonel Brownlough. 'Good of you to come! Very pleased. Very pleased.' He took Lucia's hand between both his own. 'So this is your husband, eh? Very glad to meet you at last, Gethryn. Very glad. Heard a lot about you. A lot. Who hasn't, eh? Known this lovely wife of yours since she was a kiddie. Haven't I, m'dear? Yes. *So* high . . .'

He went on spraying Anthony with talk while Lucia went, shepherded by a servant, to unwrap. He was somewhere, this Colonel Brownlough, between fifty and sixty; a burly man of considerable height and great breadth and thickness, with an agility and lack of fat most commendable.

He stuck to Anthony and went on spraying Anthony, who bided his time and smiled and nodded.

They went from cloakroom to hall, from hall to library. Colonel Brownlough waved a hand at the long white-clothed table, beside it small clusters of guests in which, rather surprisingly for the times, the men outnumbered the women. 'Glass of wine?' said Colonel Brownlough. 'Or anything else you'd rather? What?'

Anthony found himself drinking a Pol Roget of excellence. He kept half an ear for the splashing talk of his host and discreetly used all his eyes and the rest of his hearing for others. What he saw he found to be what he had expected. Perhaps a little more so. The atmosphere of a Hunt Ball without its formality and with a rather larger leavening of militance than is usual at most Hunt Balls. Fully forty per cent of the men he saw were very obviously soldiers, the subaltern predominating.

'. . . and so that's how it was!' The barking rattle of his host's voice beat upon Anthony's ears. 'No sooner did I enter Betty Marston's drawing-room than I saw your wife . . . An' so here you are at my little tamasha . . .' The voice paused for a moment; then dropped to a tone of impressive confidentiality. 'S'pose,' it said, 'you won't be gettin' in any huntin' round here, what? Too busy, eh? Damn fine effort, this o' yours. Fine!' The voice went lower still. 'No business o' mine o' course, Gethryn . . . mustn't take any offence . . . just a friendly tip y'know . . . but that lovely wife o' yours . . . well, fact *is*, thought she talked a bit more than you'd like . . . what I mean, must be half round the county by this time that you're makin' this effort . . .'

Anthony, restraining his emotions, smiled at his host. He said:

'Much obliged. A woman's tongue's a tiresome thing—nearly as bad as a man's. But in *this* case, the more talk there is, the better I'll be pleased. That, you know, was my wife's reason for talking.' His voice, by stages so cleverly handled as to be imperceptible, had been rising. It was now, though unostentatiously, loud; so loud that it would carry—should they care to listen—to any of the other groups at the buffet. He said:

'I've no objection to the whole world knowing. I am, in fact, encouraging all I meet to spread my business here. The more it's known that there's a movement to save Bronson because there are people who believe Bronson innocent, the better I shall like it. And the greater the chance for Bronson. Because, as Bronson *isn't* guilty, there must be someone who is. And that someone is in this county. And the more Someone hears the more frightened he'll get, and a Someone afraid's worth two in a hush . . . Besides, the revival of thoughts about Bronson might lead to a revival in memories about l'affaire Bronson, and that'd be to the good too. Something—some little, apparently insignificant point—might be remembered for the first time—as Mrs Starbuck remembered the ashplant in the Corson business—and turn out to be the key-piece that's been missing . . .' Anthony allowed himself to become aware, for the first time, of Colonel Brownlough's now fervid attempts to silence or quieten him. He made almost petulant apology. He shrugged and said: 'Sorry, sorry! Boring you!' and plunged into small talk.

But of small talk his host would have none. He cut across it with an apology of his own.

'Not boring at all! No. Deeply interested, Gethryn. Deeply . . .' He moved closer and in hoarse whisper added: 'Feller just come in. Standin' behind me now. Ravenscourt. Chief Constable. Very proud of the way the case was handled. Don't want to upset him. Stout fellah. VC an' all that. But opinionated. Always right. Sorry if I seemed rude. Doosid awkward . . .'

Anthony permitted himself to unbend. 'Not at all. My fault entirely. Talking much too much. And I quite see your point.' Overtly now, as covertly for the past few moments, he looked at the Chief Constable of the County. He wanted to know the Chief Constable, if the Chief Constable of the County were the right sort. It was impossible, he found, to tell. If Brownlough were right, then no need to waste time in trying to get the man's help. But Brownlough might be wrong . . .

His thoughts were past this point when Colonel Brownlough, with spraying apology, left his side—'just for a moment, Gethryn.'

With half an eye, Anthony watched; saw Colonel Brownlough's quick, deft preening—a twitch to the tie, a tug to the waistcoat, a one-two, one-two up-brushing of the moustache; saw Colonel Brownlough making erect and swift and by no means ungainly passage towards his objective; saw at once the objective. He studied this for a moment. He saw a flame-coloured, startling island entirely surrounded by Man. A tall woman, but without that seeming of top-heaviness which is the marring of many tall women. A woman whose face and body, whose gown and few jewels, whose self in all guessed and unguessed aspects, not so much demanded attention as spontaneously received attention without the necessity for demand.

Anthony, empty glass in hand, drifted nearer. He set the glass down and, immediately, it was filled. He lifted it, began drifting again; finally settled to drink upon a spot from whence his view was good and less interrupted. He could see her face in detail now. A face, like the whole of her, which held attention. Not a beautiful face; but a face of that undefinable kind which, for good or evil or both of these, far outruns mere beauty in its effect upon mankind. He studied this face; its pallor, its tenseness, its long eyes whose colour seemed not static but ever-changing, its lack of paint except upon the over-full lips which stood out impossibly yet pleasingly scarlet against their background; its hardness which sometimes seemed a mask for tenderness; its gentleness which might be a veil for cruelty.

He was still looking when there came a touch upon his arm and the soft deep voice of his wife to his hearing.

'You too!' said Lucia. 'It *is* what you'd call an eyeful, though, I must admit.'

Anthony looked down at her. He smiled. 'Interest's purely the speculative impersonal. Know who it is? Or what?'

Lucia lowered her voice. 'The name,' she said, 'is Carter-Fawcett, with hyphen. The husband is alive but nearly always absent. I also gather that what money Mr Ford and the Rockefellers haven't got belongs to her. She's got a house near here, a few castles in Scotland, a palace in Rome, a flat some-where W1, a yacht and a racing-stable . . .'

Anthony interrupted. 'Got it! Racing-stable did it. I thought the Carter-Fawcett sound was familiar . . . So she's that one, is she? Well, well!'

'Well-well what?' said Lucia. 'Why well-well?' She studied her husband with intentness.

He shrugged. 'Couldn't tell you. Have a drink, dear.' He turned from her to the buffet. When he turned back, a wineglass in his hand, it was to find his wife in speech with their host, now sundered from the Carter-Fawcett group. There were, too, a young woman of the usual prettiness and a younger man, plainly military.

It became clear to Anthony, after mumbled introductions, that he was to dance with, talk to or supply with food and drink the young woman. Lucia, the subaltern beside her patently congratulating himself upon his luck, moved off. To Anthony the girl said wistfully:

'They're going to dance . . . Colonel Gethryn, isn't your wife *lovely*! Oh, I'm sorry, I shouldn't 've . . .'

'Why shouldn't you?' Anthony smiled upon her. 'I know it, but that doesn't mean I don't like hearing it. Shall *we* dance?'

'Please,' she said. She had a voice as pretty as herself. Blue eyes looked with frank pleasure at the lean length and quiet splendour of Colonel Gethryn. They walked side by side from the room, weaving a path between clusters of their fellow-guests. To almost every group the girl smiled and nodded. Anthony, his eyes keen beneath sleepy-seeming lids, picked up hope. He said:

'I'm very sorry. I didn't catch . . .'

She laughed. 'You wouldn't. It's Brocklebank. But when Colonel Brownlough says it, it sounds Polish.'

They had come out into and across the hall. Before them the pleasantly-decorated dining-turned-ballroom showed itself. An orchestra of three was playing, softly and with good enough rhythm, the latest foxtrot but three. The floor was crowded with couples. Anthony swung his partner into their midst. They got on quietly but with smoothness. For two complete circles of the big room they did not speak, and then the girl broke the silence. Just as Anthony was about to play his gambit, she said from his shoulder:

'You must dance an awful lot. And that's odd . . .'

Anthony glanced downwards. He could see nothing save the top of a corn-coloured head and a triangle of white forehead. 'I don't,' he said. 'But where's the oddity?'

'I'm very rude, I suppose,' said Miss Brocklebank.

'If you are you're disguising it well.' Anthony, with a sudden and adroit changing of step, avoided collision with a flame-coloured gown and its inhabitant. Mrs Carter-Fawcett and partner swept on—graceful Juggernauts. Anthony's eyes for a moment followed their progress.

'And what,' said his partner's voice, 'do *you* think of her?'

Anthony looked down again. This time the pretty face of Miss Brocklebank was upturned and in full view; its blue eyes wore a guarded, veiled curiosity which belied the pleasant smiling of the nearly insipid mouth. Anthony said:

'I daren't . . . A cyclonic lady.'

'Daren't what?' Miss Brocklebank was persistent. 'Think of her? Or say what you think?'

Anthony grinned. 'Both,' he said.

Miss Brocklebank started in his arms, and missed her step. She said, in a small and panic-stricken voice:

'I say! You don't know her, do you? I . . .'

Anthony was reassuring. 'I don't . . . Now you tell me something. Why, if I did dance a lot, would there be oddity?'

Miss Brocklebank's face disappeared again. 'Oh . . . just because . . . because . . . it wasn't . . . I mean it isn't . . . I mean it wouldn't . . . we hadn't . . .'

'I *see*!' said Anthony.

Miss Brocklebank suddenly shook with laughter. But the triangle of forehead was white no longer. She said, in a little rush of words:

'All I was trying to say was that ballrooms didn't seem quite the setting for Colonel Gethryn who does wonderful finding-out things . . . You must think I'm a fool, talking like this. But you see Father and Bobbie—my brother—and I, we're all very great admirers of yours. Ever since the Hoode case. And when Colonel Brownlough happened to tell Father you were coming here tonight, I nearly jumped out of my skin with excitement. And I badgered old Brownie . . . Colonel Brownlough, I mean

. . . till he introduced me . . . Oh *damn*, they're stopping!' And, despite Miss Brocklebank's annoyance, cease the music did.

'Clap!' said Miss Brocklebank, '*please* clap!'

Anthony clapped. There came from the room enough applause. With a sour smile, the orchestra-leader picked up again his drum-sticks. There was a pause while he consulted with his two satellites. There came suddenly to Anthony's ears, through the clattering buzz of the dancers' chatter, a voice from close behind him. A male voice which he did not know, deep and harsh and vibrant.

'*That's* the feller, is it?' said this voice. 'Don't like the cut of his jib. Looks a blighter.'

Anthony turned, casually, to see the speaker. He knew, as a man inexplicably will always know in such a situation, that this speech had applied to him. And he had seen, though he had given no sign of seeing, the effect of this speech upon his partner. Miss Brocklebank, good manners fighting a losing battle with emotions, had gone first scarlet, then very pale. And the blue eyes of Miss Brocklebank were torches of angry dislike, darting their flames at the speaker. As he turned, too, he caught a mutter from Miss Brocklebank's lips; one word, which sounded like 'Swine!'

Anthony looked, across eight feet of unoccupied parquet, into the eyes of the man who had spoken. This was, he saw, the partner of Mrs Carter-Fawcett; a black-haired, black-browed, sleek, very thick person of an age somewhere between thirty-five and forty. On the upper lip of the almost brutal mouth was a bar of black moustache, below it the mouth was twisted into a snarling sneer which showed a glimpse of white, strong teeth; the nearly over-perfect dress-coat set off a magnificent torso. The black eyes gave back a glare for the green, lazy gaze of Anthony's.

The music began; a quick tune and a noisy. The violinist had now a saxophone. Anthony, sliding his right arm about the waist of his partner, found that her body was a-tremble. He said:

'And who's the black gentleman?'

'Lake,' said Miss Brocklebank. She did not open her pretty teeth for the word.

'Yes?' said Anthony. 'Crimson, certainly. Who and what is it?'

'Captain A. D. Featherstone Lake!' Miss Brocklebank's rendering of the title and penultimate name was magnificently scornful. 'He's . . . he's . . . one of the Lost Legion—that's what Daddy calls Her . . . courtiers . . .'

'I see,' said Anthony. 'And he'd like to be all of it.' His eye was upon Lake's back; it noted the force with which Mrs Carter-Fawcett was enclasped.

'Vile pig!' said Miss Brocklebank. 'And why, why, *why* say that about you—even if he hadn't almost bellowed it? Why *think* it?' There were now two pink patches staining Miss Brocklebank's pallor.

They were abreast of the door, and through the door Anthony swung Miss Brocklebank. He looked down, smiling, at her surprise and disappointment. He said:

'D'you know what we're going to do? We're going to drink. And, if it's all the same to you, we're going out of the crowd to do it.'

'I should,' said Miss Brocklebank with fervour, 'love it . . . And I know a good place.'

To this good place, with wine, they went. It was an alcove in the western corridor. As, explained Miss Brocklebank, the conservatory was at the end of the eastern corridor, down the western corridor there was no traffic, not even of the most enthusiastic hand-holders.

They sat in wicker arm-chairs of inviting appearance and repellent discomfort. Miss Brocklebank settled herself. She looked at Anthony and she said:

'You want to ask me questions, don't you?'

Anthony smiled. 'My *dear* Watson! . . . Yes, I do.'

'Fire ahead!' said Miss Brocklebank.

'If you know I want to question,' Anthony said, 'you know why. In other words, you know what I'm in this part of the world for.'

The blonde head nodded. 'I do . . . And I think it's won . . .'

'How d'you know?' Anthony's smile robbed interruption of discourtesy.

'Everybody does. I was told by Daddy. Daddy was told by old Lady Fisher, who met your wife this afternoon.'

'So that you believe it to be general knowledge . . . at least in the county with a capital C?'

'Yes. Anyone that hasn't heard about it by now certainly will have by tomorrow afternoon . . . And I'm including the . . . the . . . everybody—servants and all. Talk goes quicker, here anyhow, from top to bottom than it does upwards.'

Anthony surveyed this girl with approval. He saw now that the usualness of her healthy, ordinary, prettiness was belied by the intelligence of the blue eyes. He said, after a pause:

'And this party? Everyone under this roof?'

'Knows as much as I do.'

'Which is?'

Miss Brocklebank fixed her blue gaze upon her questioner. She said:

'That you think Bronson wasn't guilty after all and that because you think so you've come down here to try and find some new evidence which'll save him.'

Anthony considered this. 'I see. And what's the prevailing attitude?'

Miss Brocklebank hesitated; thought deeply; said at last:

'It's not evenly divided . . .' she hesitated again.

Anthony, watching her, laughed. 'You mean that ninety-nine point five per cent say I'm crazy; and I expect some of 'em would add—Captain Crimson Lake for instance—that if I'm not crazy I'm a-hunger for publicity . . .'

Miss Brocklebank flushed. 'I'm afraid you're right,' she said. 'Fatheads!'

'Lake now,' said Anthony; 'Lake interests me. People who dislike me always seem so much more interesting than the others, especially when they say so without being properly introduced. I could, you know, bear to know a whole lot more about Lake.'

Miss Brocklebank pulled down the corners of the mouth which was not insipid after all. She said:

'He doesn't belong. He comes here in the hunting season . . . for the hunting and . . . and . . .'

'And Mrs Carter-Fawcett,' said Anthony.

She nodded.

'And he *never* comes during the non-hunting seasons?'

She lifted white shoulders. 'Not unless She's here. And that's not often except during the hunting.'

'And our Crimson friend,' Anthony asked, 'he stays . . .'

'At Weydings . . . that's her house. *Lovely* place, about four miles from here.'

'Many . . . er . . . other guests?'

'House,' said Miss Brocklebank, 'is always full. Not that that means anything . . . unless it makes it worse. There's always a platoon or so of the Lost Legion there . . . Miaou-*miaou*!'

'Cats,' said Anthony, 'are truthful beasts more often than not. What's Lake's rank in the Legion?'

Miss Brocklebank pursed her lips. 'I can only talk from hearsay, and what I've happened to see . . . I should say he's fairly high up. Sort of favourite Lieutenant who knows he's all right so long as he doesn't object when someone else is temporarily on duty.'

Anthony looked at her. A little smile twisted his mouth. 'You don't like the lady, do you?'

The girl flushed hotly. 'I do *not*! Shouldn't like myself if I did. I know it's the 20th century and all that rot—but there *must* be a limit. At least, *I* think so. And so does Daddy. He's the only one, though, that lives up to what he thinks. All the others kow-tow to her with one hand and backbite her with the other. *I* say they're as bad as she is. Worse. She *has* got the courage . . .'

'Of her predilections,' finished Anthony. 'Quite. But that's fairly easy when there's all that money. Yes . . . This Legion now, any others here tonight?'

Miss Brocklebank shook her head. 'Not to speak of. Two recruits. Jack Borstowe and another boy.' Miss Brocklebank allowed a small but heavy sigh to escape her; then angrily bit her lip. She said, in a tone exaggeratedly level: 'Pity about Jack. He was a nice boy. He is still. But he won't be long, if he ever gets out of the Recruit class . . . I say!'

'Yes?' said Anthony.

'You said, at the beginning of this conversation, that you wanted to know a lot about Captain Lake . . .'

'Yes,' said Anthony.

'And we've really been spending all our time on That Woman . . .'

'Yes,' said Anthony.

'Oh!' said Miss Brocklebank. 'Was it Her you really wanted to know about?'

Anthony got suddenly to his feet. He smiled. He said vaguely:

'Yes and no. In a way . . . I'm going to be very rude. I'm going to ask you to give up the rest—or almost all of it—of this party to me. Will you? I should be very . . .'

Miss Brocklebank interrupted. 'Can,' she said, 'a duck swim? . . . Of course I will, Colonel Gethryn.' She looked up at him with her blue eyes shining.

'Don't,' said Anthony. 'Please don't. Anything but "Colonel". I never could bear it. And in this atmosphere it's worse than ever. The place is alive with the things.'

The girl laughed. 'It is, isn't it? They're all soldiers . . .'

'I . . .' began Anthony. And then stopped. His mouth closed. His whole body stiffened. His eyes became slits, the frown between them carving deep creases between his brows. He said beneath his breath, 'Good *Lord*!'

Miss Brocklebank regarded him. 'Forgotten something?' she said.

He shook his head. He laughed, and that sudden alertness, like the sudden alertness of a pointer, went from him. He said:

'No. Rather the other way. Perhaps . . . Miss Brocklebank, give further proof of your angelity. Stay here while, for a moment, I go and speak to my wife.'

'Right.' Miss Brocklebank smiled serenely. 'I always said,' she murmured, 'that I'd make a Watson.'

'Watson,' said Anthony, 'nothing! You're the answer to the Detective's Prayer!' He was gone, his long stride, with its seeming laziness, taking him down the corridor and round its corner, out of the girl's sight, quicker than she would have thought possible.

Anthony was in luck. Turning into the hall, he came face to face with his wife, and his wife at the one moment, between partners, when she was alone. The hall was full; the music had just stopped, and stopped for a real interval while the band might drink. The dancers were making, in eddying blocks, for the buffet in the library. Lucia said:

'So you *are* still here. I thought . . .'

Anthony took her by the arm. He steered a way for her through the press. Back to the ballroom he went. He said:

'We'll be alone *here*. Only got a moment, dear. Want to tell you: keep one of those eyes of yours on someone for me. The Carter-Fawcett woman. Let the other eye go everywhere, but one on her *all* the time. And pick up anything you can about her, too.'

'Yes, sir,' said his wife. 'Why?'

'No time now. Just for oddity generally. Look out for anything unusual. She's sure to give you something to tell me about, whether it's what I want or not . . . G'bye!'

Lucia watched his back as he made swift, easy way across the hall again. She was still looking, though the back had gone, when a voice came in her ear; the voice of her next partner.

And down the western corridor, Anthony sat again to face Peggy Brocklebank. He said:

'Now. Ready for questions. Lots of 'em? About lots of people?'

She nodded eagerly.

II

It was at about the time when Anthony's first of this second batch of questions was being announced—or perhaps a little earlier—that there entered the Saloon Bar of The Horse and Hound, from the interior and not the street door, Mr Walter Flood.

There were two other men in this bar; Mr Dollboys, quiet and self-contained on the settee which was drawn, cornerwise, close to the glowing fire in the brick fireplace; and, at the other side of the fire a man, erect upon a small chair, who was hidden by the evening paper which he read.

Mr Flood sauntered to the bar and stood leaning, not without grace, upon it. His ruddy face shone with health; his fair hair was sleek and gleaming. His tie was very beautiful and the jacket of his plus-four suit a quiet advertisement for his tailor.

Mr Flood ordered a brandy and soda. Mr Dollboys stared at him. Mr Flood, glass in hand, turned from the bar towards the fire; became suddenly aware of Mr Dollboys' presence; smiled genially; wished Mr Dollboys good evening.

Mr Dollboys was amicable. He returned almost heartily Mr Flood's greeting. He said, after this:

'Pleasant t'see a friendly face.' His speech was a little blurred; ever so slightly thickened at its edges; his words showed a tendency to run one into the other. He glared over his glass at the other man, still behind his barrier of paper. 'Some folks,' said Mr Dollboys, 'can only just bring 'emselves to pass the time o' day. An' after that . . . well, that's where their speakin's finished.' From Mr Dollboys' face, which was pale beneath its tan, his small eyes glittered balefully.

'Join me?' said Flood. His tone was soothing. He held up his glass.

'Don' . . .' said the other, 'don' . . . mine if I do!' He rose to his feet and walked, with a rather solemn care, to the bar counter. Flood joined him. He studied Mr Dollboys. He came easily to the conclusion that Dyson was right. The man was scared. Or had been scared . . . Well, he was about to be scared still further. He looked actually smaller; there were pinched lines about the corners of his mouth. And the eyes—bright with the glaze of alcohol—would not be still. Flood remembered their steadiness of the early afternoon. Now they darted quick, furtive glances this way and that.

'What is it?' said Flood blandly.

'Whis ... whisky.' The man pushed his glass towards the barmaid with fingers which shook. He watched, with the painful concentration of the unsober, while the girl held his glass beneath the tapped bottle. Behind his back Flood cast a glance back at the bar's other occupant. Who now put down for a moment the paper from before the face of Pike, and held up a hand with all five fingers out-stretched. So Dollboys was on his fifth double since Pike's entrance an hour before. And there must have been some before that ... Flood turned back to his guest; in his wide blue gaze there was something like admiration.

To Dollboys' owlish salutation he raised his own glass. He was very affable. He said:

'Good luck! And I hope our little deal this afternoon may bring you a slice. What?'

Mr Dollboys did not like this. Mr Dollboys put an unsteady finger to his mouth. He said:

'Ssh! Ssh! No talk o' that.' His voice was a hoarse and penetrating rumble. 'Not here, mister. No bus ... bus'ness here. No.'

'Sorry indeed,' said Flood. His round face wore a look of solicitous concern.

'Comansiddown!' said Mr Dollboys, still in his penetrating whisper. He fastened fingers to Flood's coat sleeve and led him, slowly but with commendable accuracy, to the settee. He let go the sleeve and sat heavily. Some of the whisky slopped out of his glass and splashed down over his waistcoat. He rubbed at it with an uncertain palm. He sat straighter, suddenly, and seemed to take a grip upon himself. Flood marvelled, for when the whisper came again much of the slurring and thickness had gone from it. It said:

'After you'd gone s'afternoon, mister ... that other cove turned up ... the one you bade me keep eye open for ...' Once more the fingers of Mr Dollboys fastened themselves upon Flood's coat-sleeve. 'Jest 's you said, mister ...'

'Shame,' said Flood indignantly. 'That fellow Marable's a public nuisance. If I had my way, I'd have him locked up. Can't stand the creeping hound!'

Mr Dollboys almost smiled. 'Thass right!' he said. He nodded and forgot for nearly a minute to stop nodding. 'Thass right!' he said. The hand which had been gripping Flood's coat sleeve turned into a patting hand.

Flood bore the caress with fortitude, as also the blasts of stale spirit which were wafted from Mr Dollboys. He knew there was not long to endure.

There was not. Before Mr Dollboys could speak again, the door from the hotel passage swung open. Dyson came in with a rush. And Dyson said to Flood, in a voice which might have been heard for a hundred yards:

'There you are, Flood! Been looking all over for you. They've lighted a fire in our sitting-room. C'mon up!'

Mr Dollboys had his back to the newcomer. But at the sound of the voice he started violently. More whisky splashed down upon his clothes. His face became, instantly, of a palish, slatey-grey colour. He began slowly to turn in his seat. It was as if a magnet which he resisted were pulling him.

But his turning did not prevent him from seeing the actions of Flood, who sat beside him but leaning in the angle of the settee so that almost directly he faced the newcomer. And Flood was making frantic, and patently would-be secret, signs to the newcomer. Signs which meant 'Go away! Go away! . . . Before he sees you!'

And Mr Dollboys, having taken this in, finished his turning. And he saw his long, thin, disturbing visitor of the earlier evening. Who stared at him, gaped, muttered 'Good God!' darted a glance of apology at the man beside Mr Dollboys, and fled.

The glass fell from Mr Dollboys' hand and smashed into many pieces upon the brick floor. It lay like a ruined star at his feet.

Flood jumped up. He looked at Mr Dollboys.

Mr Dollboys rose. He stood like a sober man. He was, very

nearly, a sober man. And the grey of his face was like ashes. He said:

'You . . . you . . . *you and him!*'

Flood shrugged. Flood smiled. Not a pleasant smile. Flood walked to the door and passed out. The door banged behind him. Over the bar looked the puzzled, broad, big-eyed barmaid. She gazed at Mr Dollboys, with unwinking eyes, like a cow.

Mr Dollboys put a hand to his head. He looked once, across at the chair upon the far side of the fireplace. But still he only saw the evening paper.

Mr Dollboys made for the door. He looked like a man who wishes to run but dares not.

'I say!' said the barmaid. 'Thet glass!' She pointed accusingly to the smashed and wetly glittering star upon the red floor.

Mr Dollboys put a hand into his pocket and threw a florin upon the counter . . .

The street door swung to behind Mr Dollboys.

The inner door opened again. Flood came in, cautiously, Dyson behind him.

Pike threw down his paper and rose. They went up to him. Flood said something.

'*Scared*?' said Pike, 'Frightened stiff. More 'n that, frightened *sober*!' He pulled a cap from his pocket, clapped it on his head and went out, but not by the street door.

'Have a snifter?' said Dyson.

Flood nodded.

While they were drinking there came the sound of a car starting, a nerve-racking grinding of gears, a spluttering engine . . . and then a chug-chug which died rapidly away.

Dyson grinned over his glass. He said:

'We'll *both* call in the morning. Together. He'll be easy.'

'Clay,' said Flood, 'under potter's thumbs. Wonder what we'll squeeze out, though . . . Chin-chin!'

'Chin-chin!' said Dyson.

III

Colonel Brownlough's 'little tamasha' was drawing towards its end. Guests had gone; guests were going. Dance-music spasmodically continued, but only six or seven couples danced. The hall was full of overcoated men and cloaked women. From the darkness without came muffled sounds of motor-engines racing to achieve warmth. The buffet held still a few adherents, now exclusively male.

Into the hall, from the western corridor, came Anthony and his partner. To meet them strode a tall, stooping man of sixty with white hair and imperial. From under pleasantly incongruous black brows a pair of bright brown eyes looked youthfully out. Miss Brocklebank introduced her father and her partner.

'And, Daddy,' she said, 'we mustn't call him "Colonel". He doesn't like it.'

'I never,' said Sir Richard Brocklebank, 'call anybody Colonel—if I can help it . . . How d'ye do, sir.' He held out a hand. Long, slim fingers gripped Anthony's with quite astonishing power. The brown eyes twinkled. Anthony said:

'I've a lot to thank you for, sir . . .'

The black brows were raised; beneath them the young eyes twinkled. 'Thank *me*? How's that?'

'For your daugher's intelligence and kindness,' said Anthony. 'I've thanked her. Or tried to.'

Sir Richard turned his bright gaze upon his daughter. 'Intelligent?' he said. 'And kind? . . . What have you been up to, Peggy?'

Miss Brocklebank cast a look about her. She said, in a lowered voice:

'I've been a Watson. At last!'

Anthony shook his head. He looked at Miss Brocklebank's father. 'Watson,' he said, 'is self-libel. Watson asked idiot questions and got no answers. *I've* asked difficult questions and received more than adequate answers.'

'Watson,' said Miss Brocklebank, 'never knew what Holmes was driving at. *I* didn't know what you were driving at. I am, therefore, Watson.'

'Holmes,' said Anthony, 'always knew his own mind. I hardly ever do. Tonight I certainly don't. As I didn't know what I was driving at myself, you couldn't have done so. *Ergo*, you are no Watson. Bad logic but as good as yours. Anyhow, again thank you.'

Sir Richard Brocklebank looked at his watch. His daughter said:

'All right, Daddy. I'm coming.' She turned to Anthony and held out her hand. 'Good night,' she said.

Anthony shook it. Before he had spoken there came a sudden, angry exclamation from Brocklebank *père*, and, atop of it, a sudden flurry and a shock. A man's shoulder, hard and heavy, caught Anthony. He swayed but did not stagger. Behind him a deep, harsh voice growled:

'Sorry. Clumsy.' It did not seem by its tone to be altogether applying the second word to its owner. Anthony turned. Captain Lake was facing Sir Richard. As Anthony saw him, he was stepping aside to pass Sir Richard, and saying as he stepped:

'Excuse me, sir . . .'

'Why?' said the old man. His brown eye had now a reddish tinge to its glitter.

Anthony, turning back to speak with Miss Margaret Brocklebank, seemed suddenly to stumble. He recovered, but in recovery took three backward steps. And the last of these brought his heel down, with force, upon the toes of Captain Lake.

Anthony turned again. He said:

'Sorry. Very clumsy!'

There came a choking sound, immediately repressed, from Miss Brocklebank, and the neat beard of her father twitched as his thin lips curled to a smile undisguised.

Lake and Anthony faced each other. Lake's dark face was darker, with a dull, ugly flush beneath its tan. The full lips of his brutal mouth had almost disappeared. His black eyes were slits. His big hands were fists at his sides.

The Brocklebanks watched. The father's white head was to one side; the little smile still curved his mouth, his bright eyes darted their curiously eager glance from one man to the other and back again. The girl was white, and her breath came fast. Her eyes, after one furious glare at Lake, fixed their gaze upon Anthony.

Anthony's hands were in his pockets. His green eyes, steady upon those slitted black ones, were lazy-seeming but with something very different from laziness somewhere behind them.

There was no movement in the group for a half-minute which seemed many minutes. And then Sir Richard Brocklebank sighed, groped for his cigarette-case and said:

'Tableau. Very interesting indeed.'

Lake, with the ghost of a movement, instantly repressed, towards Anthony, muttered something, turned on his heel and flung off.

They watched him; saw that, with little care for the manner or manners of his progress, he turned in at the library door; the door through which there still came the clinking of glass and the deep buzz of masculine gossiping.

'It wasn't,' said Anthony, '*me* who stole his marbles. But he seems to think so. Wonder why?' He still gazed out across the hall.

'The thing,' said Sir Richard, 'is a nasty thing. It probably has no reason for its action, beyond Brownlough's champagne . . .'

'Beast!' said Miss Brocklebank with conviction. 'Good night. Colonel Gethryn . . . Oh! I'm sorry.'

'Good night again,' said Sir Richard. 'And, if you will, come and see us. Any time. Stoke House. Not four miles from Farrow. Take the Malling road.'

They went. Anthony stood where he was. He looked about him for a sign of Lucia, and found none. He glanced at his watch. One-fifteen. He walked towards the library door. As he reached it there came a touch upon his shoulder, and a male voice which said his name. He turned to see a man taller than himself and of much the same age. An erect man, of the best type of military good looks—the County's Chief Constable.

'It *is* Gethryn, isn't it?' said the pleasant, decisive voice.

Anthony held out his hand. 'It is. And you're Ravenscourt.' His hand was shaken. Ravenscourt said:

'I've been dancing with your wife. I said I wanted to meet you. She told me to seek you out.'

'Did she say,' said Anthony, 'that I wanted to meet you? And badly wanted? Because I did and do.'

Ravenscourt smiled. 'You have. Let's go and find a drink. Old Brownlough's got a good brandy there.'

They went into the room and up to the buffet, whose attendance was now reduced. The extra waiters had gone; behind the long table was now only the ex-soldier-servant of the host. In the middle of the group nearest to where they took their stand was Lake. Anthony eyed him. But Captain Lake was at last showing discretion. He did not see Anthony; most broadly he did not see Anthony.

Ravenscourt ordered drinks, for himself liqueur brandy, for Anthony a brandy-and-soda. He took the two glasses when they came and bore them to a table in the room's far corner. He said:

'May as well sit down . . . Good health!'

Anthony raised his glass. When he had drunk, he said:

'I want to get straight with you, Ravenscourt. I won't waste time. You've heard what I'm at down here.'

Ravenscourt nodded his fair head. 'Yes,' he said shortly. His voice had changed. Now it was a non-committal, official voice. Anthony looked at him. Anthony said:

'If I want it, do I get any help from you? Officially, of course, I can't; for officially Bronson's as dead as he may be on Tuesday morning. But do I, *un*officially?'

Ravenscourt raised his eyes from the finger-nails he had been studying. There was a pause. He said at last:

'I don't know. Damned if I do. Ever since this evening, when

I heard about what you were trying to do, I've been wondering how I'd answer if you asked me just the question you have asked me.' He cupped his glass in both hands and began slowly to roll it, watching intently while the oil of the brandy left its aromatic trail higher and even higher. He was silent; he waited for Anthony to speak but Anthony did not. So himself he spoke again. He said:

'It's like this, Gethryn. Here's a perfectly straightforward case, on which I and my fellows 've done a neat, straightforward job. A man's killed and we find the man who's killed him. And that man's tried before every court; given every possible chance of proving his innocence; but he can't do it; he's convicted by three courts and a coroner's jury, and our case—the Police case—isn't shaken at any point whatsoever. And then, months later, you come along—a private individual—and say you "don't think Bronson's guilty" and ask whether I'll use—because this is what it comes to—whether I'll use my official knowledge or status or both to help you . . . I don't know what to say, Gethryn, and that's a fact. If it wasn't you . . . I mean if I were asked what you've asked me by just an ordinary person, I tell you frankly my answer 'd be a polite version of go-to-the-devil. But it *is* you who's asking—and you *are* a man who's pulled off some extraordinary bits of detective work. So I can't count you as "just an ordinary person" . . . *But*, and it's a big one, I'm dead, cold, utterly certain you're wrong. I *know* you're wrong. After all, I was on the spot, I know more of the leading characters than you do, I did the work or directed it, I know . . . D'you follow me?'

Anthony nodded. 'With ease. And you're quite right, y'know . . . except for one thing, and that is that you're quite wrong. No; let me finish. I mean you're wrong at the start. Bronson *isn't* guilty. I started this business making myself—forcing myself—to adopt that as a creed, because if I hadn't I shouldn't have been able to start. But now I have started, and more than started, I'm getting somewhere. And I know now that the hypothesis of Bronson's innocence was right. I don't have to make myself believe now; there's no need.'

Ravenscourt's rather cold blue eyes were alight now with interest. He said:

'You say you've got somewhere . . .'

Anthony interrupted. 'Yes. But where it is God knows. I don't. What I do know is that there're so many oddnesses about that there must be something behind 'em. Follow?'

Ravenscourt nodded. 'Can't be more than a certain amount of smoke without a fire.'

'Exactly. There's a fire all right. And I've got to find it. And I've only a limited time—very limited, by God!—to find it in. It's that time-limit that forces me to ask considerable things of people that in other circumstances I would barely beg a match from . . .'

He was interrupted. Suddenly Ravenscourt threw back his head and laughed. An infectious sound. He said:

'All right; don't rub it in.' He went on laughing.

Anthony grinned. 'Sorry. But I'm not mincing words. And I wasn't necessarily referring to you, you know . . .'

'And that's another!' said Ravenscourt. Then his tone changed. Laughter faded from his voice and face and eyes. He said: 'Look here, Gethryn! Will you swear to me that you're in earnest; that you *know* you're not deluding yourself; that you have real and solid reason for believing that, in spite of all appearances, Bronson was not the murderer of Blackatter; that if I put aside my natural feelings and prejudices and promise to give you within reason any help I can, you have hope of saving Bronson?'

Anthony looked at him; across the little table the blue eyes and the green held each other. Slowly, Anthony nodded. He said:

'See it wet, see it dry! I give you my word.'

Ravenscourt swallowed the remains of his brandy. He got to his feet. He leaned his knuckles on the table and looked down at Anthony. He said:

'Right. Call on me when you want me. Sooner, if you like; because I've got to admit that I'm interested. Though, believe me, entirely unconvinced.'

Anthony got up. He held out his hand and the other took it. Anthony said:

'Thank you. And suppose we meet tomorrow, if you can.'

Ravenscourt nodded. 'Yes. Morning. Come and see me. No; that won't do, because you must want all the time you've got and then some more. I'll come and see you. You're at Bronson's pub, aren't you? S'pose I come there about ten?'

'Ten it shall be,' said Anthony. 'And thanks again.' He watched while Ravenscourt strode away to the door, a wide-shouldered, graceful figure with decision in its every movement, its fair head held like a boy's.

Anthony, standing, finished his brandy-and-soda. He looked at his watch. At it he raised his eyebrows. He set down his glass and made for the door.

In the hall he found Lucia, and to her hurried. She said:

'No, I haven't been waiting. I've just come. We ought to go, oughtn't we? Did Colonel Ravenscourt find you?'

'Good. Yes. He did, thank you,' said Anthony. 'Where's the host?'

Lucia shrugged white shoulders. 'No idea. Other people 've been looking for him . . . I'm going to get my things, dear.'

Anthony looked after her. She had been very quiet; quite properly tired seeming and just a little bored. But he knew this woman. Something there was up the sleeve she had not got. There had been about her a certain suppressed excitement, concealed so cleverly that certainly no one else in the world would have seen it. He said to himself:

'She's got something, bless her!'

He went in search of hat and coat. He was back in the hall with these before Lucia had emerged. The big doors were open now, and a cold night breeze was playing havoc with tobacco-fumes and jaded air. The ballroom was dark and empty and quiet; and the library lights went out, one by one, until only a single centre lamp was burning. By the open doors there now stood Colonel Brownlough and with him a group. A male group, Anthony saw, posed about the central figure of Mrs Carter-Fawcett. He looked in vain for the burliness of Captain Lake. He stood, hat in hand, waiting for Lucia.

But he was not to wait unheeded. From the fringes of that group, his host detached himself. To Anthony he came hurrying and seized an arm of Anthony. He sprayed Anthony with speech; speech, gathered Anthony, indicative of Mrs Carter-Fawcett's desire that Colonel Gethryn should be presented to her.

'Well, well!' said Anthony. He suffered that hand upon his arm to lead him across to the group.

In the hoarsest of whispers Colonel Brownlough spoke on the journey. 'Charmin' woman!' he said. 'Wonderful woman. You'll be glad to've met her, Gethryn. Unique woman . . .'

A segment of the group, most reluctant, made way for them.

'Here he is, my dear lady. I have him!' Colonel Brownlough was heavily facetious. It did not suit him. And his voice, thought Anthony, had changed most unpleasingly. Gone its martial throatiness, its full-blooded, vintage-port, be-damned-to-you-damn-you rattle; it was, when its owner addressed the woman, an unctuous and discordant cooing.

'She's got something, bless her!'

Anthony, straightening after his bow, looked into the odd eyes of Mrs Carter-Fawcett. They were cold; but with the sort of coldness which may easily become a ravenous flame. She looked tired. She also looked, thought Anthony, a good four years older than she had as many hours ago. She said, in an insolent and deep and rather beautiful voice:

'*You're* not the Gethryn that won the Grand Military on Firespring last year.'

Anthony shook his head. 'Alas, no. A cousin. A young cousin.'

'Ah,' said the lady, 'thought you weren't. Pity. Like to meet that boy. He can ride.'

'After a fashion,' said Anthony, 'yes.' He was very much at his ease; perhaps a shade more than good manners would usually have allowed.

The slanting eyes opened widely for a second. They surveyed him; their coldness blazed for a moment into iced fire; but instantly they were veiled again. She put up a hand to the crimson mouth and yawned behind five fingers whose two rings were worth a fortune not so small. She turned a shoulder to Anthony. To the youth who was next to her she murmured:

'You drive, Jack. I'm sleepy.'

The boy crimsoned with pleasure. The group broke; drifted down the steps and out into the darkness. By the doors Anthony was left with his host. A voice, her voice, drifted up to them:

'Thanks for the party, Brownie. Not so bad.'

Colonel Brownlough waved his hand. He turned then to Anthony. He seemed to find some difficulty in finding words. And his eyes did not meet Anthony's. He was saved by Lucia's arrival.

They got away from him quickly. He stood at the head of his steps as their shoes began to crunch on gravel and he waved. But he was not waving to them. Lucia glanced back at him. She saw his strong figure silhouetted against the lights of his hall. There was a droop to it now. She said:

'Is he *rather* pathetic? Or not? P'r'aps not.'

Anthony found his car. From just before it, two others started, viciously. A spurt of gravel thrown up by the off back-tyre of the nearest car stung his cheek. He swore beneath his breath.

'That's a pig in that Bentley!' Lucia said.

'Or sow,' said her husband. 'Hop in!'

Neither spoke again until the car was out of the drive and fairly upon their homeward road. Anthony drove slowly—a rare thing, a phenomenon. The speedometer needle pointed to twenty-five—figures it had, perhaps, never seen before save in passing. Anthony said:

'And now! . . . Shoot, Pinkerton!'

'Beast!' said Lucia. 'How did you know?'

'Your face told me. What was it, darling?'

'The Carter-Whatsit woman. I kept that eye on her. But it wasn't the eye that gave me the only oddity I've got to tell you about. It was both ears. And—I've got to confess it—utterly by accident. I was sitting out in that conservatory. A very nice boy. He wanted to hold my hand. I let him. He did it very firmly. Sweet. And then I was thirsty and rather than lose seclusion he darted to fetch me a drink. I stayed. I was glad to. He was quite a long time gone, which was a good thing. It was terribly hot in that place and when we first went in he'd opened a window for me—a transom thing. I was sitting right underneath it. I was wondering how much longer that drink was going to be, when I heard—just like George Robey—"footsteps upon the gravel outside". Two pairs. And they stopped just outside my little window. And a woman spoke. I very nearly squeaked, because it was the Carter-Fawcett female. There's no mistaking that croaking, *rather* attractive voice. The man's I didn't get a chance of recognising for the simple reason that I never heard it. Two growls were all that came from *him*; they were just human enough and male enough to make me know it *was* a man; but otherwise . . .' She broke off; she half-turned in her seat and looked at her husband with wide eyes. 'Dear,' she said, 'I . . . it's rather awful . . . now I've got to the point of telling you, I feel it's really all nothing . . . I mean it may all have been about something else and I may've been working myself up for no reason at all . . . and you . . . What are you doing?'

Anthony was drawing the car in to the side of the road. It came gently to a standstill. He switched off the headlights, but left the engine running; it purred softly in the chill, bright darkness. He turned in his seat now; his hands came up and each gripped an arm of his wife. He said:

'You tell now; or there'll be trouble.'

She laughed a little. 'Well . . . what she said first was: "It doesn't matter what you say, I *know* there was something!" ' . . .

That's practically word for word. I know it's the sort of thing that men and women say to each other, all over the world, at the rate of about a thousand a minute; and I know it's said, equally, about tiny things, and middle-sized things and very, very important things. But the way this was said, and the person it was said by, made me know at once—absolutely *know*—that whatever it was was an important thing; something vital . . . And then there was a sort of growling "Ssh!" from the man . . . And then *she* said: "It's all right, there's no one about . . . Why won't you *tell* me? let me help you; I probably could" . . . And then another sh'shing growl from the man, and another sort of impatient noise from her; and she said: "All right, damn you, if you won't tell! But don't make me sick by saying there's nothing! And *don't* deny this man's coming hasn't upset you; because I know better . . ." They walked off after that; I heard their feet on the gravel. They went round, past the conservatory, to the left . . . And that . . . that's all.'

She fell silent; her dark eyes searched her husband's face in the faint light cast by the little lamp upon the dashboard; but she could not read the face, except to half-see, half-guess, that it was set in lines she knew, with the jaw muscles standing out beneath the skin and the deep V of a frown between the eyes.

Anthony was silent too. Very silent. He sat motionless. At last, still without speaking, he switched on the headlights again. With a muffled throbbing the car moved forward. And now it did not move slowly; it was travelling on its fourth gear within a hundred yards; the needle on the speedometer dial quivered and began to race round the last segment of its glowing circle.

They were almost home before Lucia spoke. She said, raising her voice to carry above the engine's humming roar:

'I wasn't a fool, then? To be excited, I mean.' She saw a little smile twist down the corner of Anthony's mouth. He said:

'You know you weren't . . . I'm thinking . . . We'll talk when we get in.'

And in very soon they were. The car in its garage, they stamped cold-footed way across the cobbled yard and so into the warmth of The Horse and Hound. Anthony's watch showed the time as one-fifty.

In the Smoking Room, beside a fire of magnificence, were Dyson and Flood. They rose. Flood in graceful hurry took Lucia's cloak; set for her, facing the fire, a chair. Dyson looked on. He said to Anthony:

'Have a drink? Cold outside.' His head darted out like a bird's from between his lean, stooping shoulders; it pointed with its beak to a small table upon which were glasses and a whisky-bottle.

Anthony nodded. 'Thanks. Where's Pike?' He crossed to the table and poured whisky; he looked across at his wife. She smiled, shaking her head. Dyson said:

'PC Pike's on his beat. Where that is, God knows.'

'He rushed off,' said Flood, 'just as soon as comrade Dollboys had gone.'

Anthony set down his glass. 'About Dollboys now? What happened?'

Flood smiled; not without complacence. His round, fresh face seemed rounder and fresher. He smoothed his sleek, fair hair. He said:

'We frightened him according to plan. I might say I've never seen a man more scared.'

'Tornado,' said Dyson round his pipe, 'vertical!'

'Absolutely!' Flood beamed. 'It went off very well, I think. Eh, Mogul? I met him in the bar. I was pleased to see him. He was delighted to see me. He was a bit on; he told me the terrible sleuth-hound reporter I'd warned him against *had* turned up. He didn't like him; not at all! . . . And just then in pops Dyson; it turns out, most convincing, that he and I are really thick as thieves. Comrade Dollboys got the shock of his life. It actually sobered him . . . And he buzzed off, scared as a hare in the Waterloo Cup . . .'

'We know now,' Dyson said. 'Bloke was so scared there *must* be something to him . . . Collusion between two press men wouldn't blister him all that much if there's nothing to him.' He dropped his dishevelled lankiness into his chair on the last word; it seemed that the length of his last sentence had exhausted him.

Anthony, an arm upon the mantel and a foot upon the fender, stared into the fire's crimson heart. Flood said, looking at him:

'And you, sir? Find anything?'

Anthony straightened himself. He turned to face them.

'Nothing so definite,' he said, 'as Dollboys . . . But I wouldn't say we found nothing. No . . .'

'Perhaps,' said Lucia from her chair, 'too much . . .'

Anthony shook his head. 'Couldn't do that. But nothing'—he looked at Dyson and then at Flood—'we found was positive. Nor negative . . . Just oddity. I said I was looking for oddity. And I found it. Too much of it for my mental digestion.'

'Atmosphere only?' Dyson asked. The words came from his mouth like reluctant bullets.

'Not only. As my wife would tell you. But won't, because I'll ask her not to. Not just yet. No good talking until I've got a bit straighter . . . But I've got jobs for you tomorrow . . .'

Dyson sat up with a jerk. 'Tomorrow? What about Dollboys?'

'After Dollboys,' said Anthony. 'We're coming into the open with Dollboys tomorrow. Early, you and Flood and I interview Mr Dollboys. And what you've begun with Dollboys I'll finish. You two'll be free as soon as Dollboys and I've begun our chat.'

Dyson squirmed in his chair. Behind his glasses his eyes were tight shut. His lank black hair seemed more than ever like a disorderly and badly-attached wig. His thin-lipped mouth opened as if he were about to speak. But he shut it again before sound had escaped him. At him Flood gazed with a smile which grew into the widest of grins. Still grinning he looked at Anthony and winked. He said, in a stage-whisper:

'He's not used to it.'

Dyson opened his eyes. They blazed at his friend.

'Shut y'r mouth!' said Dyson.

Anthony looked down at him. 'Dyson,' he said, 'I'm running

this business. Possibly you'd run it better. Only it's no use running at all if we don't run one way.' His voice was very pleasant.

Dyson shut his eyes again. His mouth emitted a sound which may have been the word 'Quite!'

Lucia did not allow the silence which followed to remain.

'Wherever,' she said, '*is* Mr Pike?'

Flood shrugged. Dyson made no reply of voice or gesture.

'I can guess,' said Anthony. 'No; I won't say. I might be wrong, you know.'

Lucia glanced at the clock upon the mantelpiece. 'It's so late,' she said.

The clock struck the quarter-hour past two. And on the last of its strokes the door opened.

Pike came in. He wore no overcoat, but the collar of his tweed jacket was upturned. At sight of Lucia, who smiled at him, he snatched from his head the cap which had been pulled down almost over his eyes. Despite the cold of the outer night his face was flushed beneath its tan, and there was a gleam of sweat upon his forehead. His boots looked sodden; and to the tweed trousers there stuck blades of grass, a burr or two, and traces of mouldering leaves.

Dyson opened his eyes, squirmed round in his chair, said 'Enter bit of Big Four!' and closed his eyes again. Pike, fumbling at his collar to turn it down, came near to the fire. To Lucia he made a slight, stiff, pleasing little bow. He said, looking at Anthony:

''Fraid I'm a bit late, sir. I've been with that Dollboys, only he didn't know.' He chuckled a little. 'These two'—a little circular movement of his head indicated Flood and Dyson—'frightened him so much, I thought he'd be none the worse with an eye on him, as you might say.'

Dyson snorted. 'He's not suicidal. Wrong sort of guts, if any.'

Flood nodded.

Pike gazed from one to the other of them something in the

manner of a parent proud yet irritated by precociousness in offspring. He said drily:

'Maybe. Or maybe not. But he *is* the sort that might do a bolt. Quite easy too. And s'pose he'd flitted tonight, where'd we have been? It would've made us surer still that he knew something, but it also might've made us too late finding out what it was that he knew . . . This isn't any ordin'ry case; we're up against time, time, *time*! . . . And I didn't want what you two had started—and none so badly either—spoiled for a ha'porth o' tar.'

Dyson grunted. But Flood said:

'Believe you're right, Lestrade.'

'Entirely right,' Anthony said. 'Good work, Pike. And Dollboys is all right till the morning, is he?'

Pike nodded. He looked down, rather ruefully, at a rent in his jacket. 'I've been atop of a shed he's got there next his house. I could see right into his bedroom. He took a long time getting to bed, but he's there OK . . .' He broke off to stare at Flood, who was looking at him speculatively; he returned the look. His tone changed to one of cheerful truculence. 'What's up with *you*?' he said.

'I was wondering'—Flood was bland but curious—'exactly how you got to Dollboys' house. And back.'

Pike smiled; a grim, small smile with triumph somewhere within it. He said:

'I walked back. That's why I'm late. I went there by motor-car. Dollboys's motor-car. I was in the dickey, though he didn't know that. I shut the top behind me. You see, Mr Flood, they do teach us just one or two things in the Police. And one of 'em's to think quick. And another's to take a chance . . . Thank you, sir.' This as he took the proffered tumbler from Anthony's hand.

Dyson's voice came again. It said:

'This other job for the morning, after Dollboys? . . .'

Anthony turned. 'Yes. One, for you or Flood or both, according to what the morning brings, is to rout out everything you can about a woman. Decent reticence to be jettisoned . . .'

'Haven't got any,' said Dyson.

'Mine sloughs,' said Flood.

Anthony smiled. 'The name,' he said, 'is Carter-Fawcett.'

Dyson opened his eyes. Flood whistled. Anthony surveyed them. He said:

'Thought you'd know the sound. She's news, I suppose?'

'With two capital Ns.' Flood had got to his feet. 'You don't mean to say *she's* mixed up in this business?'

'I don't,' said Anthony, 'know myself what I mean to say. Except that I could bear to know about her.'

Dyson grinned. 'Tall order. Don't suppose she does herself. I'll have a slap at it.'

'Or,' said Flood, 'me.' He looked at Anthony. 'What's the other job? Or jobs?'

Anthony shook his head. 'That I'll tell in the morning. I may change my mind about it—if I've got one to change . . . And now we'll sleep. All of us. May not be much time for it soon.'

Lucia got to her feet. She was pale, though not with fatigue. Her eyes were enormous. She said:

'*I* shan't sleep. I'm too excited.' She took a step towards her husband. Her hand came out and rested long, slender fingers upon his arm. 'If . . .' she began. She hesitated; tried again. 'If this man Dollboys . . . if you see him in the morning and . . . won't you be able to—to make him tell? And if he tells, isn't it . . . well, over? I mean . . . oh! You *know* what I mean!' Her voice broke a little on those last six words. Her fingers gripped at the arm they held. She looked up into her husband's eyes. She had forgotten the other men.

Anthony smiled at her. 'Of course I do. And you might—you may—be absolutely right, dear. But we daren't count on that. That's the obvious, easy solution. So obvious and easy that the chances are against its coming out that way. Never mind what they tell you, its not generally the obvious that happens in this sort of business. Especially in real life, which is very nearly always true to the canons of Wallace. Edgar, I mean.'

He turned to the three men. 'Dollboys early,' he said. 'Before breakfast Dyson, Flood and myself'll go down there. Six-thirty start. Dyson and Flood, we'll fix up your other jobs definitely on the way. Pike, will you wait till I come back?'

He received three nods. Lucia, with an effort, smiled and said 'Good night.' She smiled once and spoke once; but somehow each of the three was sure that he, at least, had not been overlooked. She slipped a hand through her husband's arm. Flood held the door for them.

At the head of the stairs, Anthony felt upon his upper arm a sudden, convulsive little squeeze. Lucia shrank against him. He looked down; she was pointing, her arm fully outstretched, at the door to the left of the stairhead. Beneath it showed a thin blade of yellow light.

In the semi-darkness Anthony nodded. He freed his arm and slipped it about soft shoulders. 'I know,' he said. But there's nothing to do, except what we're doing. And we're getting on.' The lighted room was the room of Selma Bronson.

They were in their own room before either spoke again. And again it was Lucia who broke silence. She sat, heavily, upon the bed's edge. She said.

'*Think* of it! Just think . . . I don't suppose she's slept for . . . even since the Appeal . . . Poor thing! Poor, poor thing!' Her voice was dull and heavy. In her lap her hands twisted about each other.

'Think,' said Anthony, 'of what I just said. We've done something. We're doing something. We've done better, really, than we'd any right to expect. It won't do us, or her, any good to get overwhelmed by pity.' He put a hand beneath her chin and tilted up her face. He smiled down at her. 'Don't forget Dollboys,' he said. 'And what we're going to find out tomorrow . . . today, really. We're going to be a lot further on before we go to bed again. Dollboys, you know, is a gift from the gods. I don't know what we'd do without our Dollboys. And that's the truest thing I've said tonight. You get to bed and dream of Dollboys and what Dollboys will bring. He might even—I didn't say it wasn't a possibility—he might even give a complete solution. He *might* say: '*That's* the man!' and tell me X's name . . . I'm afraid he won't go quite as far as that, but he *might*. There's no denying he might . . . But whatever he says, and whatever he does, you can bet your small and expensive shoes it's going to put us on the right pair of rails.'

Lucia's face had changed. The despair of hopeless pity had gone from it. Her colour had come back. Once more she was eager. She interrupted. She said:

'But . . . but all that tonight? All the what you call oddities?'

'Won't,' said Anthony, 'be oddities any longer. Not in the end. When Dollboys talks, I daresay most of the oddnesses 'll be smoothed out at once. And any that *are* left 'll drop into place just a bit further up that line that the talk of Dollboys is going to put us on to.' He was not looking at Lucia now, but above her head and out into nothingness; there were lines in his face which had not been there before he began to speak of Dollboys.

Lucia studied him. She drew in her breath sharply. She said, in a smaller voice:

'What are you going to do to that man? . . . Suppose he won't say anything?'

Anthony brought back his gaze. He smiled. 'He's got to say something. And say a lot. He will, all right.'

Lucia kept her eyes upon his face. She shuddered a little. 'I don't think,' she said uncertainly, 'that I like you looking like that. And yet I do . . .'

Anthony pointed, towards the western wall of their room. 'Remember her,' he said. 'I was telling you not to just now. But in a different way . . . And remember Bronson himself . . . It's up to us to . . .' He left his sentence unfinished. His tone changed. He said: 'But just at present don't remember anything—except that I've got to be out of bed in four hours and that if you're not in bed within three minutes I'll beat you. And once you're in bed you go to sleep and dream dreams about the trustworthiness of your Uncle Stalky.'

CHAPTER V

I

THERE was heavy mist in the morning. It lay like white, heavy wool over the land. Down a road which might, for all the three men could see of it, as well have been a river, crawled Anthony's car. Anthony drove. Beside him, huddled in an oil-stained, creased and ancient weather-proof of an astonishing yellowness, was Dyson. Upon the nearside running-board, clinging to door-top and windscreen, stood Flood. He was bent half-double, peering at the road's left-hand edge. Every moment he gave hoarse directions. By them Anthony steered.

The first two miles and a half of the four-mile journey took them twenty minutes which seemed an hour. Dyson said, drawing the yellow coat yet more closely about him:

'Quicker walk. Let's try it.'

Anthony shook his head. 'Might clear up any moment. And anyhow it'll have gone by the time you want to come back.'

They went on. In patches, the mist began to lift, so that they could sometimes see as much as fifty yards ahead of them. And then would come a dense patch, seeming denser than ever by comparison. But progress became faster. The mile and a half to the lane to Dollboys' farm was done in under the ten minutes, and Flood did not miss the turning.

The big car left the macadam of the high road for bumps and ruts and miniature pot-holes which it took with creditable smoothness. The lane was an incline of steepness and, suddenly, with the level, unhurried wonder of a miracle, they came out from the white night of the mist into the clear grey light of an

early November morning. They blinked, looked, and gave
thanks. Straight before them, and to their left, the countryside,
wrapped in the sedate stillness of a steel-engraving, rose sharply
to the crests of the three hills called collectively The Share.
Down in the valley was nothing for the eye save the white,
smoking sheet of the dissolving mists.

To their right, the other side of the once-white post-and-rail
fencing, was the land and square stone house of Dollboys. In
the yard was no stir of man nor beast. The only sign of existent
humanity was a bicycle—a new and shining and heavily-built
bicycle—which rested against the house's wall to the right-hand
side of the main door. And this door, they saw as the car came
to the gate in the fencing and swung inwards, stood ajar. Anthony
looked at the clock upon his dashboard. It showed the time to
be ten minutes short of seven. He looked up at the chimneys.
There was no smoke. He shook his head, like a man puzzled.
He brought the car to a standstill in the centre of the yard.

Flood jumped down from the running-board. He stamped his
feet upon the stones and beat cold hands against his sides. Dyson
got out stiffly and stood flapping his arms like an eagle disguised
as first cabman in a musical comedy. Anthony shut off his engine
and stepped over the car's low door and stood back to survey
the house. His eye kept returning to the bicycle against the wall.

'Next move?' Dyson said. 'Walk in or wait for invitation?'

Anthony did not reply. But the question, almost before it was
out, nevertheless was answered.

The door that was ajar was flung suddenly wide. A man
stood in the doorway and surveyed them. Upon his round,
bucolic face, now pale where normally it was almost crimson,
there dawned slowly a look of incredulous relief. A tall man,
this, and a portly. A man in clothes of blue, with many shining
buttons down the coat, and shining letter-badges upon the
stiffly-upstanding collar. A man whose gleaming baldness of
head prevented them, for one puzzled half-second, from seeing
what he was. Then:

'Bobbie, by God!' said Anthony, and was at the door in three long strides which were leaps.

II

'Y'see my trouble, sir,' said Police-Constable Murch. He looked at Anthony, and jerked his bald head towards the corner where the old woman, Flood bending over her, was huddled moaning in the high-backed oaken chair. 'Can't 'ardly leave 'er. An' yet it's my dooty to notify the Inspector. All cases of sooicide 'ave to be notified immediate.'

Anthony nodded. Behind an impassive face, his mind was racing. He said, raising his voice:

'Flood: can Dyson drive a car?'

Flood straightened his back. He kept a hand upon the old woman's shoulder. Over his own he said:

'Very well. Any sort, too.' He turned his body again, and once more stooped over his charge.

Anthony turned to the policeman. 'Right,' he said. 'My other friend will drive you where you want to go. Quicker than your bicycle; you can put that in the back. This gentleman'—he waved a hand towards Flood—'and I will stay here and look after the woman till you get back . . . That suit you?'

Mr Murch beamed. His round face seemed in an instant to slough the lines of care which had been making it like a mask of unhappy infancy. He said:

'Thank'ee very kindly, I'm sure sir, Takes a load off'n me mind like. T'wouldn't 'a been so bad if that girl what came an' reported would 'a come back with me. But the kid were so scairt like, it wouldn't 'a been no manner o' use forcin' her t' come along. An' 'ow was I to know there wouldn't be not another soul in a 'ouse o' this size an' what men as the deceased 'ad over away to Blackfan? What I mean t'say, sir . . .'

Anthony dammed this flow by retreating from it. He strode to the door and through it out into the yard.

'Dyson!' he called.

Dyson came, lounging but with some celerity, round the side of the house. He was shaking his head. Behind the great glasses his eyes were puzzled and resentful. He said as he came up:

'It's all *wrong*! Not suicide type. But he goes 'n does it!'

Anthony was brief and explicit. Within two minutes his car, Dyson peering over the wheel like a savage bird, was carrying Police-Constable Murch and Police-Constable Murch's bicycle out of the yard gates.

Anthony went back into the house. In the old chair in the square hall's corner, the mother of Dollboys still moaned and twisted and alternated dumb and safety-seeking clutches at Flood's hands with harsh, screaming efforts to beat him off. She would cry, only half-articulately, so that her sounds were like those of an animal who miraculously has acquired speech; and then the crying, in which the only words distinguishable were 'boy' and 'Andrew' would cease as suddenly as it had begun. And the whimpering, more distressing still, would begin again.

But Flood dealt with it; most surprisingly Flood dealt with it in a manner entirely efficient; it was as if for a great part of his life he had been controlling the hysteria of women. He was kind always; adamant at times, soothing at others. He exhibited neither impatience nor distaste, too much sympathy nor too little. He was wholly admirable.

Anthony left him to it. Anthony crossed the stone floor of the hall upon noiseless feet, went again down the dark, narrow passage to the kitchen. The kitchen door he shut behind him. He leaned back against it and looked at what he had already seen, but not statically and not alone.

He was in the room to which, upon the night before, Dyson had made his deliberately dramatic entrance. And the room, save that the table was laid with breakfast and not supper furnishings and that in the big grate was grey ash instead of glowing fire, was, in regard to itself, as Dyson had seen it.

And Dollboys was in the room. Or what was left of Dollboys. He lay flat upon his back and his eyes stared up at the blackness of his ceiling. His left arm was doubled beneath him; his right half-outstretched beside him. In the fingers of his right arm's hand was a heavy, brown revolver. His feet pointed to the fireplace; his head towards the door against which Anthony leaned. Shapeless trousers of heavy grey tweed clothed his legs and middle, and upon his feet were thick brogues with soles of crepe rubber. But upon his torso was only an unbuttoned and rather dirty pyjama jacket of greyish flannel, and the twisting of the right leg had so dragged up the trouser that between turn-up and shoe-top there showed a white patch of naked ankle. The laces of both shoes were untied and hanging. On the left side of the scalp was a round but ragged-edged hole to the edges of which clung, sticky with blood and other matters, wisps of the sparse sandy hair. From this orifice, which had been the exit of the bullet, a few drops of blood had trickled to the floor, where they now were a dark pool, swiftly congealing. They had left behind them, across the temple, a little trail. If a man knelt down beside this deadness, so that he might see the right ear of it, there was no further to seek for the place of the bullet's entrance. Anthony, thirty minutes ago, had so knelt. Now, as he leant against the door, his eyes went to and from the sprawled body to this and that within the room. They saw, first, the hole of the bullet in the far wall, a hole whose height showed that Dollboys could not have been standing for the shot. They stayed upon this hole for awhile, but their owner did not move. And then, finished with the bullet, the eyes sent their quick frowning glance this way and that. Not long did that glance rest anywhere until, upon its fourth journey to the table, it suddenly widened; became a fixed stare.

He leant back against the door no longer. He jerked his long body upright and crossed to the table in three strides, the second of which took him over the body of the table's owner.

He stood before the table and stared down for a long moment

at its breakfast furnishings and their arrangement. The tenseness of his stance, the gleam in his eyes, unsubdued because
of his solitude, showed an interest developing into excitement.
He swung away from the table. He went down upon one knee
by the still body. His hands moved about it, exploring. They
pried into pockets; they lifted each a dead hand . . .

He was sitting upon a corner of the table, his pipe-smoke
blue in the room's chill air, when, heralded by trampings, there
came into the room a thick-set Inspector of Police, behind him
the burly roundness of Constable Murch.

Anthony got to his feet. He nodded to the Inspector and
gave Murch a smile.

The Inspector neither smiled nor nodded. His small eyes,
of a cold grey, were fierce and yet deprecating. He spoke from
behind a clipped moustache which seemed perpetually to bristle
with fury. He said:

'You're the gentleman who lent the car.'

From his tone, it was difficult to classify this remark; it was
neither question nor accusation nor plain statement. Anthony
nodded.

The hairs of the Inspector's moustache seemed to be reaching
out. 'You arrived in the car,' he said, with a sort of dead brisk-
ness, 'and found this officer'—he jerked a spatulate thumb at
Murch behind him—'and loaned him the car.'

Anthony nodded. His eyes, apparently full of a mild curiosity,
met the fierce grey ones.

The Inspector found himself, inexplicably, to be blushing.
His tone grew undisguisedly savage. He said:

'Who was that driving the car?'

'A friend of mine,' said Anthony. His tone was mild as his
gaze.

The Inspector grunted. He jerked his thumb again, this time
to indicate the hall from which just now he had come.

'Who's that out here with the woman?'

'A friend of mine,' said Anthony.

The Inspector's eyes were now frankly angry. He said, his lips twisting beneath the bristling moustache:

'And that other in the car; the one we picked up at Farrow? Who's he? Another?'

'Friend of mine?' said Anthony. 'Quite.'

The Inspector came a step nearer, so that the still thing on the floor was now within a few inches of his boots. But he did not look down at it; as yet he had scarcely glanced towards it. He kept his gaze fixed upon Anthony. He said:

'Lot of friends, haven't you?'

Anthony took his pipe from his mouth. 'I'm *so* popular!' he said. He kept his eyes, still mildly curious, gazing into the Inspector's; but he pointed downwards, with his pipe-stem, at the body asprawl between them upon the brick floor. 'Better have a look at him, hadn't you? Must know my face by this time. I shan't be in the way here, shall I?' He sat down again upon the table's corner.

The Inspector opened his mouth as if to speak; visibly changed his mind; snapped his jaws together with a click of strong teeth. He unbuttoned a tunic pocket and pulled out his notebook. His final glared seemed to say 'More for you later!' He stepped back from the body and for the first time really surveyed it.

He revealed himself, while Anthony smoked and watched, as an officer of thoroughness and capability. In the notebook he made a firm, capable sketch or two; entered details of the essential measurements, which he had taken with swift accuracy, necessary to establish the body's exact position; asked crisp questions, further to those he had already asked upon the journey, of Constable Murch, and entered condensed notes of the replies; found the bullet-hole in the far wall and from it probed the little lump of flattened lead; examined, without in any way disturbing the body, the two wounds of the bullet's entry and departure; and finally, after examining the body's odd-lot of clothing stood, silent, looking down at it in faint puzzlement.

Anthony spoke. 'Seems odd at first, doesn't it?'

The Inspector started as if something had stung him. He glared. But he said:

'Mean the clothes? Why "at first"?' He switched his glare from Anthony to the heap that had been Dollboys; he gazed down at it, from over the bristling moustache, as if in a moment he would order it to rise and explain its trappings.

There came, breaking the silence, the sound of feet marching down the passage from the hall. Constable Murch opened the door some twelve inches; peered round it; flung it wide; said to his superior:

'Doctor Cave, sir.'

There came in a stumpy, bustling little man in a grey, square-topped bowler. His face was round and red, with a roundness and redness far exceeding Mr Murch's. He was clean-shaven and also, when he took off the square hat and flung it to a chair, completely bald. But he gave, by reason of a pair of shaggy eyebrows, an impression of general hairiness. He grunted pleasantly at Murch; shot Anthony a quick look from beneath the forests and nodded to the Inspector. He said:

'Mornin', Rawlins. What's all this? Dollboys done himself in?' He marched straight to the body and stood, hands on hips, looking down at it.

The Inspector, Anthony saw, stiffened a little. He plainly was inclined to resent Dr Cave and Dr Cave's ways but, also plainly, was determined not to show this any more than he might. He said:

'Good morning, Doctor . . . Yes, it's a suicide; though what *he* wanted to do away with himself for's beyond me. Always heard he was comfortable enough.'

The doctor was on his knees by the body now, his hands professionally busy about it. He did not look up to answer.

'No telling!' he grunted. 'A close devil, he always was.' He sat back upon stocky hams and cocked his head to one side. 'And why, Rawlins, did he come down here to do it?' He bent forward and pointed to the pyjama jacket and to the top of the pyjama-legs which showed just above the trouser-band. 'Must've been to bed, got up, come down here an' shot himself. . . P'r'aps he didn't want to wake the old woman. By the way, who's that young feller with her now, out there?'

The Inspector froze. 'A friend,' he said, 'of this gentleman.' He nodded towards Anthony. 'This gentleman, and it seems a whole regiment of his friends, called here this morning, very early, to see Dollboys. And they found Murch, here, and . . .'

The doctor cut him short. Still squatting, he twisted his short neck round until he looked straight at Anthony. He said:

'Good boy, that friend o' yours. Wonderful way with the old woman.'

The Inspector cut in. His notebook was open. He was sharply official. He said:

'Excuse me, doctor. How long would you say life had been extinct?' He was talking of the body, and standing almost atop of the body, but he did not look down at the body, sprawling there—an ugly shapelessness upon its own floor.

But the old doctor did. He straightened his legs, coming from his squat to his full height with the ease of an athletic boy. He looked down at the husk of Andrew Dollboys for a long moment before he spoke. He said at last:

'That don't matter much to *him* . . . I'd say, roughly, not less than four hours, and not more than seven.'

The Inspector made a parade of his note-taking. He shut the notebook with a snap and returned it to its pocket. He looked again at the doctor and said:

'I can make arrangements for its removal now?'

The old man nodded his bald head. 'Far as I'm concerned, most certainly.'

Anthony slipped off the table, stood, and stretched himself with wide-flung arms.

'I shouldn't touch it just yet,' he said.

Six eyes came round to his as one. The mouth of Murch

gaped. The mouth of the doctor smiled a puzzled smile. The mouth of Inspector Rawlins showed strong white teeth but did not either gape or smile. There was a silence. Anthony said:

'No. Really I wouldn't.' He looked down at the thing on the floor. 'He must stay where he is. For a bit, anyhow.'

Rawlins found his voice. It said:

'Oh, *must* he? And might I ask until when?' His harsh tones were laden with a sarcasm so close to rage as to make them thick and throaty.

Anthony nodded. 'Certainly you may. Until I've had a word with someone in authority. Colonel Ravenscourt, say. Dollboys isn't a suicide. He's a murderee.'

The gape of Constable Murch widened ludicrously. The doctor's smile vanished. Beneath those terrific brows his red-rimmed eyes stared at Anthony's face. And Rawlins, after a moment in which his face grew dark with a rush of blood beneath the skin, put back his head and laughed.

His laughter went on. It shook the square thickness of him. The three watched him, Anthony mildly, the doctor in controlled bewilderment, Murch almost in horror.

Rawlins took hold of himself. His laughter ceased, but the tears of it still stood in his eyes. He said, speaking to the doctor and jerking a thumb towards Anthony:

'He's seen the revolver.' The laughter showed signs of returning, but again was mastered. 'There's some initials scratched on the handle, and they're not Dollboys'. They're K.R.B. So Mister here thinks the gun's someone else's. But it isn't. And I *know*. I know because Dollboys brought the gun in to the Station 'bout six months ago to register it, and I did the registration. He told me then he'd just bought it, second-hand.' Again he put back his head, and again laughter came out of him. By the doorway, Constable Murch, so bewildered by unusualness that no longer was he even trying to understand the words he was hearing, gave himself up to horror at this levity in a room where a dead man, with a hole through his head, sprawled about under the very nose of the laughter.

But the laughter cut off with almost uncanny abruptness. Again there came the sound of a man's tread—now a jingling, long-striding tread—in the passage. The door, Constable Murch notwithstanding, was flung open.

The Chief Constable, in the green-collared pink of the Brunton Hounds, stood just inside the room. His quick eyes went first to the dead man, then in turn to the three who faced him. He nodded, curtly. He said:

'Morning, Cave. Morning, Gethryn. Rawlins, what the hell were you laughing at?'

He did not wait for an answer. He took two strides and stood looking down at the body of Dollboys.

'Poor damn fool!' he said. 'It's a fool trick.'

'To get shot?' said Anthony. 'By a man so close that he must've been unsuspected?'

Ravenscourt jerked his head round. 'What's that?' he said. 'They told me it was suicide.'

Rawlins made his endeavour. He stood very stiff at attention. He began:

'I beg your pardon, sir. It . . .'

'Shut up!' said Ravenscourt. 'Fire away, Gethryn.'

'Dollboys,' said Anthony, 'was killed, and not by himself.' He stood away from the table and pointed to it. 'Look here. Here's the order for breakfast. That's his mother's place, where the teapot and cups are. And here's his place. Look at it. One fork, one large knife, one small knife. And the knives are on the left, and the fork's on the right.' He walked round the table and stood at the body's feet. 'Look there, now. He was in bed. Someone comes. He pulls on trousers over his pyjamas and jams his feet into a pair of quiet shoes, and slops down as he is. But he's not a careful man. He's left, as always probably, his keys in his trousers. See the key-chain, with the button-loop still over the button. And the keys are on the other end of that chain, in his left-hand pocket. And pick up his hands and look at 'em. Even to a lay eye, there's a marked difference; once you've looked at 'em you'll see the left's much bigger . . . If you're going to believe that Dollboys killed himself, you've got to believe (a) that he got up and half-dressed in the middle of the night and came all the way downstairs in the cold to do it, and (b) that for this, his last act upon earth, he deliberately chose to use his right hand when the easier, natural, simple, ordinary and therefore far surer way would have been to use his left, and (c) that he neither stood nor sat nor knelt to shoot himself, but squatted or bent down as if he were looking for something he'd dropped. One might believe (a) alone or (b) alone or (c) alone. But (a) plus (b) plus (c)'s too much . . .'

'By Gad!' said Ravenscourt under his breath. 'He *was* left-handed.'

'And so he was; so he was!' The little doctor was excited. 'And it's me that's the fool for not having remembered it. But I've had little to do with the man. But I ought to've seen, that I ought.' Excitement was bringing to his speech traces of the brogue and idiom of his birth-place. 'And where were me eyes that I didn't get the truth of that bullet bein' down there in the wall. It's right; how should a man put lead through his head in such a position as that position he must have had?'

Ravenscourt said: 'Thanks, Gethryn. You're right. Anything more for us?' The half-resentful curtness that he had shown at first sight of Anthony was gone.

Anthony shook his head. 'Sorry, nothing.'

More speech burst from the doctor, still aboil with this excitement born of unusual event. 'But I'm wanting to ask you, sir, how is it you're sure as you are that the man was ever a-bed? The clothes of him make it seem so. But seemings mayn't be what they seem . . .'

Anthony shot a glance at Ravenscourt; a swift, nearly imperceptible glance. He said to the doctor:

'I knew he'd been in bed. I can't . . .'

Ravenscourt took his cue. He said, with curtness:

'That'll do, now. 'Fraid we must get on with the job. Rawlins, get back to a 'phone and get Fox to come along at once. He'll be in charge. You'll work under him. Understand? While you're gone this Constable stays in charge here. No one to be allowed into this room, or into the house, without permission. Cave; you've finished, haven't you? Gethryn, you won't want to stay. Right. Now get off, Rawlins. And be quick. You can use my car: tell the chauffeur. Gethryn, p'r'aps you'll give me a lift back in yours. I was coming to see you this morning anyhow. Rawlins, when you've done with my car, tell Peters to bring it to The Horse and Hound in Farrow and wait.'

Rawlins was the first to go, with a stiff salute and precisely military right turn. The old doctor, his Irishness dropped from him, was next; he appeared to have for Ravenscourt a respect tinged with affectionate awe. But before he went he insisted upon shaking hands with Anthony. He said:

'Wondered who you were, sir, until I heard Colonel Ravens-court use y'r name. Very *proud* to've met you!' He bustled off in the Inspector's wake.

Ravenscourt looked first down at Dollboys, then about the cold, bare room. He said:

'Let's get out of this. Nothing to do yet, and Fox is the best man I've got.' He turned and made for the door. His spurs clinked, and the heels of his hunting-boots were loud on the brick floor. He said a word or two to Murch, rigid at attention, and went out into the dark passage.

Anthony followed. They came out into the hall together. And together they halted to watch. Flood and the old woman were still there; but they were not now near to each other. Mrs Dollboys had not moved from the great chair; still she was huddled, a wrinkled heap of drab clothes, in its hard embrace. But Flood was at the window beside the front door. He was standing upon a table, which tottered beneath his weight, and was reaching precariously up to touch the rod from which had parted some of the rings of the faded curtain. He was saying over a hunched shoulder:

'This? This what's wrong?' He shook the loose-hanging stuff.

Ravenscourt took three steps out into the hall. At the sound of his tread, there was a swift movement in the oak chair. Out of her wizened face, looking now like that of a terror-stricken monkey, the woman stared. Anthony, too, came out into her sight. He went towards her. She cowered, her hands pressed to her face. A harsh, rattling cry burst from her.

Flood jumped down. The table which had been his support crashed to the stone floor. He crossed with rapid steps to his old position. He bent over the chair and laid a hand on her shaking shoulder. Under his touch she quietened. The hands came down from her face and clutched at him. He looked at Anthony and shook his head, which now had lost much of its sleekness. He put up one hand and smoothed back his disordered hair; with the other hand he patted the bony fingers which were gripping and kneading at his coat. He murmured, over his charge's head:

'Not a bit of good. She won't have anyone but me. But she keeps asking for an Alice. And something about some curtains keeps worrying her. She's not coherent. But she may get. *If* the crowd goes.'

Ravenscourt, rubbing his chin, looked at Anthony. Who said, out of the corner of his mouth:

'This is Flood. He's helping me. Good man. I'd suggest leaving him with her. She's taken a fancy to him. Leave him, and give instructions she's not to be questioned yet, except through him, and not at all unless he says so. I'll tell him to get what he can. But if she's worried she'll go *moost*. And then she'll only confuse us.'

Ravenscourt nodded. 'If he'll stay,' he said doubtfully.

Anthony took out pencil and a small notebook. 'He'll stay all right. He's on the job.' He wrote upon a leaf from the notebook, tore out the leaf, screwed it up and threw it.

Flood's free hand caught it neatly, and neatly unrolled it. Flood's eyes read the message. 'D. was murdered. She may know something. Stay with her. You're in charge with authority. Get what you can. Can we use your car?'

Flood nodded. His eyes rested upon Anthony's for a moment before they turned back to his charge. They showed no surprise, those eyes; their look conveyed an impression that to surprise their owner much more than all this would have to happen.

Ravenscourt turned on his heel and went back down the passage. From its end Anthony heard the crisp voice giving orders, and when it ceased the rumbling, very respectful murmur of Constable Murch.

Anthony, taking cap and coat from the hall's centre table, went to the main door and through it and out into the air. All traces of the mist had now vanished. A yellow sun, bright and cold, made the world sparkle like a nursery picture. He drew in draughts of the earth-scented, sharp-cutting air.

From Anthony's car, the loose figure of Dyson detached itself; it came to meet Anthony with long and flapping strides. Leaning against the car's bonnet was Pike.

'What's *on*?' said Dyson. His voice was querulous.

Anthony smiled with one corner of his mouth. 'You were right, Dyson. No suicide, Dollboys.'

Dyson rubbed together his ungloved hands. Almost he smiled. He said:

'Murdered, was he? Excellent! Knew *he* wasn't a *felo de se*.'

Pike came forward now. 'Got your message from Mr Dyson, sir. And here I am.' His tone added wordlessly: and what's to do?

Anthony answered the unspoken. 'A lot and a hell of a lot.' He no longer smiled. 'While they've all been gabbling in there, I've been thinking. Or trying to. Where are we now? Up against it? It's time again. If there wasn't this time-limit, I believe we'd be better off; because this elimination of Dollboys is another confirmation for us. We know now that Dollboys knew something or everything, and we know too that he wasn't X. At least, we know this, if we assume, as we've got to assume, that

Dollboys' murder is a direct sequel of our activities. If it isn't
we're done anyhow; so it's got to be. And we're near to knowing
that if we get the killer of Dollboys we'll find that he equals X.
But, though we're ahead that way, we're really astern. Now, we
can't talk to Dollboys and twist the truth out of him. We've a
double job instead of a single. And only time for half a single.'
His tone was savage. His eyes looked at the men he talked with,
but did not seem to see them. There was a silence, broken only
by the scraping of Dyson's shoe upon the frozen earth. Dyson
was tracing an invisible pattern with his toe. Pike said:

'But what'll we *do,* sir?' There was urgency in his voice.

'Everything,' said Anthony. 'And all at once.' His tone had
changed again; the savagery had gone from it; it was eager and
decisive. 'Pike; so soon as we get back, take Flood's car . . . can
you drive? . . . Yes? . . . Good! Take Flood's car and do this:
from the man himself, or any other, find out what a Captain
Lake, at present staying with the Carter-Fawcett woman . . .
anyone'll tell you where her place is . . . find out *what* this man
is and *why* and *who* and *how.* That's in general. In particular,
find out whether, after that party of Brownlough's last night,
Lake went to bed—properly or improperly; in other words, is
it possible that he was out and about? Got that?'

Pike nodded, once. A new seeming had come to his face as
he listened. It seemed to have grown longer and sharper. The
lantern-jaw was out-thrust like the prow of a punt. His eyes
were very bright. Dyson said:

'What for me?'

'We get off back now, sir?' said Pike.

Anthony said: 'I'm taking Colonel Ravenscourt back. He's
giving the bobbie a final word. We must wait.'

'What,' said Dyson again, 'for *me?*'

The little smile twisted Anthony's mouth. 'This.' He took out
his wallet and from the wallet a folded sheet. 'I made this out
in bed last night. This district creeps with soldiery, past and
present. This paper's got all their names, and as much of their

particulars as I could get. I want their War Service records. Get up to town on that machine of yours, go to the War Office and ask for General Beaumont. He'll see you're attended to, and properly. Friend of mine. I'll ring him up before you get there. Whether the job's finished or not, report back at the pub tonight. Any time, but come. Also, ring me up there between one and two this afternoon. I might have more for you. Got that?'

Dyson snorted. 'But what's the idea?'

'I'm damned,' said Anthony, 'if I know.' He looked at Dyson. 'But I want it done.'

Dyson was unshaken. He tried again. 'Mean t'say: like to know what's behind . . .'

Anthony cut him short. 'You'll hear tonight. Perhaps. Or perhaps not. According to whether or not I've got my present Irish Stew of a mind sorted out. But do it! Blast you, Dyson, do it!' There was no sting in the curse, and there was a smile with the words. But Pike, watching covertly, felt rather than saw the brief combat of two minds.

Dyson shrugged. 'Right!' he said at last. His voice had no sulkiness in it.

Behind them, the door of the house shut with a bang. Ravenscourt came towards them. They turned. Dyson surveyed the tall figure in its red coat beneath which the dazzling white of the breeches merged into the glossy black of the boots. Beneath his breath Mr Francis Dyson, who had somehow to assert again his complete contempt for all men except Mr Francis Dyson, made an impolite noise. There came from his lips, after this, a muted parody of the hunting horn.

'Shades,' said Dyson, who had never in his life enforked even a seaside donkey, 'of Surtees!'

Anthony went to meet the resplendence. Pike looked at Dyson sharply. He said:

'You in France, Dyson?'

Dyson looked over his great glasses. 'Great Bore?' he said. 'A little. Three years, nine months.'

Anthony and Ravenscourt, having halted a moment in conversation, now were coming towards the car. Dyson, his head to one side, birdlike surveyed them. Pike said, lowering his voice:

'Don't jeer then. That's the Varolles VC that is.'

Dyson's face for a moment displayed interest. ''Zat so?' he said. And then, recovering, again made the horn noise. 'A-hunting,' he murmured, 'we will go.' He turned back to Anthony's car, whistling *John Peel*, and stripped the radiator of its rug.

III

Ravenscourt followed Anthony into The Horse and Hound's Smoking Room. From without there came to their ears, and their eyes when they looked from the side-window, the sound and sight of Pike starting the small, wicked-looking and dusty car of Flood, and Dyson, upon his motor-bicycle, leaving the yard at a speed which must have been near to thirty miles an hour.

'Have a drink?' said Anthony. 'Or too early?'

Ravenscourt nodded. 'I will. Not too early today.' He jerked his neat head to point the window and the yard without. 'Who are those two? I've seen that . . . whatsaname? Pike? . . . Seem to've seen him before.'

Anthony smiled. He pressed the bell by the fireplace. He said:

'You have. He knows you by sight. You've seen him in Scotland House. As a Chief-Detective Inspector CID.'

Ravenscourt threw himself into a chair. 'Of *course*. But how . . .'

Anthony interrupted. 'Easy. He's on holiday. And he heard of my pursuit of very wild geese and just came along to help. He's a good line in men, that. I've worked with him. He was on the Lines-Bower job.'

Ravenscourt nodded. 'And the other two of your . . . er . . . staff?'

'They're press men. Ever see *The Owl*?'

Ravenscourt nodded again. 'Always. Regular subscriber. And

I get the Specials if there happens to be one when I'm in town. Good little paper. And not so little.'

'Partly mine,' said Anthony. He turned and pressed the bell again. 'And partly Hastings' who edits it. Friend of mine. Those two, Dyson and Flood, are on the "Special" staff. Hastings lent 'em to me.'

'And you all . . .' began Ravenscourt, but checked in mid-sentence and was silent. The door had opened. The girl Annie came in. Ravenscourt wanted brandy and soda. Anthony gave his order: coffee for himself. 'And is Mrs Gethryn up?'

The girl fingered her apron. 'Yes, sir. And she's not had breakfast yet. She's ordered it in half an hour, sir, in the Coffee Room. Should . . . should I tell her you'll have yours then, sir?' Her speech was quick enough, but somehow there was about it an uncertainness, as if she were talking upon one subject but thinking of another.

'Yes, do.' Anthony looked at her. Her china-blue eyes, round and large and polished like a doll's, seemed to have in them a question; a something odd and appealing and tinged with fear. He held these eyes with his own; the green gaze probed the blue. She went scarlet; then, quicker than it had come, the colour ebbed, leaving an ashen paleness.

She turned with a flutter of apron. As she walked to the door, there seemed to Anthony's eye to be an unsteadiness about her gait, the shadow of a wavering.

'Pretty child,' said Ravenscourt from his chair. 'But as I was going to say when she came in, you and your . . . er . . . staff all called on Dollboys this morning? Mind if you say why?' The tone was curt, but devoid of offence.

Anthony suddenly grinned. 'You know why. But that Inspector didn't. Although he thought Dollboys was a suicide, he was worried about this regiment of callers. And callers of that sort at that hour . . . Now he knows it's murder, he'll be thinking a lot more. And possibly talking. Don't worry. None of us killed Dollboys.' His smile was gone now; and his tone changed. 'I told you I *knew* Dollboys went to bed last night. But that was because Pike was watching over him to make sure he'd be safe for us this morning. I wish to God he'd watched all night.'

'Watching?' said Ravenscourt. 'How?'

'On the roof of that shed at the end of the house nearer the road. The window above Dollboys' chamber. Pike watched him go to bed; waited till he judged him asleep. We'd been frightening Dollboys, you see. To loosen that tongue. And Pike thought we might have so frightened him that he'd bolt. Hence the watching, and the early call.'

Ravenscourt laughed—a sound not free from annoyance.

He said:

'Don't know that I ought to listen to this. You're breaking the law all round. And you insist on telling *me*. Why?'

Anthony's answer was delayed. Annie came back, with a tray against which the cup and saucer of Anthony's coffee and the glass and small soda-water bottle of Ravenscourt's brandy seemed to beat a trembling tattoo not to be accounted for by her careful gait. She served them in speed and silence and was gone. Again Anthony's eyes followed her to the door; again he detected that hesitant flaw in her gait; it was as if she walked every third step with closed eyes.

Ravenscourt drank. 'That's good. Thanks. Good health. Carry on, won't you? Why tell *me*, I said.'

Anthony carried on. 'I tell you because you're going to help me. You may not've been sure last night. But you're sure now. Dollboys has been killed. By the man—my X—who killed Blackatter and who'll get away with his third killing—Bronson— if we've not found him within seventy-two hours . . . Seventy-two hours! Think of it, man! Seventy-two hours to save a man from hanging—a man who deserves hanging much less probably, than you or me . . .

'You can't doubt *now*. We scared Dollboys. What happened then must've been that Dollboys got in touch with X, because he was scared. He wanted support and instruction. He got, for

X's safety, a bullet through the head. We're surer now, if more sureness was necessary. But, by God, we're up against time still, and with much larger odds against us. I can convince *you*, here, now, in this room. But what sort of a case have I got to postpone Bronson's hanging to give me *time*? None. You know it and I know it. Bronson's deader than Dollboys unless we get X; get X and haul him up by the scruff of the neck and make him say "I did it! I did it because of *this*, like *that*." Follow me? 'Course you do! . . . You've *got* to help me, Ravenscourt.'

The other man got suddenly to his feet. Glass in hand he walked over to the fire and stood looking down into it. His face was overcast; his brows met in a frown and beneath them his eyes seemed to have sunk back into his head with the conflict of his thoughts. Anthony watched him, seeing a struggle between human and official nature. Watching each phase as one watches a fight between two men.

And then, with a change complete in an instant when it did come, Ravenscourt put back his head and laughed. Real laughter this time; a young and joyous sound. He said:

'We're a couple of fools. I can't help helping you. My job now's to find out who killed Dollboys. And you say that when you've got *him*, you've got your X. There you are. We're on the same job whether we like it or not.' He laughed again.

Anthony said: 'That's not all I meant. And you . . .'

'And I know it, you're going to say. All right, I do. You want more.' He straightened himself. He held out a hand and Anthony took it. He said:

'You can have it, Gethryn. I'm with you; officially so far as I may—that's confining things to the Dollboys case; and unofficially with no hesitations . . . But don't forget, if you think I've been slow coming round, that you're asking me to help to prove myself wrong; to expose myself as a fool who, with all his underlings, was hoodwinked; to make myself known as the sort of feller who "doesn't mind who they hang so long as they hang someone" . . . Don't forget that . . . But I'll help. I've said so and I will; though I suppose this is the first time in my life I've ever gone back on my own opinion on a big issue . . . And I'm not utterly convinced yet, you know. But you've made me feel there's a doubt and a biggish doubt. I thought it all out last night. I kept seeing that feller Bronson waiting. Just waiting . . .' He broke off abruptly. He finished his drink. He set the tumbler down and said:

'Anything you want of me *now*?'

Anthony nodded. 'Yes. This is the unofficial side. What d'you know of one Lake? Called Captain?'

Ravenscourt's brows came together again. His face set in hard lines. '*That* thing!' he said. 'What the devil . . . well, you know what you want. Lake? All I know about him is that he's got much money, damned bad manners and a foul face. Magnificent horseman, though. I've hardly ever spoken to him. But he's about these parts quite a bit. With the Carter-Fawcett crowd.'

'Captain?' said Anthony. 'What in? Is or was?'

Ravenscourt's lips twisted in a sneer. 'Was. Temporary gent. Don't know what in. But he did well, I believe. Guts of a lion, I should say. But a damn' nasty job otherwise.' Through the smoke of his cigarette he surveyed Anthony with curiosity. 'Why Lake?' he said. 'D'you think? . . .'

'Hardly,' said Anthony, 'at all.' He smiled. 'No, I mean it. I daren't *think* yet. But I could bear to know about Lake. Thanks. I've also got another string on to him. Pike.'

Ravenscourt raised his eyebrows. 'So?' He looked at his watch. 'Anything else? Anything official?'

'Not yet. Now you're on my side, I'm easier though. I had to get you to say you were, more in case of almost certain future need than anything in the present. Can I always get you quick?'

Ravenscourt gave two telephone numbers. 'One or other of those is pretty certain always.' He picked up his silk hat and gloves and moved towards the door.

Anthony stopped him. 'Stay and have some breakfast. Late but good.'

Ravenscourt shook his head. 'Thanks, no. Had mine early.' He looked down, a little ruefully, at his splendour. 'There's a meet at Copthalls, only a few miles off. I was going. Matter of fact, that's how I came to get down to Dollboys' at all. I came here early to see whether I could get our talk in and be off by ten-fifteen. When I got here I heard Dollboys had shot himself. So I went straight along.'

They went out together by the inn's front door. Ravenscourt's car, a large and powerful but by no means new limousine, had just arrived. Its owner got in. 'Home, quick,' he said to the chauffeur; then to Anthony: 'Hear from you soon. If anything happens on our side, I'll telephone.'

'So long,' said Anthony. 'And thanks.' He watched as the car curled carefully way out into the road, accelerated and slid smoothly out of sight round the corner.

He went back to The Horse and Hound and breakfast.

IV

The cell door was not quite closed. Those two in their blue uniforms were not inside the cell. But he knew where they were. They might as well have stayed on their little chairs. They were outside—only just outside—the door which seemed shut but wasn't.

He sat upon the edge of the bed and looked heavily, without expression, at the man who sat, to face him, upon one of those chairs. A man, this, whose clean-shaven face wore a look of gentle tolerance and earnest kindliness well-nigh insufferable to the man upon the bed. The earnest one had been talking; the resonances of his deep voice seemed to be still hanging in the air, that air which was never stale, but which never seemed *alive*: he leant forward, his steady gaze bent upon the man on the bed, his hands clasped between his knees; his whole attitude expectant of answer.

Bronson looked up. His blue eyes, cold and steely behind their mask of deadness, stared until the gaze of the brown was lowered. Bronson said:

'Padre: there's no manner o' use to it. If it's kindness you want to do . . .' he paused a moment, and jerked a thumb towards the door . . . 'let *them* come back an' d'you go away about your business.'

The Chaplain stirred, uneasy, upon the small chair. He began to speak, but the other would have none of it. Suddenly the veil over the blue eyes was gone, like a mist before breeze. Those eyes became vital and more than vital; they bored into the mind of the Chaplain as they had been used to bore into the minds of opponents in the ring.

'Get out!' said Bronson. The voice was low, scarcely more than a whisper, but the Chaplain's plump cheeks lost much of their ruddiness. He rose, and, rising, tried once again. He said:

'Bronson: I have come to offer . . . to ask you to consider . . . to . . .'

He cut off the sentence in mid-speech. He backed, involuntarily, two paces.

For Bronson, too, had risen. He stood, and the cell seemed to shrink. A thick, immovable, menacing giant of a man. He raised his voice and called:

'Warder!'

The door which had seemed shut swung open with the word. Bronson said, his voice low again:

'Take him away!'

The Chaplain went. Once more the two chairs supported the pair of blue-clad figures. Blue-clad figures who now were so accustomed to the silence of their charge that almost they started when his voice came.

'Christ!' said Bronson, 'he was going to talk about God!'

He began to laugh.

v

Lucia Gethryn poured coffee for herself. She said:

'After all, I did eat.' She looked across the table at her husband with some wonder. 'You said I would. I owe you five shillings, don't I? . . . You know, you've got *the* most exasperating habit of being right. I'm not used to it yet, and I don't suppose I ever shall be.'

Anthony smiled at her. He put away the notebook he had been using. He said:

'Time for Sister Anne yet?'

Lucia shook her head. 'Five minutes.' Her tone was lightly despondent. 'That was a failure, wasn't it? I did think I'd be able to get her to talk. But all I got was your name babbled at me like a parrot.'

Anthony lit a cigarette. 'I'm worried about that girl. Her demeanour's magnificent—from our point of view; if ever anyone went about with a guilty secret in her bosom, that one does. And she wants to get rid of it. Trouble is, what weighs so heavy on her may really be the smallest of new potatoes. I . . .'

He broke off sharply. Wide-eyed, Lucia met his look. They sat motionless. They listened. Lucia lifted her chin and gazed at the ceiling; it was from above that the sound had come.

No further sound came. Lucia lowered her head. She began to speak.

'It sounded . . .'

'Ssh!' Anthony raised a hand.

And they heard it again. The choking fragment of a scream. Then silence. Then a shuffling, scraping noise on the floor of a room above their heads.

Anthony's chair fell with a soft crash to the carpet. He was out of the room before Lucia had moved.

He crossed from the door of the Coffee Room to the stair-foot in a stride and a leap. He took the stairs four at a time. At the stair-head he paused and stood without movement, all other senses subordinated to that of hearing.

For a moment which seemed ten times its length he heard nothing, and then there came again that shuffled scraping, with it the murmur of a voice whose low pitch did not disguise its tensity.

Anthony, in two strides, was at the door of the house's mistress. He put his fingers to the handle and twisted. At the same instant he smote the door with his shoulder, all his weight behind the thrust. But the door was unlocked. Almost he fell, but recovered in two staggering steps which brought him well within the room.

There was a group in the recess of the room's bay window. Two women. Mistress and servant. Selma Bronson and the girl Annie. And the throat of Annie was between the hands of Annie's mistress, who towered over the girl like a Norn. And Annie, the uppers of whose shoes were their only parts to touch the floor, would have sunk to a huddled heap had it not been for those hands about her throat.

Anthony, even as he jumped towards them, heard Selma Bronson's voice. She was saying, in a dull yet dreadful whisper:

'Tell. Tell. Tell! You *shall* tell! Tell.'

She had not heard him. That crash of the door as it had hit the wall, his stagger as he had saved himself, no sound had penetrated to her consciousness.

The feet of Annie beat out, once more, that little scraping tattoo.

Anthony's hand came down, heavy yet gentle, upon the shoulder of Bronson's wife. Over the shoulder came his other hand, to loose the clutch upon the girl's throat.

He had expected resistance. But none came. At the touch her grip loosened. She stood utterly still. She did not even turn her head. The limpness of Annie slid to the floor with a rustle, ending with a soft bump.

Anthony, his hand still upon the shoulder which might, save for its warmth and softness, have been marble, turned his head. He had heard a sound behind him. He saw his wife. She was pale and her breast rose to hurried breathing and her dark eyes were wide. But she was calm and herself. Anthony looked at her, then at the woman who stood so still. To Lucia he said:

'Stay with her. I'll come back.'

Lucia came close. She stood where Anthony had stood. She laid a gentle hand upon Selma Bronson's arm.

Anthony bent over the huddled girl. She was breathing fast and jerkily, and over her doll's-eyes was a glaze of terror. One hand rubbed gently at her throat. Anthony looked up at his wife. He said:

'Fright's the most of the damage.' He bent down and lifted the girl like a child. He went from the room, carrying her against his chest. To Lucia his voice came back from the passage.

'Shut the door,' it said.

Lucia shut the door. By it she stood for a moment. She heard her husband's footsteps going along the corridor towards their room; then a pause; the opening of a door and another pause; the door closing. She turned and went back to the window. The woman still stood, motionless, where she had been. It was as if she had been deprived of the power of movement.

Lucia shivered. She went past that statue and sat herself upon the curtained window-seat. She looked up at the statue. She said, in a low soft voice:

'Sit down. Sit here.' She patted the seat beside her. 'You poor, poor dear!' she said.

The statue moved. A tremor shook it. It melted and became a woman. She staggered; it was as if her stance had been a rigor suddenly fluxed. Lucia put out a quick hand. It was clutched. The woman sat. All rigidity had gone from her now. She shook. Lucia could feel the shaking of her though their bodies did not touch.

There was silence. Such silence that Lucia fancied, once or twice, that she could hear the murmur of Anthony's voice though two rooms separated them. She did not speak; the woman beside her did not speak.

Lucia laid her hand, firm and strong and healing upon an arm that quivered without its owner's volition. There was no word; no change in attitude; but there seemed to be born into the room a warmth. Presently the woman's head drooped, drooped . . . Lucia, imperceptibly, moved nearer, an inch at a time. She kept her hand upon the arm. The quivering, though it did not cease, grew less and lesser. Presently Selma Bronson's head was resting, almost without knowing that there come to rest it had, upon Lucia's shoulder.

When Anthony came back, they were still like this, only Lucia's right arm was about the shoulders that still quivered and Lucia's cheek was resting against that smooth hair whose real colour no man might tell, so level was its balance between the palest gold and the warmest silver.

He came in softly, and softly closed the door behind him. As he crossed the room towards them, Selma Bronson stirred; she was making effort to sit erect—perhaps to stand. But the arm about her shoulders tightened.

'Lie still, dear!' Lucia said. 'Lie still.'

She looked up at her husband. There was anxiety in her glance, but no more. She waited.

Anthony turned an armchair to face the window-seat. he dropped into it. Except that he had, to save the chair's owner from the need of speech, not asked permission for his sitting, his manner was that of a man who 'drops in for a chat'; he was ordinary-everydayness incarnate. He said:

'The girl's all right. She's gone up to her room. But before she went she told me all about it.'

In spite of their meaning, these words were clothed in a voice which might have been discoursing of weather and watercress. To her husband Lucia flashed a smile so lovely that for a moment he lost all thought of anything save her. He said, after that moment:

'Yes. It turned out almost as I thought, you know, Remember I said I was frightened those potatoes would be very, very small? Well, small they were. Not so small, mark you, as to be worthless. But small. The secret heavy in Annie's bosom was Dollboys . . .'

'Dollboys!' said Lucia, between white teeth. 'It's always coming back to Dollboys. *Dollboys!* The name'd be silly if it weren't terrible.'

Anthony glanced at her, a warning glance. 'Go easy!' said the glance. Himself he said:

'Dollboys, you see, had fallen for Annie. Some time ago it started. Over six months. Apparently his intentions were most strictly honourable—or, at least, became so after acquaintance with the firm principles of Annie. He wanted to marry Annie; he wanted to marry Annie very badly. Annie kept him dangling; she was only a little between-maid, but oh, how she called the tune. But at last she said yes. That I gather, was about four months back. Having said "yes", she wanted, naturally, to know roughly the date of the wedding. She was then told that this could not, just immediately, be fixed. Suitor was forced to admit that he was pushed for money. He'd have to tide over a bit; things hadn't been going well; farming wasn't what it had been; things would, of course, be delightful after the tide-over, but ... Annie, frankly disgruntled, agreed to wait a while before insisting upon a fixed date. Privately, she thought that she would have to wait at least six months. There was every indication of such a period; a longer one wouldn't have surprised her. But what did surprise her was, that within six weeks or so, Dollboys was telling her that no longer was there any need to hesitate in fixing a date; no longer, even, any need to delay actual wedding. They could—and would she—get married tomorrow ...

'But Annie held off. Wouldn't make herself cheap. Made Dollboys consent to wait two months. And during the two months, she began—being, apparently, shrewder than most would guess—to wonder. For the announcement of the sudden change in the prosperity of Dollboys had taken place almost immediately after'—Anthony nerved himself here for continuation of his even, conversational tone—'the conviction of Mr Bronson ...'

He broke off. He had to break off. That head was no longer

on Lucia's shoulder. Selma Bronson sat upright; there was in her pose something again of that strange rigidity. She said, in a curiously toneless voice:

'Dollboys had been paid to . . .'

Anthony interrupted her. 'The inference is certainly that he was paid for something—some work or action, or refraining from action—in connection with the murder of Blackatter and the fixing of that on your husband. But *all* he did or didn't do we can't tell. Not yet.' He paused for a moment, and he smiled at Bronson's wife and looked steadily into her eyes. 'But,' he said, 'we shall . . . To finish: Annie didn't, of course think so clearly as that at first, or even really along those lines. But think she did. And went on thinking. And the more she thought—for in a childish sort of way she is devoted to you, Mrs Bronson— the more she disliked having anything to do with a man whom she didn't really love anyhow, and whose fortunes seemed, to say the least, to have risen with the downfall of yours . . . I think that's as far as she really got until *we* came down here; she was obeying an instinct, a superstition, more than a reasoned thought. But whatever it was, it was strong enough—perhaps I should say her affection for you was strong enough—to make her throw Dollboys over. She did that—it was as easy for her as she had kept her engagement secret—about a fortnight ago. Dollboys, as you know, went on hanging about here. But he got no change from Annie. And then we arrived, and I suppose, as we took no trouble to hide our intentions, she found out what we were up to. And that put it into her small head that there was "a chance for the Master after all". And *that* filled her head with thoughts of *how* there could be that chance. And she thought: *if* there's that chance, it means somebody else did it . . . And if somebody else did it, there was a plot. And a plot means funny goings-on . . . and Dollboys' sudden reversal of fortune was a funny going-on . . . She thought and thought. Sometimes it seemed silly, and Annie likes no more to be laughed at than any of us. Sometimes it seemed important—

terribly important—so that she grew scared of telling in case she might find grave trouble for herself through not having told before . . . But she decided to tell. She was to speak to me, at her own request, this morning. But somehow . . .'

Lucia said swiftly: 'Oh, *that's* all quite simple. Mrs Bronson had seen her hanging about us. And saw her, just now, waiting outside our room. And she wondered and asked her and the silly child got frightened and behaved so extraordinarily that Mrs Bronson, having got her in here, began to think she knew something—had been keeping back something vital. And she—Mrs Bronson—couldn't bear to wait to know—it came just like that—and then . . . and then . . .'

A harsh, painful sound, somewhere between laugh and sob, came from Selma Bronson's throat. She said:

'And then I . . . I . . . I might have killed.' She looked at Anthony. 'But you saved me. I . . . I . . . will go to the girl.' She stood up. She took the half of a step forward and then she crumpled.

Lucia's arm was there. Lucia's arm guided her so that her little fall brought her, sitting again, to the window-seat.

Selma Bronson sat huddled, rather dreadfully, with her shoulders bowed and her hands squeezed between her knees. She began to laugh; a sound that sent Lucia's hands, before she could control them, flying for a moment to her ears.

Anthony stood up. He crossed to the window-seat. Selma Bronson stopped laughing. Her body shook and the flaxen head nodded with jerky nods and quivers. Her teeth chattered together. Through the chattering teeth she forced out words. She said:

'I . . . I should like . . . to lie down. I . . . am . . . sorry . . . This is foolish . . . But I have not . . . this is not . . . a happy time . . .' She began to laugh again.

Lucia looked, with eyes of agony, at her husband.

'Ger her on to the bed,' said Anthony, and was gone.

Somehow, Lucia obeyed. The bed shook with the shakings

of its burden. Anthony came back. In one hand was a flask, in the other a small bottle. He took a tumbler from a table. He unstoppered the bottle and shook out into Lucia's hands two white tablets. He said:

'Make her swallow them.'

Lucia made her swallow them. Into the tumbler Anthony poured brandy; added water from a carafe. He sat upon the bed's edge and slid an arm beneath the shaking head and raised it and put the tumbler to its lips. She drank, her teeth beating out a tattoo against the glass.

Anthony let the head gently down to the pillow. He stood, looking down at his patient. Lucia, beside him, slipped a hand through his arm and pressed it. They saw the eyes close, the head sink into the pillow, the twitching and shaking grow less and die away save for an occasional tremor of the whole body. Selma Bronson, who had not slept for days and nights which were carved into her mind like decades, slept now.

They covered her. Anthony nodded at the door. They left upon silent feet.

VI

They had reached only the head of the stairs when the maid who was Annie's understudy came lumbering up to meet them. To Anthony she gasped:

'Pleezir, there's a lady and a gentleman, sir. In the Smoke Room they are, sir. Name of Bricklebrock, sir.'

'Brocklebank?' Anthony lifted an eyebrow.

'Yezzir, Bricklebonk?' She turned and lumbered down the stairs again and was lost to sight.

'You come too,' said Anthony to his wife. 'If it's a party call, I'll leave 'em to you.'

In the Smoking Room they found Sir Richard Brocklebank and his daughter, both pink-cheeked, heavily-coated and smiling. Miss Brocklebank was urgent. With no pause from her introduction to Lucia she seized upon Lucia's husband. She said:

'Colonel . . . sorry, I mean Mr Gethryn: I *do* hope you won't think I'm being a perfect little fool of a busybody; but I asked Daddy and he did seem to think it wouldn't be *too* ridiculous if I came and anyhow I can't be doing any worse than wasting two minutes of your time. Only when I heard, I simply *had* to tell you; because, you know, whatever you didn't say last night, it was perfectly obvious that you *must* be interested in the beast, specially as he was so foully rude to you . . .'

'Lake?' said Anthony swiftly, planting the word, so to speak, in between the ribs of the girl's speech.

She nodded with violence. 'Yes. Sorry. I'm excited. I was talking too much like a woman. Yes, Lake . . . Colonel Gethryn: he's *gone*.'

Anthony raised his eyebrows. 'Has he now?'

Again Miss Brocklebank's emphatic nod. 'And I believe he's bunked; from you.'

Sir Richard's laugh came then, like a low-pitched and musical neigh.

His daughter flushed. 'Don't be a beast, Daddy. You think so too, only you're such a coward you won't say anything just in case you're wrong.'

Anthony looked at the baronet; found those bright keen eyes were watching him. Anthony said:

'*Do* you agree with your daughter, sir?'

The bright eyes twinkled. 'I'd like notice of that question, I think. Go on, Margaret.'

Miss Brocklebank was not loth. 'I heard about it from one of the servants. She'd been sent down to the village, early this morning, six-thirty, about some parcel expected off a train. She bicycled. She was just at the bottom of Pedlar's Hill—there's a nasty almost right-angled turn there—when a great green car, she says: "swep' roun' at a t'riffic speed and all but 'ad me". But she's a brightish sort of girl and in spite of the "t'riffic" speed she saw the driver. It was Lake, Captain Lake. He was alone. He was travelling very fast. He was heading London-wards. His luggage—it's an open car and she could see—was piled up in the back. Not one or two bags but a huge collection . . .' Miss Brocklebank paused—for effect and breath.

'Fast,' said Anthony. 'Lot of kit. Heading for London. Six-thirty a.m.' He smiled at Miss Brocklebank. 'Pretty certain he's going away. But nothing to prove he's running.'

Miss Brocklebank smiled a triumphant smile, again, bringing that soft and musical neigh from her father. She said:

'But I've got something else to tell you. I was intrigued by this story . . .'

'*Intrigued!*' groaned her father.

'Intrigued by this story, in view of last night,' said Miss Brocklebank magnificently. 'So I took matters into my own hands and I did a little telephoning. I rang up the Carter-Fawcett number—this was at about a quarter to ten, p'r'aps a bit earlier—and I was a Miss Gayley who wanted every so badly to speak, at once, to Captain Lake. I had a pleasant and refaned voice. The butler answered. He was sorry, but Captain Lake was not available. Miss Gayley persisted; it was very, very important. I was in the neighbourhood; would there be any chance of seeing Captain Lake a little later in the day if I were to motor over? . . . That did it. There would be no chance of seeing Captain Lake a little later in the day if I were to motor over, as Captain Lake had suddenly been called away . . . No. Very sorry; it was *not* known where Captain Lake had been called away to. There!'

Miss Brocklebank ended. Miss Brocklebank waited anxiously. She was not disappointed.

Anthony looked at her. 'Watson couldn't 've done that, he wouldn't 've thought of it, and if he had he'd 've got the wrong number.' He smiled at her. 'Thank you very much,' he said. 'And I mean that.'

Miss Brocklebank turned upon her father, now deep in talk with Lucia. Miss Brocklebank said:

'Did you hear that, Daddy! I *was* right to come. Again Colonel Gethryn's told me I'm too good to be a Watson. I'll believe it soon. You ought to've had me on Intelligence with you, Daddy!'

Anthony turned. To the baronet he said:

'You on Intelligence during the War, sir?'

Sir Richard nodded. His bright eyes gleamed. 'And I am intelligent,' he said. The eyes twinkled. 'Strange.'

'Home?' said Anthony. 'Or overseas? Or both . . . Hope I don't seem inquisitive. But I had S.I. III for a bit.'

'I know,' Sir Richard nodded. 'No. Matter of fact I was pretty nearly all the time in France. Well, I might say, behind the lines.'

'Daddy!' said Miss Brocklebank reproachfully, 'you do fib!'

Anthony looked at his watch. Sir Richard glanced at his daughter. Who took her cue, though with some reluctance.

There were goodbyes. Sir Richard raised Lucia's fingers to his lips. With Anthony, Miss Brocklebank shook hands fervently.

'You *will*,' she pleaded, 'let me know about . . . about everything. Won't you?'

Anthony answered her. 'I couldn't,' he said, 'do otherwise. Even if I wanted to. And I don't want to.'

'And if,' said Miss Brocklebank a moment or so later, her foot on the running-board of her father's car, 'there *was* anything I could do . . .'

'Of course!' Anthony smiled. 'Ring you up at once!'

'And come and see us!' said Sir Richard out of the car's window.

Lucia watched the car out of sight. 'Nice girl!' she said.

Anthony nodded. But his thoughts seemed elsewhere.

'Daddy,' said Lucia, 'is a bit of a lady's man. But a very good one.'

Anthony grunted. He said absently:

'Old enough to know better.'

Lucia shook her head. 'He's not the kind that age affects. He'd never be gaga. He'll remain attractive till they bury him.'

'Attractive?' said Anthony. 'Well . . . yes. I suppose I can see it.'

Lucia nodded. 'It's there. With that kind—I admit they're rare—their age simply doesn't count with women . . . What're you going to do now, dear?'

They went back into the house.

VII

It was half-past twelve when Dyson rang up. Anthony answered the ring. To his ear there came a harsh, grating voice.

'Dyson here.'

'Gethryn,' said Anthony.

'Any more names for the list?' said the voice.

'One,' said Anthony, and gave it. 'How're you getting on?'

'Quick,' said the voice. 'G'bye.' There was the click of a replaced receiver.

Anthony went back to the Smoking Room. He was restless. He smoked pipe after pipe. His tongue began to smart. He smoked cigarettes. He sat down. He stood up. He wandered about the room. His every movement was aimless and hesitant. But his mind worked. It raced. His eyes were blank, their greenness almost startling. But behind their blankness was a furious activity. He was alone. But he spoke once aloud. He came to a halt in one of his wanderings. He said:

'Blast it! It might be wrong.' The door opened. Lucia came in. He did not hear her. 'So easily might be wrong!' he said.

'What?' said his wife softly.

He grunted. 'Theory,' he said.

She left him to his silence. She sat mute and relaxed in a chair near the fire. Behind her he went on with that aimless prowling.

And then, at one-fifteen, came Pike.

'He's gone, sir,' said Pike. His voice was hard.

Anthony nodded. 'I know. Why?'

Pike shrugged.

'Where?' said Anthony.

Pike's jaw was out-thrust. 'Gave out it was London. I got that much. But that probably means it's anywhere but. Unless he's a doubler. How did you know he'd gone, sir?'

'People I met last night. They were here just now. Servant had seen him in a car. What's your full tale?'

Pike told it. He had gone to the house called Weydings. He had been humble. He had called at the servants' quarters. He was inquiring for a friend of his—a valet whom he believed was staying in this house with his master. He was disappointed, none knew the valet's name, nor the master's. But they were hospitable. Mr Pierce was asked in. Mr Pierce—it says much for Pike's powers when he set himself to use them—was refreshed. And Mr Pierce, by that inevitably, crushingly tedious and roundabout way which is necessary, had learnt quite a lot about Captain A. D. Featherstone Lake. But nothing (Pike was dismal) worth anything, you might say. He'd got notes of all that stuff. Sat in the car a mile from Weydings ('My Winkey! That's a beautiful place, sir!') and jotted 'em down in his notebook while memory was green. No; so far as he could find out, no telegram or telephone message had come for Captain Lake. He had just left, talking of urgent business. He had tipped all right, but then he always did. Those servants whom, owing to the earliness of his departure, he had not seen he had provided for through their fellows. No; it was impossible to find out where Captain Lake had spent such of the night as came between the return from the dance and this early departure. Captain Lake might've been in his own bed, or in someone else's—or in no bed at all. Mr Pierce's informant had been a footman, who had said, winking: 'It don't do for *us* to get curious of a night in *this* house!' Captain Lake had certainly come back after the dance; but whether he'd gone out again . . . well, he might and again he mightn't . . .

Anthony interrupted. 'How did you camouflage?'

Pike smiled, a dry, hard smile. 'I'd been hearing gossip, sir. Something about a girl in one of the villages. Little birds 'd told me Captain Lake was out and about last night.'

Anthony nodded. 'And what you've told's about all you've got?'

'Yes, sir.' Pike's tone was despondent. 'That's all . . . Except for a queer thing that happened after I'd left the place. I went out by the way I'd come. Walking, because I'd left the car some distance off—not in the main road, that's a good mile from the house, but tucked away on the road through the park, well out of sight. When I got back to it there was still no one about and I drove off for the gates—that's the East Lodge entrance. Just as I got up to the gates and pulled up for a chap to open 'em, there was the blazes an' all of a hooting behind me and along comes a great limousine—biggest car I've ever set eyes on. It drew up, as the keeper'd just begun to open the gates, right beside me. There was a chauffeur in it, and a lady. Very handsome she was, if you like that sort of handsome. I don't myself . . .'

'Dark?' said Anthony. 'Tall?'

'Both, sir. 'Least she seemed tall as she was sitting . . . Well, sir, there were the two cars side by side. There wasn't more'n a foot between the wings; the great thing towered above Flood's car like a battleship. I looked up, casual-like, and saw the lady was looking down at me. *Most* intent, she was, sir. I said to m'self, "you'll know me again", and looked the other way. And then the gates 're open and I slip into gear and pop out. I swung in to the road and eased up. It's narrow just there and I made sure the big car'd want to pass. I slowed right down, but nothing happened. I stopped and looked round. The big car was still inside the gates. The lady'd got out and was talking to the lodge-keeper. They both kept looking out into the road at me. I got out, and fiddled about under the bonnet . . . And presently I heard the gates shut, and by Cripes, when I looked up—very casual—there's the car goin' *back* towards the house. And it *was* going, too. Well over fifty, I'd say . . . So I moved on, stopped again, and wrote up my notes, and then came back here.'

Anthony rubbed at his jaw. 'Odd!' he said.

Pike brightened. 'That's what *I* thought, sir. Nothing queer, o'course, if you look at it one way . . .'

'The other view,' said Anthony, 'is always better.' He fell silent a moment. After a while he said: 'And what it all means is that we're Lakeless, and don't know where to find him.'

'We could try, sir,' Pike was urgent. 'Not so easy to hide yourself when you're wealthy and a polo-player and all that. If it was an official job now, we'd know where he was before he did himself.'

Anthony smiled; a brief smile which vanished before it had properly shown itself. He said:

'But it isn't an official job. And we've not got anything, yet, to make it so. But I might have a word with the Chief Constable.' He dropped into a chair and began, with an abstract air, to fill his pipe.

Pike looked at him: the eyes of Pike were intent and curious. It did not seem to Pike that Colonel Gethryn was quite himself. Colonel Gethryn seemed . . . tired, was it? Or dispirited? Or . . . no, Colonel Gethryn could not, possibly, he bored. But the longer one knew him, the harder it seemed to be to diagnose his moods; sometimes even his words. Had it not been, thought Pike, for a certain indefinable . . . how should he put it? . . . H.C.F., he might have thought, taking Colonel Gethryn's demeanour in the Lines-Bower case as compared with his demeanour from the very beginning of this present business, that here was not Colonel Gethryn at all, but some other man of his voice and seeming and habits.

But Pike trusted. He stuck out that long jaw a little further and tried to project himself into Colonel Gethryn's mind. He said:

'Try Colonel Ravenscourt, sir? . . . That's an idea. If he didn't get . . . er . . . well, touchy, as you might say. He's an . . . he's got the reputation of being an opinionated gentleman.'

Anthony put the match to his loaded pipe. 'I've won him, Pike.' He spoke through a little cloud of silvery blue. 'He's on our side now.'

Pike smiled. But his small brown eyes were anxious behind the smile: he was still endeavouring, without success, to get into Colonel Gethryn's mind and mood.

He became aware, quite suddenly, and with something of a shock, that Colonel Gethryn's gaze was fixed upon him through the film of smoke from Colonel Gethryn's pipe.

And Anthony smiled. He said:

'It's no good, Pike. Not a bit of good! I don't know where I am myself. That's honest. I've either got a long way or nowhere at all . . . It's different, this business. Most of the other jobs I've done in this line were like games: in a way, anyhow. I mean, they didn't affect me very closely, except in a spirit of "damn-it-I-*will*-do-this-puzzle-and-win-the-big-balloon". But *this* one . . . well, there's that woman upstairs. And in that prison there's a clean, decent, bewildered first-class man waiting to have his neck snapped by a rope for something he didn't do! . . .' He got to his feet with a sort of savage jerking of his whole body and began to pace the room.

Five strides took him from fireplace to door; five strides from door to fireplace. His pipe-smoke hung about his head like an erratic nimbus. He said, suddenly, midway between the two poles of his walking:

'And here am I, sitting on my stern. *With* the beginnings of a theory and a whole higgler's parcel of uncoordinated facts. What are we to do if my theory's tripe and the fact won't ever coordinate? What am I to *do*?' His voice was harsh with self-accusation. His long, lean length seemed to tower inches above its normally great height. His keen face seemed dark with savage thought. And, for once, the lids were lifted fully away from the strange eyes, which blazed now with a fire which changed their greenness almost to yellow.

Pike was dumb. But his heart bounded. This, although he had not seen it before, was patently a side of the Colonel Gethryn whom he knew.

Lucia's voice came suddenly from the chair before the fire. It said softly:

'You're not fair, dear. Not to yourself, I mean. Look! We came down here—only a few *hours* ago really—knowing nothing, expecting nothing. And there you are, with a theory in your head and all these facts you talk about. You ought to be glad. *And* proud of yourself and Mr Pike and the others.'

Anthony took up his pacing again. He said:

'You're heartening. And you're not exactly wrong. But it's *time* that's worrying me. Time!'

He broke off; stood looking at the door. In the silence came the repetition of the double knock which had interrupted his speech and movement.

In answer to his call there came that understudy of Annie who now lay up in her small room, feeling every now and then the tender fingers at a bruised throat.

'Pleezir!' said the understudy. 'There's a lady. Outzide. Innacarzir.' She was very ruddy of cheek, and her speech and manner were flustered out of the common.

Anthony's glance went to the window. But the car was not within this field of sight. He said:

'All right. Coming. What name?'

The crimson cheeks went pale and then flushed again. The girl's breath laboured. She was much excited. She gasped:

'Pleezir, it's Mrs Garter-Foorsit, sir.'

Anthony's glance met Pike's. Lucia rose and sauntered, with a quite admirable seeming of casualness, to a window.

Anthony nodded dismissal. The door closed behind Annie's understudy. There came a low whistle from Pike's square mouth. Anthony walked slowly from the room and into the hall. The porch door stood open, and as he went towards it he could see some part of the great car which Pike had said was like a battleship.

He pushed the porch door fully open and went out into the hard, bright sunlight. His breath made small and instant clouds upon the frosty air. By the limousine's door stood a chauffeur in a dark-green livery. Through the window of the car there showed a dark and fierce and lovely profile framed in the black and white of small velvet hat and vast collar of some costly fur.

At that window, which the chauffeur—an automaton of more

than human good-looks—lowered at his coming, Anthony
bowed. There was no bow in return; but the profile became a
full-face view. A harsh yet somehow pleasing voice came from
it. It said, with no pretence at civility:

'We met last night, so we can cut the cackle.' Thin black
brows met over flashing eyes. 'I want to know,' said the voice,
'what the *hell* you mean by sending your filthy spies to nose about
my house.'

Anthony was suitably astonished. 'My filthy spies? Nose
about your house?'

Rage broke through and distorted the white mask. The face
was beautiful still, but yet not good to look upon. A different
voice came from its twitching lips. It said, thickness marring it
yet not slurring its words:

'Cut that out! Tell me what you think you're doing—sending
your damned spies!'

'Spies?' Anthony was all bewilderment still.

A hand in a glove whose beauty was fit setting for the hand's
beauty came up. It reached through the window. It pointed a
finger which trembled at the white, low bulk of the inn.

'Yes, *spies*!' she said. 'The man's in there. Now!' In three
short sentences she described Pike. A cruel description, untrue
in adornment, excellent in essential; a description illuminated
by three words in particular, seldom heard even in these times,
from a woman's lips. 'What,' she said at the end, 'd'you mean
by sending him? Damn you, how *dare* you!'

'A man,' said Anthony, 'who is staying in this inn, where I
too am staying, chooses to visit the servants' quarters of your
house. What's that to do with me, madam?' His tone was bland,
his speech slow. He waited for what these irritants would bring.

'To do with you!' Atop of the words came a sudden flurry
within the car, and gloved fingers fumbled at the handle.
Anthony stood back. The chauffeur came out of nowhere, and
his gauntletted hand swung the door wide and held it.

She came out of the car with a rush which yet did not cost

her dignity. The chauffeur vanished again. She came close to Anthony, very close. Almost the great white collar of the beautiful coat brushed against him. She stood straight and tall and trembling with a passionate rage. She said, very low:

'To do with you! You know very well. You set your spies on to ferret out things about a guest of mine—about what he was doing and when. And how and why. And all because you're a publicity-seeking, press-toadying, jumped-up busybody who's taken it upon himself to come down here and fidget round to try and prove that a foul dog who shot another, as bad as himself, through the back of the head, ought not to be strung up . . . I know all about you, you see. Not that I wish to! . . . But leave my household alone another time. Because a guest and good friend of mine chooses to leave unexpectedly, am I to endure your attentions? And visits from your plug-ugly staff? How the hell does it concern you and this self-imposed Sherlock-Holmsing of yours if Captain Lake *does* go away without proper leave-taking? Can't he go where and when and how he likes? *I* didn't know he was going, nor did anyone else in my house; but just because, for some very good reasons of his own, he *did* have to leave suddenly, I don't conclude that he's a criminal. *I'm* not a fool . . . By God, Mr What's-your-name, I've a damned good mind to stop your game for good and all by reporting you to the Police. I will. I'm not on good terms with Colonel Ravenscourt—can't stand the man—but I know him. And he'd listen to *my* complaint . . .' Her words, all of them clear, had been coming faster and faster. Now she seemed to stop for breath.

Anthony took his chance. 'I was just about,' he said mildly, 'to ring up Colonel Ravenscourt. Perhaps, if I get the number, you would like to speak first. My business is different business.' He put up a hand and rubbed gently at the tip of his right ear, which was smarting with the cold.

The woman, for one infinitesimal fraction of time seemed about to strike him in the face.

He stood his ground. His greenish eyes held her gaze. There

was silence, broken only by her hurried breathing. She said at last:

'You damn' *dog*! . . . It won't be Ravenscourt I'll see. He and you are the same kind.'

She turned on her heel, drawing that coat about her. Again the chauffeur materialised. He opened the door; settled a rug about her knees; shut the door; went lightly and with speed to his driving-seat. His face—the mask of a dead Apollo—was blank beneath his peaked cap.

The great car slid, without sound, away from the inn, gained the high road, and disappeared.

Anthony stood gazing after it. There was the look in his face of a man who sees beyond what, ostensibly, he looks at. He was motionless for a full minute. His hand which had gone in search of his pipe to his jacket pocket stayed, still as the rest of him, suspended half a foot away from the pocket.

At last he turned. His eyes closed; opened again to the present and the concrete things before them. He saw that at the windows of The Horse and Hound were many curious heads; from the Smoking Room Pike and Lucia, shoulder to shoulder, looked out at him. Suddenly he grinned. He winked at them and ran up the steps of the porch and so into the house.

Before he got to them, there was speech between Pike and his wife. To his astonishment—and utter delight when afterwards he came, as still he frequently does, to think of it—Pike felt the lady's fingers gripping his arm.

'Oh!' breathed Lucia. 'Oh! *What's* happened? He . . . he hasn't smiled like *that* since the beginning.'

Pike nodded; he had not yet properly realised that clutch upon his arm. He beamed. 'You're right!' he said.

Anthony came in to them. There was difference in the whole of him. He had sloughed five years in as many minutes. He strode to the fireplace and pressed long and hard upon the bell-push which was beside it. He said:

'Oh frabjous day! Calloo and most certainly Callay. We will

now all have a little drink.' From Annie's understudy, who came hurrying, he ordered whisky for himself and Pike, a glass of sherry for his wife.

The understudy gone, they beset him with questions. He smiled upon them but would not speak. They gave him up. He said at last:

'Don't take my spirits without any soda, will you? I mean I'm disproportionately elated. That jigsaw in my poor head's suddenly given itself a shake. And it looks like making a picture. Very much it looks like making a picture. What's been making me like a sore with two bare heads has been that cold hot-pot I've had up here.' He tapped his forehead. 'So that now I've got it sorted, I'm full of bounce and egotism. All zeal, Mrs Easy!' He looked at his wife. His tone changed. He said:

'But you're not to go running away with the idea that I'm bound to be Deus ex Machina. I'm not. I'll be frank. It's a toss-up. Fifty-fifty . . . I'm just happy because I can see my way. I've been wandering about in the dark, being very clever about it and all that, but in the dark. And now I've seen a bit of light, it's gone straight to my head. So don't be too optimistic. Don't be optimistic at all, in fact.'

'I won't,' Lucia said. But her radiance robbed the words of meaning.

Anthony groaned. 'I meant,' he insisted, 'exactly what I said. Exactly.' His tone was incisive. Once more that atmosphere of impending horror, though less heavy, less enveloping than before, settled upon Lucia's spirit.

Anthony watched her face. He crossed to her chair and sat himself upon its arm and laid a hand upon her shoulder. He smiled down at her. A small and grave and intimate smile that Pike could not see. His fingers pressed the shoulder. He said:

'I'm a fool. I should never've done the song and dance. But I couldn't help it. And you can bet your boots, my darling, that now I can see *something* you won't at least be bothered by that dread sitting-about-and-doing-nothing sort of feeling.'

Lucia looked up at him. Her shoulder lifted itself to return the caress of the hand which rested upon it.

'But, sir,' said Pike suddenly, 'what *is* this something?' His eyes were eager but apprehensive. 'Be best for us all to be abreast of you, wouldn't it?'

Anthony shook his head. A smile twisted his mouth. 'Sorry!' he said. 'Not yet. It's not ripe. And I'm constitutionally unable to spill beans before they're properly cooked. P'r'aps I ought but I can't. That's all there is to it. I wouldn't, mind you, Pike, keep you or anyone else in the dark at a point where your being in the dark might prejudice the chance of success. But until that point, or until I'm dead, cold, utterly *sure*—whichever is the earlier—my beans remain unspilt. Sorry and all that. Expect it comes from reading too many detective stories. My subconscious ego—a monstrous brute—wants to indentify itself with Lecoq and Rouletabille and Gore. They all hold their tongues till page three hundred and four. They've got to, or no one'd read about 'em . . . Come on, it's late, let's go and have some lunch. You order while I use the 'phone.'

They went luncheonwards. From a table near the fire, Pike and Lucia heard Anthony's voice at the instrument in the hall.

"Lo . . .' it said. Pause. 'That the War Office?' Pause. 'Right. Colonel Beaumont, please.' Pause. 'That Colonel Beaumont's secretary? . . . Oh, it's yourself, Piggy.' Pause. 'Yes. Is he still with you?' Pause. 'No. No. That's what I'm ringing for. Stop him. Tell him to wait where he is. I'm coming up. He's to wait till five. If I'm not with you then, he's to go to White's and wait.' Pause. 'Thanks. G'bye.'

He came into the Coffee Room with long strides. He was whistling, very softly, a twenty-or-more-year-old music-hall ballad.

VIII

He ate swiftly, and talked not at all. The meal done, he went to the telephone again. He asked for the second of the numbers which Ravenscourt had given him in the morning. He said when he had got it:

'I want to speak to the Chief Constable if he's there. Gethryn's the name.'

There was an instant 'Yessir' and many crackling switchboard noises. Then Ravenscourt's voice:

'That you, Gethryn? I've nothing—yet. Anything you want?'

'Yes. First—as a matter of interest—d'you happen to've heard that Lake's gone?'

'Lake's what?'

'Gone,' said Anthony. 'Left us. Very sudden early this morning. All luggage. Destination unknown.'

'Damn good thing. But what's it to do with? . . .'

'Ware 'phone. All I'll say now—and I'm not pressing it—is that I could stand knowing where he could be found.'

'Might help.' Ravenscourt's voice was doubtful. 'But I can't do much—not officially. I'll try and get you something. Anything else? You sound frisky.'

'Yes. Got something at last. Tell you sometime later. Nothing at all on the Dollboys job yet, then?'

'Not a thing . . . Well, I'll do my best about Lake. 'Bye.'

Anthony heard the click of a receiver, and hung up his own. He was turning to go back to the Coffee Room, where Lucia was still at table, when there came to his ears the sudden roar of a motor-engine; then a screeching of brakes. A car had come into the forecourt and come in fast.

He went along the hall to the porch-door. He opened it and came nose to nose with Flood. At the foot of the steps stood a dusty two-seater, far from new. In it, at the wheel, was a Police Inspector. Not the belligerent Rawlins, thought Anthony, and remembered the name of Fox. He said to Flood:

'What's doing?'

'Quite a lot.' Flood was nonchalant; but his eye gleamed. He put up both hands to smooth his hair.

Anthony looked at the car and its driver, who now was starting his engine. 'Where's he bound?'

'HQ,' Flood said. 'I've got something. And they're on to it, of course.'

'Come in,' said Anthony. 'Food?'

Flood shook the disordered head. 'No. Shared a constabulary packet of sandwiches. Drink, though. Very dry work, murders.'

Anthony led the way back to the Coffee Room. At its door they met Pike. He turned back and went in with them. Flood was given a drink. He drank. He said:

'Knew I'd get something out of the old girl if I stuck it. *And* I did.'

'Photo of the guilty party?' Pike was humorously scornful.

'No,' said Flood lightly, 'only his name.' He sat back and took another drink from his glass and enjoyed the reception of this statement.

For a moment Pike's mouth opened; he shut it with a snap and once more his lower jaw protruded. But the light of astonishment was still in his eyes. Anthony sat very still; his dark face was expressionless as a mask and his eyes were blank. But his hand, clenched into fist, lay upon the table and its knuckles showed dead-white. He said, in a flat and level voice:

'Go on, Flood. And be quick.'

Flood went on. 'I got on to it like this: the old girl kept on saying something about "curtain". You remember when you and the Chief Constable were leaving she was at it and I was trying to get at what she wanted. She got much quieter after you'd gone and before the rest of the local sleuths arrived I'd managed to get her up to her room and make some tea and get it down her. Alone with me she got calmer, and gradually almost coherent. But the calmer she got the more grief-stricken she got—poor old dame!—and she was so busy weeping that she said even less than before. But I still kept hearing that word "curtain". And I began to think about it. And suddenly, after I'd tried all the curtains in that room on her and drawn blank as I had downstairs, I saw the word in my head—and it began with a capital C. I made a wild shot and began talking to her as if Curtain was a man.' Flood paused; he pushed aside his empty glass and leant his arms upon the table and over them his body. He said, with a sort of forced quietness:

'I was right. Curtain was a name. I got it out of her in bits. Curtain was a man who knew Dollboys and used to come and see Dollboys. He had business of some kind with Dollboys; what it was she never knew. The full name was Luke Curtain. She'd only seen him twice, though he'd been to the house much more often than that. But he always came in the late evening; and if she wasn't in bed already when he came she was sent there. She knew nothing about Mr Curtain and therefore nothing against him. But she never liked the . . . *feel* of Mr Curtain.'

'She *knew* this Curtain came last night?' Pike put in. He was frowning now and his eyes were glittering slits. 'Because if he did come it must've been late. Very late, because I was on that roof there till . . .'

Flood silenced him. 'She doesn't *know* anything about last night. But she just remembers waking up and hearing a movement outside and Dollboys going downstairs. She didn't know what the time was, and she just thought "Curtain" and turned over and went to sleep again.'

'That all?' said Pike. His tone said: it isn't enough.

For the first time Anthony spoke. He said, before Flood could reply:

'What does she say Curtain's like?' He had not moved; and still his voice was that curious flat-seeming sound.

Flood looked at him: 'Biggish, slouching, untidy chap. Uncertain age. Big yellow moustache and a bit of beard. Very rough clothes. Deep, surly voice.'

Anthony moved at last. He sat back in his chair. When he spoke, his voice had lost that queer tonelessness. He said:

'And where does he live? What part of the county?'

Flood shook his head. 'She doesn't know. Nor does this Alice girl: I asked her but she knew nothing at all.'

'You've told the Police?'

Flood nodded. 'Yes. They're on it, as I said. Fox has gone to see the Chief Constable.' He looked from Pike to Anthony, from Anthony to Pike. 'Funny thing,' he said slowly, 'none of the bobbies'd heard of Mr Curtain either. Secretive person.'

There was a silence. Anthony broke it. He got to his feet. 'I shan't be here the rest of today. I'm going to London. I'll bring Dyson back with me.' He looked at the two men. 'You must both get busy. Damned busy. On your own, go out into the highways and find out about Curtain. The Police'll be at it, too, but that's all to the good. Two extra cooks won't spoil this pottage; and they might cook it quicker. I'm starting at once. Pike, would you find my wife before you do anything else, and ask her to find out from the girl Annie whether she ever heard, through Dollboys or elsehow, of Curtain. If I'm not back tonight, I'll ring up.'

Pike and Flood were alone. They looked at each other. Flood's round face wore a slightly dazed look. Pike's long face broke presently into a smile. He said:

'He's more like himself than he's been since the beginning of this do.'

Flood shrugged. He looked at the door by which Anthony had left. 'What's up his sleeve?' he said.

Pike chuckled. As always when he was moved, a schoolboy oath came out of him. He said:

'Don't *know*! But, by Crops, I'll bet there's five aces.'

Outside, Anthony was shouting for his servant. Who presently came, from some nethermost region; his mouth, though he strove to conceal this, was full.

'Get the car out,' Anthony said. 'I'm going to London. Hurry, you'll drive.'

White hurried. As he hurried he muttered: 'Thank God!'

Anthony went to the telephone. Again he gave the second of Ravenscourt's two numbers. Again he was in luck.

'Hullo,' said Ravenscourt's voice at last. 'Just off. You caught me.'

'Good. Tell me a thing. What was Blackatter's unit, or units, in France? He was in France?'

There was a pause. 'He was in France all right,' said the telephone. 'Can't remember what with, though. Hang on.'

Anthony hung on. After two minutes the telephone spoke again. 'Second-Fourth Prince Edward's Rifles,' it said. 'All the time. That is from 16th January '15 to Armistice. Three leaves during that period. A week in September '15; a weekend in May '16 and a long leave—six weeks—in January '17. And a fortnight in hospital at Barrigny in May '17. That do?'

'Thanks,' said Anthony. 'Many thanks.'

'About Lake,' said the telephone, 'I've nothing for you yet. But might have later. Heard about this talk of the Dollboys woman? Some man called Curtain? I'm off there now.'

'Thanks about Lake,' said Anthony. 'Don't forget about him. Yes: I've heard of Curtain. Odd business. Very odd. Who is Curtain, what is he, that no one seems to know him?'

'Mare's-nest probably,' said the telephone. 'G'bye.'

Anthony hung up the receiver. He pulled an envelope from his pocket and upon it scribbled the details of the dead Blackatter's years in France.

Lucia came down the stairs and found him putting on his greatcoat. He kissed her. He said:

'See Pike. I'm off. Back sooner or later.'

He was gone. Within what seemed an impossibly short time there came to Lucia's ear the boom of the car's exhaust. She turned to find Pike at her elbow.

Anthony sat, buried in his great frieze coat, in the seat beside the driver's. His eyes were closed, his head sunk between his shoulders.

'Fast, sir?' said White.

'Push her along,' said his master.

White pushed her along.

Only twice upon the whole journey—and those times within three or four miles of its beginning—did the eyes of Anthony open and show him to be awake. Upon each occasion it was another car that they looked at. The first, Mrs Carter-Fawcett's limousine; the second, the sedate coupé of Sir Richard Brocklebank. The first, going their way, they passed. Anthony's eyes took in the emptiness of the car and the immobile, inhuman beauty of the profile of the silent Apollo at the wheel. The second car was travelling against their way. The road curved here and narrowed; White slowed down for the passing. Miss Brocklebank, driving, raised a hand to Anthony in salute. He raised his hat. Beside his daughter was Sir Richard. He waved airily. Anthony nodded and smiled. The car passed. His had gone perhaps fifty yards when Anthony leaned out and looked back, to see that the baronet had done the same. Even at that distance, Anthony imagined that he could see the twinkling of those brown and eternally youthful eyes.

White took the sharp S bend at Woodman's Corner and was out on the arterial road. Anthony said again:

'Push her along.'

White put down his right foot.

IX

The Horse and Hound did not see Anthony again upon that Saturday. At eight they fetched Lucia to the telephone.

'That you, dear?' said the telephone. 'I shan't be back till tomorrow. Probably evening. Dyson's staying up with me. Look after *her*.'

'I am, dear,' Lucia said. 'She slept until nearly six, d'you know.' Her voice was strained. 'It's done her good, of course. But only in one way. She . . . she . . . she can *feel* more now . . .' She broke off.

'Stick it!' said Anthony's voice. '*You* all right? . . . Good . . . What did the girl say about Curtain?' His voice gave hint of eagerness repressed.

'Sorry, dear. She'd never heard even the name.'

'Don't be sorry.' The telephone's voice was not a downcast voice. 'Could you get Pike?'

'He's waiting,' Lucia said. 'And Mr Flood.' And presently Pike spoke. He said:

'We've been over the whole countryside, sir. So far as *we* can find there's not a soul knows anything of any Curtain. The name's not known. I saw Inspector Fox in the late afternoon. I couldn't pump him—very discreet these country policemen—but it doesn't look to me, sir, as if they'd had any more luck than we have.' Pike's voice did not commit him to either sorrow or pleasure at the work's result.

The telephone grunted. Pike's hearing, strained for a note, a tone, to indicate Colonel Gethryn's feelings, was strained in vain. The telephone said:

'Try this for me. You and Flood. Find out if the Carter-Fawcett woman's at Weydings or gone. If she's there, keep an eye on the place and her if she leaves it. Only for tonight, though.'

Pike's eyes shone. 'Right, sir. Anything else?'

'No. In a hurry,' said the telephone. ''Bye.' The click of the receiver came to the listener's ear. He went in search of Flood.

Lucia Gethryn went slowly up the stairs and into the room where this morning she and Anthony had watched a woman fall into her first sleep for many days.

Selma Bronson was no longer asleep. She was walking the small room. The light, firm sound of her heels was steady and rhythmic like the beat of an engine. She went from door to window . . . window to door . . . door to window . . . Up, down . . . up, down . . .

Lucia sat upon the window-seat. The walking went on.

CHAPTER VI

SUNDAY

It was a grey day and hopeless. The frost had gone, and so had the sunshine. There was a high wind from the south-east, and the country was dim behind a veil of constant rain, fine like needles. The wind, driving this curtain of rain before it but never driving it away, had risen in the night, and throughout the day remained.

There were idleness and depression and misery behind the walls of The Horse and Hound.

'It would,' said Flood, gazing out of the Smoking Room window, 'be a Sunday.' He watched the rain while it hissed in a myriad tiny rivers between the cobbles which paved the yard. 'No news; nothing to do; a hanging over the house; a vile day. It only wanted the usual, decayed feeling of a British Sabbath to put the lid on it. And it is on; and it's damn' well *tied* on.'

Pike was slightly shocked. 'Nothing to do with Sunday,' he growled.

Flood laughed, a sound dismal and hollow. 'Have a drink?' he said. 'We'd better get tight.'

Pike grunted. 'By yourself!' He jerked himself out of his chair and wandered from the room.

Flood gazed after him. Flood shrugged, and walked to the bell and pressed it. While he waited for his drink he kept glancing up to the ceiling. Faintly, there came down to his ear the sound, steady and rhythmic, of light, firm steps which went, across a small space, up, down . . . up, down.

Lucia was again in that room whence came the sound of pacing. Once more she sat upon the window-seat. A book lay open, face downwards, upon her lap. She said once:

'Would you rather I stayed. Or went? Do I worry you?'

Selma Bronson did not pause in her walk. She answered, but her eyes though they looked into Lucia's eyes did not seem to see them. She said:

'Stay. Please stay. I would rather . . . I should not care to . . . I would be glad if you stay. Please.'

Lucia, not trusting her voice, nodded to show that she would. She felt suddenly a need for action; for any movement; any *doing*. She rose and crossed to the hearth and knelt beside it and stirred and fed the blazing fire.

She turned from this task with a quick movement. The sound of the footsteps had ceased.

Selma Bronson was standing beside her writing-table which was in a corner near the bay window. She was as motionless as just now she had been mobile. She was staring down at a sheet of paper which lay upon the blotting-pad. Lucia, watching, saw that there was a pencil in the hand upon which the woman was resting her weight. And now the body straightened and the pencil made one stroke upon the paper.

There was a little clatter as the pencil, discarded, rolled from desk-top to floor. The paper still between her fingers, the woman began again her pacing. Lucia, kneeling yet, watched her with an ache in her heart which seemed to send pain to the whole of her body.

Up, down . . . window, door . . . door, window . . . up, down . . .

Lucia found herself to be growing half-hypnotised by her watching of this ceaseless, never-varying movement. But she could not move, and she could not speak. Merely could she go on watching, turning her head . . . left, right; left, right . . . to follow that marching figure; that tall figure whose very beauty made its agony the more dreadful.

And now, as the march brought her abreast of the kneeling Lucia, the sheet of paper fluttered from her fingers. She did not notice its falling; she went on . . . window, door . . . door, window . . .

The sheet lay, a white square upon the dark carpet, by Lucia's knee.

She stretched out a hand and picked it up. Unconsciously, using it as a lever to bring back her mind from this dazed state of watching, watching, she looked down at it. There seemed to be writing upon it. Still unthinking, she raised it nearer to her eyes. And she saw that there was no writing but a series of strokes—plain, upright strokes in ink. Three lines of them there were, each line stretching across the page. And all these, save only the last two, had been cancelled with the cross-stroke of a pencil.

There swept over Lucia a sudden, appalled rush of pity. Where a man might have pondered over these hieroglyphics and not seen for many moments their significance, Lucia understood with her first glance. How often, as a schoolgirl, had she not planned a chart such as this? Every stroke a day; every cancelled stroke a day gone. But her charts had been to mark a happiness to come! And *this* . . .

Again the pacing stopped. Selma Bronson stood over this woman who stared, white-faced, at the little paper. There came from Selma Bronson's throat a sound which was a dreadful travesty of laughter. She said:

'You know that? . . . It is silly . . . Very silly. But I do it because it hurts.'

Once more came the sound of her feet; a sound light and firm; a ceaseless and unchanging sound . . .

The day wore on. And nothing happened save the wind and rain. At two o'clock came the Chief Constable, driving himself in his battered-seeming car. He looked weary and dispirited, and a heavy frown marred his fair good-looks. He asked for Anthony. Pike spoke to him; told him that Colonel Gethryn was not expected before evening. He grunted thanks and went out to his car again. Pike followed him. Pike ventured:

'Anything turned up, sir?'

Ravenscourt climbed into his car. He shut its door with a slam. He shook his head. He said, through the open window:

'Nothing. Not even about this Curtain.'

Pike was left alone in the rain, his trousers were spattered with mud from the big car's wheels.

The afternoon dragged itself by. The weather did not mind; if anything it grew worse. With the going of daylight, the wind, as always it does, seemed to increase in violence. And still the steady, slanting curtain of rain draped the world.

At six, Ravenscourt came back. Lucia saw him. She shook her head at his question.

'But if he doesn't come,' she said, 'he'll telephone. He's certain to. Shall I tell him to ring you up, too?'

Ravenscourt smiled; a tired twisting of his pale face. He said:

'If he's got anything.'

He would not stay for a drink. Once more his car roared out of the yard.

At six-thirty the telephone-bell pealed. Flood was at it first. But it was not Anthony who called. Sir Richard Brocklebank wished to know if Colonel Gethryn . . .

'Sorry,' said Flood shortly. 'Not in. Any message?'

There was no message.

But Anthony did ring up. At half-past seven. This time Pike answered.

'That you, sir?' Pike said. 'Good.'

'Not coming down tonight,' said Anthony's voice. 'Anything doing?' He was curt. He sounded like a tired man in a hurry.

At the transmitter Pike shook his head wearily. 'Nothing,' he said. 'Colonel Ravenscourt's been here after you twice. Would you ring him if you've got anything. And Sir Richard Brocklebank telephoned, sir. No message from him . . . Is there . . . How're you getting on, sir?'

'Can't tell.' The voice was very curt. 'It's a slow job. Slow, slow! . . . How's Mrs Bronson?'

'Same, sir. Wonderful, that control. But it's pretty awful too. Mrs Gethryn's with her all the time; shall I get her?'

'No. Give her my love. And make her have a good dinner, Pike . . . The Carter-Fawcett, what about her?'

'Nothing to report, sir. She didn't leave the house all last night.' Pike's voice was savagely dismal.

'Well, well!' said the telephone. 'I'll be down in the morning. If you want me, ring Buckingham 87X4 or Mall 1736.'

'Right, sir,' said Pike. He hung up the receiver and wrote the numbers in his notebook. He went slowly upstairs and knocked upon the door at the left.

Again the dull, looming silence filled the house. It was, somehow, not broken by the screaming whistle of the wind and the rain's unending hiss; rather was it intensified by them.

CHAPTER VII

MONDAY

I

ANTHONY and Dyson came back at nine-forty-five upon the Monday morning. Anthony drove; Dyson like a sleepy eagle huddled beside him. At the back were White—his face in keeping with his name—and, secured ingeniously to a running-board by rope and straps, Dyson's motor-cycle.

The morning was grey and cold. The rain had gone, for the wind was now dead in the East and a roaring, tearing gale.

In the doorway beneath the faded sign Lucia looked at her husband. There was a question aching in her eyes. He kissed her. He smiled; but it was not the smile she had longed to see and yet had known impossible. He said, though she had not spoken with her voice:

'Might be worse. Might be a whole lot worse. But I'm not shouting, dear.' The smile had gone. He took her by the shoulders and turned her face to the light. 'You look nearly played out.'

Lucia shook her head. 'I've been with her all night—It . . . she likes having me . . . She was silent all day yesterday . . . She walked . . . walked up and down that room. Up and down . . . But suddenly, last night, she stopped that. She . . . she got more—what shall I say?—*natural*. She began to talk. We talked all night.' She wriggled free of Anthony's hands; in her turn she inspected him. 'And you're tired, too. Very, very tired.'

Anthony suddenly grinned. 'I, too, have not been idle.' He took her by the arm and led her into the house. 'Let's go and have breakfast. Several breakfasts.'

After the meal he rose and stretched himself and went, with

murmured excuses, to the telephone. He asked for his number and got it in a time unusually short.

'I want,' he said, 'Colonel Ravenscourt . . .'

The blurred official voice at the other end became galvanised into something sharper and quicker. It said:

'Colonel Gethryn, sir? . . . Yessir . . . One moment.'

The moment passed. There came Ravenscourt's voice, sharp and short, but with weariness blurring its edges. It said:

'Gethryn? Good man! Been waiting to hear from you . . . Got anything?'

Anthony lowered his voice. 'A bit. I know a lot about Mr Curtain.'

The voice at the other end of the wire grew, on a sudden, thick with astonishment. 'You know . . . What the hell are you talking about, Gethryn?'

'What I said . . . Look here: I want to set a few wheels working here and then come and see you. Give me an hour. Or two hours. Will you be there just before noon?'

'If you've got all this, I'd be here at Doomsday!' The voice of the telephone was brusque and eager.

'Right!' said Anthony. 'Wait.' He rang off.

II

Anthony's car came to a sudden and gravel-kicking stop rather hard upon its tyres.

Anthony said, to the constable before the small door at the head of the steps:

'Chief Constable? Appointment.'

He was led, with a speed which showed his coming more than adequately prepared for, into the Chief Constable's presence.

Ravenscourt got up behind his table. He held out a hand which Anthony gripped; he was paler than Anthony had seen him and there were black half-circles beneath the blue eyes. He waved Anthony to a chair and dropped back into his own. He said at once:

'I want you to know, Gethryn: this business has got me

down. I'm on your side now—without any reservations. I've been doin' a lot of thinking. I'm with you. You *might*—I don't know—have persuaded me anyhow, but *now* I'm persuaded without your efforts. This Dollboys business has got me . . .'

He rose with a swift, jerky movement and stood, leaning over his wide table, supporting himself by palms flat upon the table's top. He said:

'*Did* you say, on the 'phone just now, that you knew where Curtain was? And who?'

Anthony's face, graven into its leanness the deep, hard lines of fatigue, was lighted then with a sudden smile; almost a grin. He said:

'I did, sir. But what I *meant* was that I *thought* I knew; was fairly certain . . . That's what I've come about.'

Ravenscourt dropped back into his chair. He rested his hands upon its arms and stared across the table at Anthony.

'The sooner,' he said, 'that you do tell me, the better.' Suddenly he clenched his right hand into a fist and with it beat once upon the table so that in their wells the ink-pots leapt. A dark splash marred the table's top.

'Sorry!' said Ravenscourt. He smiled. The harsh lines of fatigue about his mouth were lost in the blander lines of humour. He said:

'But do tell . . . I'm sick of my fellers. Not one with more than half an ounce of brain. Hours they've been at it! And what do they bring me? Nothing and worse than nothing! A blistered lot of bloody fools! They want three-quarters of a year—all of 'em—in a continuous barrage. That'd either kill 'em or quicken 'em.'

Anthony said:

'Listen. You've got to take me for granted, Ravenscourt. This much, I mean: I'm not going to say anything yet about *who* Mr Luke Curtain *really* is. Because, though in my own mind I'm sure I know, I want to be certain and dead certain before I speak. You understand that . . . I want you to follow me blind just as far only as will induce you to give me some men tonight, to go where I want 'em and wait. Wait until they see . . . something, and hear a signal from me to grab someone . . . Follow me? If the something happens, and I signal, *then* you'll have Mr L. Curtain. If it doesn't, I shan't give the word and you won't have Mr L. Curtain. Will you trust me?'

Ravenscourt smiled. A smile which lit up his stern, perhaps ordinarily too regular face. He said:

'Will I? . . . I'm only too glad to. But I'm coming on this job myself.' He leant forward over the table, his chest borne up upon his folded arms. 'That be all right?'

In his turn Anthony smiled. 'All right? It's just what I'd like.' He hitched his chair a little closer to the table. 'I wouldn't,' he said, 'have worried you about this job, except that I've sent all my helpers on another, auxiliary, bit of work and that I thought, if it *did* come off, we'd be all the better for an official arrest.'

Ravenscourt nodded. The wearied, glazed seeming that his blue eyes had worn at the beginning of the interview was now vanished. The eyes were bright and keen; interest and excitement made them almost blaze.

'It's night-work,' Anthony said. 'I know, or think I know, where Mr Luke Curtain will be at some time between eight and ten tonight. And that's the cattle-shelter shed on Dollboys' third field—the last one up the hill to the west of the farm. I've been there—this morning. And there I found something. So easily did I find it that for a moment I thought he'd meant me to find it. But I've ruled that out now. I think he was just hurried. And I think, too, that he'll come back to get it. And he won't come back in daylight . . . Follow me?'

Again Ravenscourt nodded.

'Bit of paper?' Anthony asked, and drew a pencil from his pocket. A piece of paper was pushed across the table towards him. He began, with firm and accurate lines, to draw a sketch map. Ravenscourt rose and walked round the table's end and came to stand at the drawer's shoulder.

'Here,' said Anthony, 'is the main road. Here's Dollboys' farm. Here's his first field—the large one. Here's the second, at the foot of the slope up to that copse . . . And here's the third. And here, up next to the easterly hedge, is the shelter . . . Follow me?'

Ravenscourt smiled. 'I'm ahead of you.' Over Anthony's shoulder his hand came, and its forefinger upon the map emphasised his words. He said:

'Here's the copse. And this hedge—here—is very thick. Suppose I come with you—wherever you're going to be—and get men posted, early, *here* in the copse . . . and *here* and *here*, along the hedge . . . How'd that do?'

With his pencil point, Anthony marked the spots where the finger had rested. He put his head upon one side and considered. He said at last:

'Very good—except for this one. And there's a gap in the hedge there. And it's through that gap that I expect Mr X—who is also L. Curtain Esquire, to come. He comes that way, you see. Or so I've worked it out . . .'

Ravenscourt laughed; a bitter sound. 'He does does he? Well, if he comes that way, he comes—he *must* come—across *my* land. Blast him! . . . That's a pill for my pride; with all my bumpkin sleuths on the job for years of hours and nothing to show for it! . . . Right! I won't have a man there: I'll move him along to here!' Again his hand came over Anthony's shoulder, and a finger pointed to a spot.

Anthony marked the place. 'That'll do well.' He got to his feet. 'There's nothing more, then.' He held out his hand. 'And thanks for being so accommodating. I'm afraid I must seem to bounce a bit sometimes.'

Ravenscourt took the hand. 'You're entitled to,' he said. He followed Anthony from the room, and through that outer room where at deal tables two bulky men in uniform dealt with pens and paper as if still these were mediums unaccustomed. At the head of the steps he stood, and watched while Anthony went down them to his car at their foot. He called, before the engine was started:

'Where's the starting-point?'

'Eh?' said Anthony.

Ravenscourt came down the steps. 'Where do we meet tonight? I'll have the men posted just after dark. But when do you and I start?'

Anthony grinned. 'I'd forgotten.' He thought for a moment. He said: 'Meet you at the junction of the main road with the lane to the farm at seven-forty-five sharp. That do?'

'Seven-forty-five it shall be!' Ravenscourt said. He stood watching while the long black car edged its difficult way round the sharp bend of the little drive, nosed out, slowly, into the road and at last was gone, with a sudden change in the note of its deep-throated engine, from sight.

There was now only one digit uncancelled upon that chart of Selma Bronson's.

III

Anthony edged the car up into the lane. A slow business without lights. He took a rug from the body and draped it over the radiator. He walked back to the mouth of the lane upon soft feet. He stood out upon the main road, dark in the black night, and whistled between his teeth. A loud whistle this was, but the blustering wind took hold of it and whirled it away until only the ghost of itself sounded around the spot of its birth.

A dark shape loomed out of the hedge and came towards him upon feet as silent as his own.

'Gethryn?' whispered Ravenscourt's voice.

'The same, y'r honour.' Anthony's voice was a whisper too. But it was a whisper which told of high spirits.

'You're late!' hissed Ravenscourt.

'Three minutes. Sorry! The night,' Anthony murmured, 'was

dark and stormy: there was a woman in the street. Her heart was full of misery: her boots were full of feet!'

'Had a drink?' said Ravenscourt in his ear.

'Sorry!' said Anthony again. 'Light hearted. On the verge of discovery . . . Come on, now! . . . Got your men there?'

They turned, shoulder to shoulder, into the lane.

'Yes,' Ravenscourt said. 'Since dark.'

'They'll be cold,' said Anthony.

There was no reply. They were big men, but their feet made little or no sound, even upon the wet, gravelled clay of the lane. Halfway up the lane they walked, and at a fair pace. And then Anthony halted. Guarding its beam with his hand, he flashed a torch at the right-hand hedge. The circle of white light showed a gap.

'Through here,' said Anthony.

And through, Ravenscourt first, they climbed.

They went on over plough-land into which their feet sank. Anthony said, his voice still in that sub-tone which is clearer and far less carrying than any whisper:

'Heavy going. But it's quicker. And there's less risk of being seen.'

Ravenscourt grunted assent.

They plodded on. Their feet sank in and out of the soft, almost marshy plough. Above their heads the cloud-wrack raced over a dead-grey, unluminous sky. To their left bulked the farm-house. From one of its upper windows there shone a yellow light which stung the darkness.

In silence they crossed this first field and climbed a stile into the second.

'Grass here,' said Anthony. 'Better going.'

Ravenscourt halted. His hand went to his pocket. 'Have a cigarette?' he said as Anthony turned.

Anthony's fingers gripped his arm. 'Don't be an ass! The lights might show.'

Ravenscourt took his hand from his pocket.

'Sorry!' he said.

They walked on and up the grassy slope. In the darkness, the savage wind, now dead in their faces, tore at them and beat them and took from them their breath. They put down their heads and side by side fought on against it.

They reached the far boundary of the second field. There was no stile here, only a hedge, through which they forced as silent a way as they might . . .

They were in the third field. Anthony drew close to his companion. He muttered:

'Dead quiet now!'

They went on. As if wishing, inimical, to show them to whomsoever might watch, the cloud-wrack suddenly split and the pale light of a watery moon bathed the land with a silver light. Before them, as if suddenly sprung from the wet grass which squelched beneath their feet, showed the ungainly rectangle of the cattle-shelter. It stood dark and stark and gaunt against the black and silver landscape, a monument to the vileness of Utility.

'Drop?' Ravenscourt's voice was a hiss.

Anthony shook his head. 'No use now. Bear right and come up under cover of the thing.'

They bore right. Under the shelter's cover they came up at last to the shelter. They stood leaning against its boards . . .

They listened. No sound came through the racketting of the gale. They breathed deep. Anthony said:

'He's not come yet . . . There's not a sound from your men.'

Ravenscourt nodded. 'Wish we could smoke,' he said. His hand went longingly to his pocket. Anthony said:

'Let's drop and work round to the front of this thing. We can lie low inside then. More shelter. And we'd be invisible in the shadow . . . OK?'

Ravenscourt nodded. He whispered:

'You lead?'

Anthony shook his head. 'Best if we split it. Two crawlers might be seen. One on each side probably won't. You go right.

I'll go left . . . See you in Pompeii.' He dropped to the sodden ground. He lay flat on his belly. Like a great snake he wriggled towards the left-hand end of the shelter.

After a moment Ravenscourt followed his example. There was a silence save for the wind. Any rustling of the two men's progress was drowned; the wind was a roaring, tearing giant. Under its blasts the very structure of the shelter seemed to sag . . .

Anthony rounded the first corner; wriggled along the side of the shelter until the front corner was reached. The moon shone only fitfully now; the cloud-wrack was gathering again; the silver light switched on and off as if worked by a drunken stage-hand of Olympus.

Anthony pushed his head round the corner. He drew back and got to his knees, his feet. The moon vanished, and he stepped out, past the shelter's corner, into the open. He whistled softly between his teeth. He peered into the darkness and made out a form, upright, moving towards him.

'Ravenscourt,' he said in a clear whisper, 'come on, man. Inside here!'

There came a laugh. A long laugh and loud. The clouds split in the sky and the world was light.

'You *bloody* fool!' said the voice of Ravenscourt.

His hand came from his pocket. And as it came, just the fraction of a second before the noise and the small red flame which three times stabbed the moonlight night, Anthony leapt, to his right, into the black shadow of the shelter and in that black shadow ran forward.

There was an oath. The tall figure in the moonlight swung round. Three times more, so nearly together that the noise sounded continuous, came the report of the revolver and the flash of flame . . . There were thuds as the bullets bored the planking of the shelter's backboards . . .

And then out of the shadow, a long, lean, charging shape, came Anthony. This charge was a balanced charge. It began at the right moment and ended at the right moment. And as it ended the right fist of Anthony met the jaw of Geoffrey Ravenscourt.

The man went down. But he was tough. And in the uncertain light of Anthony's fist had landed an inch to the left of his purpose.

From the grass Ravenscourt rose in a bound. There came a snarling noise from his throat. He hurled himself at Anthony; and as he leaped his right arm was flung upwards and back and the pale light gleamed on the butt of his pistol; it was empty now and he sought to use it as a club.

Anthony stood his ground. Anthony's knee came up with force. There was a cry—half-groan, half-scream—from Ravenscourt and for the second time he fell. But now he did not rise. He rolled this way and that upon the grass; and when he stilled his rolling, the pain having died down, he saw that over him stood not one man but five . . .

The four had come out of that black shadow of the shelter's mouth.

'My *God*!' said a voice.

And Ravenscourt knew that voice. It was the voice of Lucas; the Lucas whom he knew as Assistant Commissioner of Police; and Lucas who was at the head of the Criminal Investigation Department of Scotland Yard; the Lucas of whom his last view had been across a dinner-table of which he himself was host . . .

He struggled to his knees. A hand came from somewhere and pulled from his unresisting fingers the revolver which he had not realised still to be there . . .

And as he got to his feet and stood, swaying a little because of the pain which still gripped him, there came another hand and laid itself on his shoulder. And a voice said words of which the only ones he properly heard were his own name and the word murder. He said, with slow, stiff lips:

'Murder? Who?'

And the voice said: 'Attempted murder of Anthony Ruthven Gethryn . . . Hold up your hands.'

He held up his hands, close together, and about his wrists slipped something cold and heavy.

The mists began to clear from his eyes. He tried to laugh. A sound came, but it was not the sound he had meant. He frowned, and thrust forward his head, peering. And he saw Anthony. He said, the words coming quicker now:

'He's not hurt anyhow. There's . . .'

'There's other charges,' said Pike at his elbow. 'Be quiet.'

Now he recognised this voice, too. His face twisted into a ghastly smile. He said:

'Thought you were on . . . on holiday!'

'I'm not; not at the moment. Quiet!' Pike's voice was hard and cold.

Anthony spoke for the first time. He took the old felt hat from his head and held it up. He said:

'Look at that!'

Through the hat's crown was a hole, burnt and jagged at the edges.

'First one,' said Anthony. 'Good shooting!'

Between his teeth, Dyson whistled. Flood grunted and looked once at the man beside Pike.

'Come on!' said Anthony.

'Where?' Lucas moved forward.

'Back to the cars.'

'But after that?' Lucas was not himself. He was still dazed by the incredibility of the night's events.

Pike came up, his prisoner beside him. It is to his credit that he said his words at Lucas. 'Straight back to town, sir?'

Lucas shrugged; he turned to Anthony. He said:

'It's your show, Gethryn.'

Anthony smiled. 'And it's not quite over.' He pondered. 'Can't go back to the pub . . . His own house is the nearest; and he'll want things anyhow.'

The party began to move: Anthony first, with Lucas; and

then Pike and his prisoner. Flood and Dyson, talking in whispers, brought up the rear.

They were in the Tower room at Friars', which was Ravenscourt's house. They had been led there by an astounded manservant, who, though he had not been permitted to see the handcuffs upon his master's wrists nor hear anything which might lead him to the truth behind this invasion, was nevertheless aware of an indefinable 'something' which was 'up'.

But he led them, in obedience to his master's growl, through the panelled hall and up the oak staircase and along to the turret-stairs in the short western wing, and up these, which were so much longer than could have seemed possible that a man was almost out of his breath at their top, and so into the Tower room.

It was a long room, and high. Its eastern wall was lined with books from ceiling to floor. Its western wall was hung with swords, and scraps of chain-mail, and an assegai or two, and a pair of beautiful curved Samurai blades. Its southern wall was all window—three windows, there were, reaching from roof almost down to floor-level. And the northern wall bore three pictures, each right in its place.

And the owner of this sat at the writing-table in the centre of the room. He rested his hands, their fingers clasped together, upon the table-top; whenever he moved them there was a little chinking sound of metal upon metal. At his shoulder stood Pike, who would not sit. Directly facing Ravenscourt, his chair, too, drawn right up to the table, was Anthony. Lucas was in an armchair to the window-side of the table, and on a couch which stood parallel with the northern wall sat Flood and Dyson, side by side like schoolboys.

Anthony was saying:

'There'll be other charges. The murder of Blackatter; the murder of Dollboys. And the attempted murder, by hanging, of Bronson.' He said this quietly; his voice was level and un-interested, and very tired.

Ravenscourt looked at him from beneath drooping lids which lent to his face a new seeming; a savage and ruthless and megalomaniac look. He said:

'You're smart, aren't you? Prove 'em. That's what I say! . . . Where *is* your proof? I call your bluff! Where's the *motive*? You . . .'

Anthony interrupted. 'Motive?' he said. 'Want me to tell you . . . and these men here? . . . I've got to go a few years back for motive. Back to wartime. Back, to be exact, to March of 1918. In March of 1918, in a sector of the front line called after the village of Varolles, there was . . .'

His speech was cut short by the clatter of a heavy chair upon the wood floor. Ravenscourt had sprung to his feet. His face worked; it was a curious grey colour, in marked contrast to the pallor which had been its hue upon the way home.

'Steady there!' Pike put heavy hands upon the heaving shoulders.

The man collapsed into his chair again. His chin fell forward on to his breast so that the lamp-light glittered upon his tawny, cropped hair. His hands dropped back to their old place upon the table. As they fell, there was a rattling, clinking thud. He spoke without raising his face. He said, almost under his breath and yet so clearly that every man in the room heard every syllable:

'You devil! You clever, clever devil!' He raised his head and his eyes met Anthony's.

There was the sound of a rustling movement from the sofa: there appeared notebooks upon the knees of Flood and Dyson.

'You *clever* devil!' said Ravenscourt again. Something, some force, seemed to have gone out of him. '*All* right!' he said and looked across at Lucas. 'We won't bother any more. I did it. He's right. I killed Blackatter and tried to get Bronson hanged for it. And I shot Dollboys and tried to make it look like suicide.' He brought his eyes back to Anthony again; he squared his shoulders. 'And I'd've got away with *that* if I hadn't been rushed and forgotten the fool was left-handed.' His voice died away.

Lucas shot a glance towards the sofa. It was answered by two reassuring nods. The confession was down, verbatim and twice for safety's sake.

Ravenscourt spoke again. There was more life in his voice now; a note almost of anger had crept into it. He looked at Anthony.

'Flukes!' he said. 'All flukes . . . but I can't fight 'em. When you caught me tonight I was done. But it's fluking that's done me.'

Anthony shook his head. 'No. You're wrong. Listen: I'll tell you. We started this case at the wrong end. We had to. So I made it a stipulation that our jumping-off point should be a belief—a rooted belief—that Bronson was innocent. It worked and worked well. We soon got somewhere; soon got to the point where we realised that the fixing upon Bronson as scapegoat was not haphazard but part and parcel of a plot. A plot by X. And what could've been X's motive? To rid himself of blackmail or what amounted to blackmail; that's the only thing that 'd really fit the circumstances.* But what was the blackmail about? And how was it that Bronson could be a blackmailer? Much more difficult. The answer to the first question slipped me for a long time; until, to be precise, about midnight at Brownlough's party. The answer to "how came it that Bronson, of all men, was a blackmailer?" I reasoned was this: that he wasn't a black-mailer in esse, but that he was in posse. He had not blackmailed and probably never would blackmail; but he *could* blackmail because he was, as well as Blackatter, in possession of information detrimental to the welfare—physical, mental or financial— of X. Blackatter was the perfect blackmailer—born to the game. Bronson was most definitely the reverse; but so dangerous to X was this knowledge, traded on by Blackatter but not by Bronson, that he determined to end the danger for all time by killing Blackatter and making it seem that Bronson was guilty.

---

* Colonel Gethryn was here only recapitulating, in brief, what can be found, *in toto*, and in his own words, early in the book.

This aspect of the scheme was useful to me in this way: it showed that X knew that Bronson was not *aware* of his own knowledge. Sounds a paradox, that, but it isn't. It means that X knew that Bronson had not *yet* associated his knowledge with X. And a trial for murder you haven't done is quite enough to drive apparently extraneous matters from your head.

'What must have happened was this: Blackatter blackmails X and tells X that there is another man—and in the district—who knows everything. X finds out, however, quite possibly through Blackatter himself, that Blackatter and this other man— Bronson—aren't on good terms. And I should say that, right atop of X's realisation of this comes the dawning of his plot.

'Soon I'm going to stop calling you X, Ravenscourt . . . Shall I go on?'

Ravenscourt's eyes were fixed in a wide stare upon this man who had found him. And curiously, the only emotion in his eyes was curiosity; an overweening desire to know. He said in a low voice:

'Yes. Yes. Go on. Get off theory. Give facts.'

'In good time,' said Anthony. 'What hindered us most was inability to think of the link which connected X—who, presumably, was in what they call "a good position" with two so utterly different men as Blackatter and Bronson. But we pegged away on other lines. I got on to Master Thomas Harrigan; my friends got on to Dollboys. I took Harrigan because he was the first to see the bodies; we got on to Dollboys, because he was, though he *seemed* perfectly above-board, the only witness *really* against Bronson. From Harrigan, who, as you know, is an instance of arrested mental development, I learned more than I had dared hope. I found that before he found the men, he had seen a light in the trees which was not moonlight. A light which I argued must have been from a car or motor-bicycle's head or spot-light, and was, in fact, on your car . . . Wasn't it?'

Ravenscourt nodded. But he never took his eyes from Anthony's face.

'That,' said Anthony, 'gave me a lot of heart. It was practical corroboration of pure theory. It showed us that X existed in fact as well as in our minds . . . And then my friends, most ingeniously, put up a stunt on Dollboys to which his reaction was not the reaction of a blameless and conscience-free man. More corroboration.

'And then—and then, Ravenscourt—I got that link I spoke of just now. I saw, because a girl said something about soldiers and I replied to the effect that the neighbourhood seemed lousy with 'em, I saw what could have brought these three apparent irreconcilables, X and Blackatter and Bronson, together. The War. I should have thought of it sooner: I shall never understand why I didn't . . .

'So now I'd something to work on besides these corroborations which Harrigan and Dollboys had given me. But first, I wanted to see Dollboys, thinking I might frighten everything—or enough of everything—out of him. As I might have. But you called on Dollboys even earlier than I did, Ravenscourt. You went to the house, to which you had entry. And you called Dollboys down, and then you dropped something on to the floor of the kitchen. And as Dollboys bent to pick it up you rammed his own gun, which you'd borrowed, into his ear and fired it. You took a big risk of waking the mother, but you got away with it. You knew the thickness and solidity of the house and you knew the old woman was deafish and a heavy sleeper, and you knew that her bedroom was at the far end of the upper floor. But you got flurried and made that hideous mistake of forgetting the left-handedness . . .

'You know, Ravenscourt, I suppose *I* killed Dollboys. Not that I mind much. If I hadn't arranged to have Dollboys frightened, Dollboys wouldn't have panicked and communicated with you—as he must have done—and you wouldn't have found it necessary to get on your Luke Curtain rig—I suppose you started Curtain in the beginning as (a) a nondescript disguise to slouch from your own land across to Dollboys' in and (b) in case you were seen—as twice you were by Mrs Dollboys—in Dollboys' house . . .

'But back to the point. There was I, with yet another corroboration but no Dollboys. I had to get to work at once on my new
line. I made out a list of the soldiers of officer-rank in the neighbourhood, and I sent it up to a friend of mine in the War Office.
I wanted all their records, with particular reference to their map
positions in France. And I got them, or most of them . . . That
was the first lot, and you weren't in it! Blackatter's record you
gave me yourself—and that was when you began to feel I was
getting too warm, wasn't it? Bronson's I had from the Scotland
Yard file. I wanted an officer, serving or retired, preferably hand-
somely decorated, who could have been at any given spot at the
same time as both Bronson and Blackatter. I'm afraid a lot of time
was wasted on that list. A lot of time. I hadn't put your name on
it. I was blind and worse than blind. I was treating you in my
mind as a policeman and therefore a non-eligible; which is a bad
case of non sequitur. And then, by the grace of God, I saw.
Something happened which showed—made *me* sure at all events—
that the very man I'd missed off my list was the only one that
need have been on it.

'I went up to town myself. It was a long job. But we got it
done. I found that you fitted. For your unit, with you in it, and
Blackatter's unit with him, and Bronson's with *him*—all were
at Varolles in March '18 . . .'

Ravenscourt beat upon the table with his clenched hands,
and the handcuffs rattled and jingled. He cried:

'Stop that! You've said all that. You've pushed home your
theories . . .' He made an attempt, rather pitiful, to sneer. 'Now
give us *facts*.'

'What *is* a fact, Ravenscourt? Do you want me to tell you *how*
you killed Blackatter and nearly made Bronson your scapegoat?
. . . I can. You killed Blackatter elsewhere and took his body in
your car up to that gate near the fringe of Bellows Wood. Quite
probably you killed him *in* the car. And you made sure that there
was no one about, and you switched off your lights, got out of
the car, and opened the gate by lifting it off its hinges. You then

drove the car in through the gate and turned it to the right, into that cart track. You then backed it until it faced the clearing. You hadn't wanted to use your lights, but you found you'd have to. The night was very dark and what moon there was was hidden. You listened carefully and at last had to risk it. You switched on your headlights—or a spot-light. You hauled Blackatter out of the car and carried him, just beside the beam of light, for you had to take care not to block it, in among the trees and down over that little bank into the clearing. You posed his body as afterwards it was found. You ran back as quickly as you could to the car. You switched off that light and you went back into the trees and waited. You were in luck. You knew that Bronson walked often this way at about this time, but you hadn't been able to *ensure* that he would come. If he hadn't come, I suppose you'd just have left what remained of Blackatter where it was and waited another chance at the second bird. But Bronson came. And he came fairly close, as you had guessed he would if he came at all, to where you were hiding. And you hit him on the back of the head, possibly with a revolver-butt, probably with a heavy stick. And you carried him across the clearing and dumped *him*, arranging it so that he would seem to have slipped and hit his head against that stump. And then you took his gun and fired it, and put it into his grip. And then you took from your own pocket the note which Blackatter had sent you that morning and you put it into Bronson's pocket. And then you went, very quick and quiet you were, back to the car. And you switched on your light again and were going to start your engine . . .

'But you didn't start it. Your lucky night, wasn't it, Ravenscourt? Just in time you heard a noise; someone crashing and crackling through the undergrowth on the far side of the clearing. That was Tom Harrigan. He'd seen the pretty light. But the light went out, and in the clearing he found something—two somethings—which drove all thought of the pretty light out of that tiny brain. And by your dark car you waited; and I expect your heart was in your mouth for a bit. But at last Tom went running and you began to breathe easily. When he was out of earshot, you opened the gate, backed out into the road, put the gate back in position and at last drove off. And that was all you had to do, except to bribe Dollboys to fake his evidence. And that was very cleverly done; for it did more to get Bronson nearly hanged than the rest of the evidence put together, and yet it was only the false-reporting of that remark of Blackatter's as he turned to leave the private bar of The Horse and Hound . . . There, that's all, I think. And that, I imagine, it was what you meant by "facts". To be exact, none of my state-ments were facts; but I'd swear to them just the same. They were developed inferential theories as to what the facts were. And, as I say, except in regard to the minute details, I would swear to them.'

His voice stopped; but the room seemed to hold the sound of the level, modulated, deliberately unimpassioned words. Anthony sat as he had sat all the time he had been speaking. The eyes of the other men went from him to that other facing him across the table.

Ravenscourt sat as if he were stone and not flesh. He did not seem even to breathe. He kept his wide blue gaze upon Anthony's face.

The silence went on. It grew and went on growing; it seemed at last to become alive, as silences will.

Pike cleared his throat uneasily, and a little shuffling of his boot upon the wooden floor sounded like an explosion. Lucas started; so that his chair creaked. He frowned and settled again into immobility.

But these small sounds had broken the spell. Ravenscourt spoke. And at his tone ten eyes brought astonished gaze to bear upon him. For his tone was the tone of a man who is free and in the midst of life and yet with all life before him. He said:

'Gethryn: I congratulate you! . . . You've found out so much, starting from so little, that it seems to me that you must know everything. But there's an envelope'—he nodded his head downwards at the table—'in the drawer there. There's some-thing in it I'd like you to read . . . after I'm gone . . .'

'*Stop him!*' roared Dyson and left the sofa in a bound.

The room was bedlam for a second which seemed many minutes.

With his final word Ravenscourt had leapt to his feet. He seemed for an instant to tower above them like a Thor. His fair hair was wild and his eyes were steely flames. His shoulder caught Pike in the chest and Pike sprawled upon the polished floor. Lucas, with an agility most surprising, was out of his chair in a bound. But the handcuffed fists of Ravenscourt took him in the chest and he fell with a crash which shook the room.

It was over. They saw—they all of them saw—what he was going to do. And none of them was in time. Dyson's fingers, as he hurled himself forward, brushed the flying skirts of the tweed coat; but brushed them only.

They saw Ravenscourt gather himself, crouch like a runner, hurl himself forward, towards the middle of those three great windows. And this window, like its fellows, was closed against the wild night.

Two paces from it Ravenscourt checked in his rush; flung his joined arms above and before his head. His pose was a diver's. And dive he did. He sprang upward and outward, and as his spring began its downward curve his arms met the glass of the great window . . .

He was gone. And the ring of that appalling smash was in the ears of the men he had left. Glass lay in glistening, jagged patterns upon the oaken floor. The wind rushed into the room.

The room was silent. To the ears of the men within it had come the ghost of a sound; a sound soft and heavy and to the senses terrifying.

Flood ran for the door, and was gone. After him went Pike and Dyson together, and, last, Lucas limping from his fall.

Only Anthony did not move. He sat in the chair from which he had not stirred. Presently he glanced down. His fingers searched and found the knob of a drawer. He pulled it towards him. It was empty save for a long, thin envelope.

He took out this envelope. In a bold, ugly handwriting there was written across it:

'*Strictly Confidential.* Open in case of Death.'

Anthony weighed the thing in his hand. It was very light. He drew out two sheets of foolscap. Both sides of the sheets had been written on. The handwriting was the same as that upon the envelope, but smaller and far neater. It had about it an air of deliberate clarity.

Anthony began to read. He read:

'I don't know why I write this.' It started like that, with no heading or preamble. 'But I'd better get it down. It's a poor little story and I'll be short about it.

'Varolles, March '18. The big Bosche slam beginning. The sector caught it very hot. The –th Brigade in particular. Hell on earth, *and* below it, for twelve days. Always fresh troops are coming. But they never did. "Jam yesterday", etc.

'Then the line went. Pouf! Like that. It went, because there was no order for retreat, in bits. Only the bits that went were very big and bits that stayed were very, very small. Damned silly little blobs of men, like futile islands in a sea of grey-coats.

'One spot in the sector. There's four men, one's a Sergeant, with a Machine Gun. Not a Vickers, mark you, but a Bosche gun they've collected, together with boxes of filled belts.

'*They* were an island all right. And a big one. Peninsula really. There were seven of 'em—all out of the Dene Foresters—at dawn that day. At nine there were four. At eleven there were three and at a quarter past only two. That Sergeant was left with one man. Good men they all were. But the Sergeant he was six good men.

'At noon the Sergeant's one man got it. And almost as he died the Bosche stopped. And that meant the noise stopped. You know the relief when the noise stops. Hurts at first.

'The Sergeant doubled up over his gun. He jerked at his water-bottle. It was empty. He split its strap with a tug of his hand and pitched it away.

'Over to the right, in some shell-hole, an Englishman began to yell. I know he was an Englishman, because I could hear some of his words. That'll tell you what the quiet was like.

'Where was I? Oh, I was an officer. I was in the trench behind the forward-post that Sergeant had made for himself and his Bosche gun. No. I wasn't in his Regiment. But then there'd been a mix-up. And an unholy one at that. Everyone was all over the place.

'That quiet seemed to last for a year. The man in the shell-hole began yelling again. The officer in the trench—that's me!—began to feel better. He screwed himself up to climb out on to the parapet.

'The home-made gun-post wasn't twenty yards away. I saw the Sergeant looking first at his gun; then at that shell-hole the yelling was coming from. He was in two minds. When, he wondered, would the Bosche begin again? Had he got time?

'I crawled out towards him. My belly shook even when it was pressed tight against the dry mud. The sun was hot. Damned hot. More like August than March. There was a stink.

'The fellow in the shell-hole went on yelling.

'The sergeant turned round and saw me. In those days you couldn't tell, unless you were right up close, an officer from a member of the Sanitary Squad. Before I got within ten yards of him he was bellowing. And he could bellow. He flung out an arm and pointed at the shell-hole. He roared, "Go an' gettim! Where the *hell* 'a you bin? Go an' gettim!"

'And then the Bosche began their music again. And in earnest this time.

'The officer didn't move. That was me! *I didn't move.* I lay where I was. I pressed my face into the ground and longed for that stinking trench. I saw the Sergeant look at me. And then he jumped up and fairly bolted for the shell-hole.

'I lay and prayed.

'When I lifted my head an inch the Sergeant was back at his gun. He was shooting like all hell. The grey Bosches were moving, though.

'I shot one agonised look at the shell-hole. On the lip of it was the man and he was crawling towards the gun.

'And the gun went on. And something clicked inside me

somewhere. The grey Bosche were nearer; some of them; hordes of them.

'In my breeches I had a white handkerchief. And it was, by some miracle of war, what passed in wartime for clean.

'I fumbled it out. I had, just like a Tommy, a bayonet. I fumbled that out.

'I tied the handkerchief on to the bayonet. I put up my arm, with this flag at the end of it, and waved. And waved and waved. Bullets which had been chipping the mud all round me slacked off . . .

'And the shell-hole man was only twenty-feet from the gun. He was calling something out to the Sergeant and pointed at me and shouting.

'I stood up. I waved and waved.

'The Sergeant turned and saw me. I began to run, towards the Bosche.

'The Sergeant, just as I was abreast of the gun, jumped up.

'His fist caught me under the ear. It was odd; I wasn't unconscious. But I was temporarily paralysed. I fell over the gun. For one clear moment I saw; saw the Sergeant hurl my flag away. Saw the wounded man from the shell-hole pointing towards the empty boxes of ammunition; saw the Sergeant, realising, snatch up his rifle—the bayonet was on it—from the ground.

'And he didn't run back. And he didn't wait. He ran forward towards those Grey Things.

'And the shell-hole man was crawling, away from the gun, back towards his shell-hole.

'And then the whole world blazed into one flame which was the Heart of Noise.

'That was *our* Artillery.

'Those promised fresh troops had come.

'And I was found, with a bullet in the shoulder which I'd never felt, lying across that German gun which, used against the Germans, had made that peninsula and kept it for half a day.

'And I got the VC for that.

'The Sergeant, I thought then, was annihilated. I tried to trace him but couldn't.

'The shell-hole man, I thought then, was annihilated. I tried to trace him, but couldn't.

'And I got the VC.

'I like having the VC.

'And the shell-hole man was Blackatter.'

There was a break in the document here. But at the foot of the page, written in a different ink, were the words:

'And the Sergeant was Bronson. I'm sure of it. I didn't believe Blackatter when he told me at first. But I've been to the inn and looked.

'It's those shoulders that convince me.'

Anthony folded up the foolscap sheets and slipped them back into their envelope.

v

Dyson came into the room. Still Anthony sat in his chair. He replaced the telephone's receiver: he had been talking to his wife, who now was running, upon winged feet, carrying up the stairs of Bronson's house the news of Bronson's safety.

Before Anthony, a buff streak on the table's dark top, lay a foolscap envelope.

Dyson, his pipe sending out thick clouds of evil-smelling smoke, came up to the table and sat himself upon the table's edge and swung his thin legs in their disreputable trousers.

Anthony looked up at him.

Dyson nodded. 'As a doornail. Not a whole bone in his body, I should think.' He puffed at the pipe and more and thicker clouds ascended. He said:

'You owe me something. You wasted my time on that list. Sweated blood. Large red drops.'

'Peccavi!' Anthony said. 'But a good cause and I didn't mean it.'

'Want some flats joined,' Dyson said round his pipe-stem.

Anthony nodded. 'Exhibit them.'

'First,' said Dyson, 'Lake. Why Lake? Who Lake? What Lake? Why did he bolt?'

'Lake,' said Anthony thoughtfully. 'There was too much Lake, after a bit. He was too often the answer. He went out of his way to disapprove of me at Brownlough's party. And then he disappeared. And then people kept on telling me he'd disappeared. And the last one that told me showed me what Lake was for.'

'What?' said Dyson.

'A crimson herring. Only the scheme was too clever, too intensive, too perfect . . . Lake's an unpleasant piece of work. But he knows no more about this business than Dean Inge.'

'Go on!' said Dyson.

'He doesn't. I thought it odd when he made a dead set for me at that party. And I thought it odder when he vanished . . . People don't vanish, if they're the guilty parties, at *that* stage of an affair . . . And when Mrs Carter-Fawcett . . .'

'Eh?' Dyson pricked up his ears.

'And when Mrs Carter-Fawcett, who'd happened to hear that Pike—who'd probably been seen with me—had been hanging round the house, thought fit to come over to the pub and rate me like a fish-wife, I began to get the Lake business straight. She wanted to know why the hell this and why the worse that. And so on and so on. It was not too badly done. But it wasn't so good either. She took *too* much trouble to let me know that Lake had gone off without so much as a by your leave. And I began to think about Lake's attitude towards me at the dance. And I soon saw— it wasn't difficult you know, when you combine it with what I learnt at the same time—I soon saw that Lake was being pushed down my throat, hook, line and a very large sinker. Lake was plainly the slave of the lady. And Lake, without being told anything, would do—if she was careful—whatever she suggested to him. And so Lake, probably being told merely that the lady disliked the sight, sound and smell of me and wished someone would take me down a peg or two, began to try and do the peg-shifting . . .'

'And his bolting?' said Dyson, puffing.

'Easier still. Sent away—I'll bet all my footgear—on some wild mission, whispered to no one else, of my lady's.'

Dyson took the pipe from his mouth, and, with the hand that held the pipe, his owl-like spectacles from his nose. His eyes blinked in the light. He thrust out his head between his lean shoulders. He said:

'But what's the Carter-Fawcett to *do* with it all? She and Ravenscourt weren't even on speaking terms. Common gossip.'

'Very common,' Anthony said. 'A bit elaborately common. Too good, in fact, to be true.' He told Dyson of the incident overheard by Lucia at Brownlough's party. 'The man, whom at first we took, because we didn't think enough, to be Lake wasn't Lake. It was Ravenscourt. They were in love. Probably the Carter-Fawcett's never been in love before, not this way . . . That talk about their hating each other was fostered . . . by themselves . . . They were waiting to declare. What they were waiting *for*, I'm not sure of. Probably, as she was serious, for some move to rid themselves, quite legally, of the male Carter-Fawcett, who after fifteen years of big game hasn't yet succeeded in being eaten or clawed or gored or trampled to death . . .' His voice died away, and there was a silence. He added suddenly:

'I'm sorry for that woman.'

Dyson was smoking again. 'Why?' he said.

'Because she killed Ravenscourt. And she loved him.'

Dyson was puzzled. 'How d'you mean?'

'If it hadn't,' said Anthony, 'been for her attempts to put me *off* Ravenscourt, I doubt whether I'd ever've got *on* to him. Not in time, I mean.'

'How?' said Dyson.

'When she came and blackguarded me. I've told you she rammed Lake down my throat; and too hard. Well, in the same breath she emphasised, just a little more than from her point of view she ought to have, her dislike of Ravenscourt . . . I can't tell you more than that how it was. But I suddenly saw light. And all the jigsaw pieces in my head shook themselves and fell into their right and proper places.'

Dyson considered this. He said at last:

'So *she* knew all the time!'

Anthony shook his head. 'We'll never really know; but I doubt it. My idea is that she guessed—probably from something he let drop in a secret and tender moment—that if he hadn't actually killed Blackatter he knew more about it than was good for his peace of mind. We know that from the bit of conversation my wife overheard that night. "The Man" she talked about was me. And she knew he was worried about me. And the more he denied it, the more—being a woman—sure she was . . . And that's that. Now you know *all* about it. And I hope you're satisfied!'

Dyson grunted. 'All,' he said, 'except what it was really about? You've forgotten how close you've been. Best Whitstable! You kept on—you and him—about France and something that happened there. What was it?'

Anthony stared at him a moment. 'Good God!' he said. 'You're right! . . . Oh, it was his VC of course. He didn't earn it. He was very far from earning it.' He took the envelope and handed it to Dyson. 'Read that,' he said. 'You'll see then.'

Dyson read. Anthony, gazing out at the troubled sky, smoked and was silent.

Dyson gave him back the envelope.

'Poor devil!' said Dyson. He paused a moment. 'There's another point,' he added suddenly. 'Why all that business tonight—getting him up to that field and having us there? I see it up to a point; but I'd like the whole story.'

'Easy,' Anthony said. 'Without that attempt to get rid of me, I'd really have had nothing cast-iron against him. I *knew* it all, but I couldn't 've hoped to prove it legally without the backing of a confession. And it struck me that the best way to get a confession—and also to provide a good backing for it—would be to shake one out of him by getting him caught red-handed trying to do yet another killing. So I worked it that he should try to get rid of me. He was already nervous about me because, what with my inquiries about Blackatter's war service and so on, it was beginning to look as if I were getting warm. I went and told him, all friendly, that I knew who Curtain was, and asked would he help me to get Curtain. That was a shock for him—for a moment. Then he saw—or thought he did—that it was all right; because as I'd come and told him about Curtain, I couldn't really be on to the fact that he himself was Curtain. But he also realised, more sharply than ever, that it was going to be very unhealthy for him if I were allowed to go on nosing . . .

'Poor devil! He did everything I'd counted on him doing. It must 've looked to him as if Kismet were handing me to him on a nice warm plate. We were alone in his office when I asked him to post his men up in that field—alone, in fact, the whole time I was there. And I'd told him all my helpers would be elsewhere tonight. And I'd arranged to go on this lovely dark walk with him. All he had to do—all he did—was to keep mum and load his gun and come and meet me as arranged . . .'

Dyson interrupted. 'When did you work all this out? And how did he think he was going to get away with bumping you off when you might've told everyone you were going there with him?'

'I worked out the battle-scheme,' Anthony said, 'during that very silent meal of ours last night; and after you were in bed I got hold of Lucas and arranged for him to come down . . . As to Ravenscourt's getting away with killing me, that would've been easy. Don't you see? It would've been the mysterious and still evasive Mr Curtain who shot A. R. Gethryn—and very nearly shot Colonel Ravenscourt too. The only point he must 've had difficulty with must 've been to think out how he was going to explain why—if I happened to tell anyone *all* about the night's intended operations—he hadn't posted his men as agreed; but you can wager he'd got a reason ready—and a good one . . .' He broke off and shook his head slowly. He stared with unseeing eyes at the smashed window. He said, after a pause:

'Odd, you know . . . There's a man who, for the sake of keeping the glory of a medal he'd stolen—or at any rate done the reverse of winning—showed enough courage and resource and cold, thoughtful recklessness to win a dozen . . .'

Dyson nodded. 'But I can see how he couldn't face the possibility of that story coming out.' He looked down at the buff envelope. 'Wonder how much Blackatter squeezed out of him before it got too much of a good thing?'

Anthony shrugged. 'Yes,' he said. 'Now . . . where 're the others?'

Dyson's smile was like the sardonic beak-opening of an eagle. 'Still viewing the body,' he said.

'Let's go down,' said Anthony and led the way.

There was a small crowd in the large hall, and on a couch a shapeless thing that was covered with a sheet. In places the grey-whiteness of the sheet was patched with dark, damp stains.

Anthony stood in the doorway and talked with Lucas. Anthony said:

'And there's one thing I'll *never* know!' He sighed.

'Eh?' said Lucas. 'What's that?'

'The night Blackatter was killed,' Anthony said slowly. 'You remember he went, though he'd been ordered to keep off, into The Horse and Hound. That was very important to Ravenscourt. It gave him the chance to bribe Dollboys to tell that lie about what Blackatter said before he left . . .'

Lucas was impatient. He interrupted. 'But *what* is it you'll never know?'

Anthony raised a hand. 'Slowly! Slowly! I'm coming to it. It's this: How did Ravenscourt induce Blackatter to enter the place. If he did so induce him, it was the cleverest thing he did. If he didn't, it was Satan's luck . . . Which? . . . Lucas, I could stand it if I knew, and I never shall know.'

They had to stand aside from the door, then. A doctor came. And men carrying a stretcher.

What was left of Ravenscourt, the Varolles VC, was carried out into the night.

CHAPTER VIII

DAY

THE wall was high and long. It was a grey, thick wall of heavy stone. In its expanse the little wooden alcove of the wicket-gate was scarcely an interruption.

The gate in the wall swung open, inwards. Through it there came a man and a woman. Their arms were linked; but not linked in the casual way of arm-linking; these arms strained each the other to its side.

There was a motor-car at the curb. Across the pavement to it they walked. The man was a great man, thick and tall, and yet he moved with a step light for all its present slowness. But big as he was, the woman's head was not far below his. She, too, walked with a light step; but her gait had in it an oddness, an uncertainty which told of some emotion too great for speech.

They sat in the car. Slowly it moved away. The long wall of grey stone was lost in the dim land behind them. The head of the woman came to rest upon the man's shoulder.

THE END